THE

BUMPER

BOOK

OF

BRITISH

BIZARRO

DEDICATION

In remembrance of Frank Key and for the Mermaids
Charity; we welcome you through the doors of wonder
into The Bumper Book Of British Bizarro!!

CONTENTS

ACKNOWLEDGEMENTS

The British Bizarro Community would like to accuse the following of crimes against editing, formatting and typesetting: Duncan P. Bradshaw, Dani Brown and Chris Meekings

Their sins shall live on in infamy throughout the ages. A pox be upon them!!!

INTRODUCTION

We live in a time when the Demiurge's power runs rampant. His fingers, made of unicorn tears and gum, are digging deep into publishing landscape. With his allies, the snake aliens in Seattle and the reptilians in NYC, He has turned the written word into a flaccid logic that longs for more. Much much more.

Bizarro is more. British Bizarro's are the prophets of more and of the strange. The British Bizarros are my Gnostic children who know the true nature of the Druids. Their words are not corrupted by the Demiurge, but through charity, where a surreal Gnostic heaven is born inside of this book.

Mandy De Sandra

FOREWORD

Dear Editor of *The Times,*

I am writing to you regarding the publication of an obscene book. I, the most important reader you have, feel that this is an aboination *(Ed. abomination?)* on all things gentile and decent.

Furthermore, you should also beware I am not crazy. I have a certificate from my doctor saying that everything I say is right and sane.

Honestly, I'm so not insane your *(Ed. you)* could use me as a flaying *(Ed. flying? Not sure)* piggy bank and everyone would be like " oh wow that's the normalist *(Ed. is this a word?)* thing I've ever seen."

I'm NORMAL*(Ed. all caps suggest otherwise)*. Doctors have studied me and my gaping brain cavity, which is totally human, and said " That's ok why are you in the hospital. Go home it's nomal *(Ed. normal – see this is what comes of typing too fast while being so normal)* for your brain to breathe nitrogen."

There is no one watching the human race. Of which I'm a part of, and if this so-called Bizarro anthology is published it will be to the detriment of all universe kind, beings of energy or not.

Honestly, I am offended and so such *(Ed. should)* be the GREAT BRITISH public. It is a travesty and so, so , so , such a bad of a thing that I'm willing to send them a copy of this rambling letter also *(Ed. Help!?!)*.

This flith will not stand! Look at it, a story of Valencian ghosts! pah! And anothur of a man with JukeboxTeeth. I nevver heard of such rubbish! A poem about a talking penis! What s the world coming to? And our beloved Magaret

Thatcher (god rest her soul) lampooned!

Who do thees people think they is?! Madaleine Swann – some sort of interweb TheyTube celebrity I am led to beleive. Leigham Shardlow, no idea, probably a communist. Duncan Bradshaw. No one called Duncan is of any rank in the cicrles I tred in. Greg James, I suspect is related to the pasty maker, and he should stick to that. Chris Meeikings? Probably a crusty-man and proto-communist. Dani Brown? Now, I do know some Brown's terribly nice people, but I suspect that this Dani person is of no relation to them what-so-ever! And the rest are no doubt neardowells and other riffraff, of beetling brows and lowbirth *(Ed. I'm giving up – it just seems like a rant)*

I dare them to put this as thier intorduction, they won't because they are coards of pink flesh .Little flowers who do not have the big green alien courage, that I also do not have, to put this in front of all thier work. *(Ed. unable to make intelligible and stay within the original writer's voice)*

Yours elegently

Self-entitled Gods of beings everywhere and everywhen
Disgruntled from Hemel Hempstead

TEETH OUT FOR PEWDIEPIE

- Madeleine Swann -

Brian's teeth felt particularly attached to his face today, their roots climbing to the top of his head. He couldn't imagine anyone reaching into his mouth, let alone yanking his pearlies out one by one with metal pliers. He'd probably die of blood loss. His ex-mate Martin knew someone whose gum had been ripped out along with his gnashers and bled out on the spot.

Brian flopped back in the grass, dandelion seeds floating into the air. Midsummer flower smells sprouted in his nostrils, and birds chirped in the forest trees. It was the perfect place for a bloodbath orgy.

The stump on his right hand twitched, reminding him of last summer's pain. It was hard to believe how fervent he'd been when he allowed the High Priestess of the Zoellas near his little finger with the nutcrackers. He'd reached ecstasy with the others that day, though, convinced he could see Zoella, vlog Goddess herself, among the roiling naked bodies and smeared blood of the initiates. Now the pink scar glinted uselessly in the sun, announcing to all how lame he used to be. Still, he'd stumbled across the PewdiePies while wandering, alone and spiritually bereft, after noticing several red flags that their Earth Mother was not the almighty being he'd been led to believe, namely that the calendar she released at Christmas was really expensive, and she didn't properly apologise.

They'd welcomed him warmly, offering him stew they'd cooked in a pot over the fire and giving him clothes without holes. His heart hurt when they spoke of their Great One, jealous of the fervour in their eyes. As the night progressed and he drank more of their mead and joined in their raucous laughter and singing, he felt the light of PewDiePie dawn inside him. These were good people, he would stay with them.

"Brian," the voice cut through the memory. It was Jim, the one he'd grown closest to, which was probably why they'd sent him, "it's time."

He led Brian through the trees into a clearing. Hundreds of eyes crept over him, and Brian folded his arms. The PewdiePies holding drums beat a rhythm while the others rotated hips, swirled feet and waved arms, faces burning with excitement. Brian imagined himself backing away, making excuses, heading back to the Zoellas or starting his own farm, alone. Instead, he watched the High Priest step free of the crowd and approach him, face almost covered by long, heavy robes. He held up a hand and spoke, his voice deep and impressive, "Respect wahmen."

"Respect wahmen," the group responded; the volume curling Brian's insides. He opened his mouth to copy them but froze when the Priest revealed his other hand holding the pliers. This was it.

He knew he wouldn't go through with it. Something would happen, he'd change his mind, or their rules would suddenly vary, anything. He had to admit, though, as he followed the Priest's instructions by opening his mouth and staying still while the first molar was restrained, that it seemed very much like he was going through with it. It wasn't until the first yank tore through his body that he realised he was absolutely, unquestioningly, allowing his teeth to be removed one by one so he could join a group.

For the next several minutes, maybe hours, the world was nothing but pain. The dancing of his friends was smothered in pain, the Priest's calming words dripped with pain, the sky needled his exposed wounds. One by one, they were ripped free; molars, canines, incisors. Then, suddenly, it was over. Brian looked down to see a pile of red and white chunks that used to belong to him and felt his blood pour onto his chest. "Keep your head back," said the Priest and, woozy, Brian did as he was told. He yelped in surprise when several arms were thrown about him, and that's when he realised he'd done it, he was a PewDiePie.

"Thank you so much," he wept, any flame of uncertainty extinguished for good.

"We must celebrate," said Jim, grinning toothlessly. "I heard there was a thot group just over the hill. The women parade in their underwear in honour of some Twitch streamer." He and the others wrinkled their noses in disgust. Jim continued, "We should gather on the hilltop and yell stuff down at them."

"Yes," they cried, "teach them a lesson," and they were off, Brian in tow, arms linked with his new brothers, the soft summer breeze beneath his feet.

MAUD'S SEQUEL GOES STRAIGHT TO VIDEO

- Die Booth -

"Baby," says Maud, "Do you remember when we met?"

"Of course I do," Tom says. He inches closer, squeezing one bum-cheek onto Maud's sofa cushion, his arm around her.

Maud smiles, in that way when she's trying to be charming. "Tell me?"

"We were in Heaven."

"Our eyes met across the crowded dancefloor."

Tom laughs. "It wasn't crowded. It was chucking-out time, we were the only ones left. You wouldn't have spoken to me if you hadn't had six lager-and-blacks."

"I would have spoken to you if all I'd had was orange squash for a million weeks," Maud says and presses the tip of her finger against the tip of his nose. She looks a little sad, though.

"What's up, baby?"

Maud sighs. The couch creaks, quietly. "I know I can remember. But I can't remember, you know?"

"Six lager-and-blacks," Tom repeats, sagely.

She nods. "I know it's in here." She taps her forehead.

Tom presses his lips together in consideration. "I bet I could find it." Her hair is lilac today, like a mermaid's. He brushes a long, crackly strand back behind her ear and peers in. "Hmmm. I can't see it from here."

"Look harder!"

Tom presses his nose to the hinge of her jaw and peers into the deep, mysterious darkness. "I think I'm gonna have to go in."

4

"Never put anything smaller than your elbow into your ear," Maud says, with a smirk.

Tom returns it, with interest. "Oh, baby – I am far bigger than your elbow." He waggles his eyebrows as he climbs inside.

It had looked dark inside Maud's head from the outside, but inside it's well-lit by thousands of strings of fairy lights, in all the colours of the rainbow and some special-edition ones from either side. They cobweb a big vaulted ceiling, like a cross between King's College Chapel, and Berghain. Tom produces his shades from his hoody pocket and puts them on.

"What can you see in there?" Maud's voice booms, sort of resonant and goddy, from all around. It feels like Tom is a marble in the drum of a washing machine.

"Not much!" He cups his hands around his mouth and shouts back. "I think I'm in the atrium or something. I'll have to go deeper."

"Bring me back a nice surprise about myself!" Maud rumbles.

"That shouldn't be difficult."

The vaulted room, with its unseen apex, stretches shadily into recesses all around. On inspection, these alcoves are doorless outlets, each onto a canal, with a vessel floating in wait for wanderers. Tom wonders briefly how much traffic there is, through Maud's mind, as he selects a rubber dinghy that seems – compared to gondolas and soap-crates and surf-boards – the likeliest prospect of remaining afloat.

There are no oars, but the canal winds down a tunnel, with close-clutching rock walls that are near enough and rough enough that he can use them to propel himself along. The stone runs with drips, echoes with it. The shushing wind through and through sounds like the sigh inside a seashell. Tom shivers. The dinghy bumps, against a quay, and he frog-leaps out, peering around. There's nothing much here, just a stifling smell of dusty rubber matting, and a man.

"Hi," Tom says, pushing his shades up.

"Drop and give me twenty." The man replies in a certain voice. He's tall and broad, with a mat of yellow hair sticking straight up off his very red forehead. Tom takes a vivid dislike to him.

"Who the hell are you?" Tom plants his feet firmly, far apart on the rubbery ground, and crosses his arms.

The man smiles, like chewing gum. "I'm [redacted]'s gym teacher from high school."

The buzzing of Tom's blood sets up an alarm chorus in his ears. "Her name is Maud. And you shouldn't be hanging around in here."

The man's bloated smile stretches. "And what's *your* name, young lady?"

"Not today, Satan." Tom raises his eyebrows and his tips up his chin. "I challenge you to a duel."

"A duel? Are you sure?"

"I smash it at the gym, now, sucker. I challenge you to netball."

"You never were any good at netball…" The words warp in pitch as Maud's gym teacher squishes and bulges and turns into-

"You!" She doesn't look exactly like Tom's high school gym mistress. In fact, she doesn't look quite human at all, but she's still recognisable from the descriptions that Tom has given of her to Maud. The bouncing blonde curls, the whistle around her neck, the big white teeth that now gnash like a garbage disposal's blades as she aims the netball at Tom's head.

"Dodgeball!"

"You shouldn't be here *at all*," Tom says, breathlessly, as he sidesteps orange missiles. "I've learnt a lot since I saw you last." He catches one of the flung balls and launches it smartly back. "It's time for you to leave."

There's the thick thud of rubber hitting rock as the ball strikes the wall behind Tom's high school gym mistress and rebounds off it, whacking her soundly in the back of the head. A sharp crack, like a party popper going off, and she explodes into a flurry of raining straw.

Tom brushes a few shreds from his sleeve, replaces his shades on his nose and steps carefully through the mess. "And don't come back!" He looks around, at the echoing chamber. There are two doors on the opposite wall, marked with familiar signs. "Oh, no." Tom glances back the way he came, but the dinghy has disappeared: unless he fancies a paddle, there's no way but onwards. He squares his shoulders, and places a hand firmly on the door marked with a little, trousered stick-man, and pushes it open.

"What the..?!" Tom wobbles for balance, as the door slams shut behind him and he finds himself suddenly teetering on the edge of a most horrible abyss. Plastering his back against the tiled wall, he gropes for a handle, hinges – anything – but can find no trace of the entrance he just came through. The only route available to him is the shiny, convex surface of a giant toilet seat, haloing the impeccable porcelain depths of a vast toilet bowl. The stench of bleach makes his eyes water. "At least it's clean, I guess," Tom mutters as he starts to navigate the lavatory.

It's treacherous going, as he shuffles along, inch by inch, keeping his balance. But if he can only make it past the cistern, then there appears to be some kind of freedom beyond. "Keep calm. You can do this." Tom wobbles uncertainly, as an ominous kind of vibration starts up beneath his feet. He holds his arms out to the sides for balance, soles slipping on the shiny surface. "Oh, no… noooo…" several feet beneath him, blue water begins to cascade from beneath the porcelain rim. The seat shakes.

It's a torrent, churning and gushing in the bowl, as Tom loses his footing and plummets. He grips the rim of the seat grimly, white-knuckled. But the pull of the flush is too much: with one last frantic gulp of air, he's sucked under.

He surfaces, spluttering and spits out bleachy water. His eyes sting: he rubs them and peers into the dim distance. More tunnels. This one tiled, like a public swimming pool, and about as pissy. Tom doggy-paddles until he feels the kick of floor beneath his feet, and he can start to wade. His waterlogged clothes make him feel like twice his normal weight. "I know I always say your mind is a sewer, baby, but this is ridiculous." He pushes his wet hair away from his face. "Where's the good stuff?"

No sooner has he spoken, than a light appears, at the end of the tunnel. He plops towards it. It's not actually the end, just more tunnel, delineated by a velvet rope. Unfastening the rope, he twists over the threshold and then drops the brass hook back into its loop again. Overhead a mirror-ball spins, scattering sequins of light across the mosaic walls. This part of the tunnel is lined with disco heels, stacked into alcoves like a glitzy Capuchin catacombs. Tom smiles. He slips off his squelchy sneakers and selects a pair of strappy platform shoes instead, in iridescent blues. They're all Maud's size, which means they're all his size. He buckles the ankle straps and does a little tap-tap-spin. "This is more like it." His footsteps clip across the tiles. After a few hundred metres, the path turns a corner. It opens out onto the dancefloor of Heaven.

"Hey there, baby."

Maud grins at him and raises a mostly-empty pint glass. Her progress is wobbly. "I knew you'd find me." Her voice comes from her mouth, and from all around.

"It wasn't easy. You were really buried in here."

The club sways and shimmies, like it's printed on gauze.

The walls are curtains of eyes. Memory-Maud bats her lashes, and cups one ear, "Tell me again?" And Tom shrugs and climbs inside.

This version of the memory is brighter. Less filmy. Memory-Maud2 welcomes him with outstretched hands. "Are you starting to remember now?" Tom whispers into her ear before he climbs in again.

Memory-Maud3 nods happily. She laughs, "Is this me cubed now?"

"I think so," Tom says.

"I think we're going around in circles." The mirror ball above twirls. The lights sail around the walls, eyes blinking.

"I can't help it," Tom says, as he climbs inside her mind again, "I'm just so into you, into you, into you."

"This is getting silly." Says Maud. Her eyes are bright, every lash in super-microscopic focus, each trickle of condensation on her pint glass in high definition. "I'm going to start to think I imagined you. You need to get out of my head and back into my arms!"

"How'd I do that?"

"I have it." She says. With thumb and forefinger, she pinches her nostrils shut. "Hold on." Her voice comes out kind of buzzy with her nose held closed. Then there's a hollow, ringing feeling as she blows down into her sinuses, and a loud pop, like driving down a hill, fast.

Tom blinks. He rubs his eyes. Maud is there, still, but now they're surrounded by their front room, instead of a deserted dancefloor. He squares his shoulders and cracks his neck. Maud says, "Welcome home, baby. What did you find?"

"Shoes." Tom raises his right leg and wiggles his ankle round. Maud tilts her head, admiring the play of light off the shiny blue pleather of his platform shoe. "There's an awful lot of shoes in there."

"Mmmm. Yeah. Those are nice. I saw them once in a shop window in Camden: they must have left more of an impression than I realised."

"And there're lots of disco balls."

"That's cool. What's all this?" Maud runs a finger through his damp hair. It comes away slippery and blue.

"I think it's love. I'm covered in love from you."

Maud's smile tips up at one corner. "It smells like Harpic."

"That's how you know it's pure. Do you remember how we met now?"

She nods. "Every last second. Clear as video."

Tom swings his legs around and drapes them across her lap. "And was it as magical as you hoped?"

"Even better, baby," Maud says. She bats her lashes. "Do you think you'll be keeping those shoes..?"

Tom smiles. "They're all yours," he says.

THE POST-MAN PAT

- Leigham Shardlow -

The charred skeletal remains of Mrs Goggins shrieked into the blood bathed sky. The air vibrated with the volume, disturbing centuries of dead brick dust, which crumbled from shadow hewn ceiling. As it slowly dissipated, the Cyborg began to awaken with a faint buzzing and a soft green light from the screen embedded into its face.

The cold black screen whirred and lit up with bold green text that read "Postman Loading sequence 100%". Thick, yellowed plastic tubes hooked into the glass-encased brain from a huge rusty steel tank affixed in the wall behind. It glugged with black life-giving fluids. Tiny sparks of electricity flashed across the surface of its grey matter, filling the air with the stench of ozone and cooking cerebellum.

Its metal limbs, infused with coarse, leathery flesh, whirred and juddered with the decay of a thousand years of neglect and abuse. Slowly and inevitably they moved in an echoing parody of life trying to remember how to stand, how to be human once again. It rose and the screen lit up showing two round eyes made up of text characters. They blinked and it wiped a thick layer of dust from optical sensors situated next to the screen. Each a tiny black camera that whirred, moving with unseen motors that laid deep within its skull. It focused on the room it found itself in, trying to make sense as everything swam into reality as its brain steadily activated.

Mrs Goggins lay on her fossilised wooden desk, face up to the decaying roof's opening. The sky roared at her with harsh nuclear fallout winds and the dust of a fallen civilisation. Her bones had bleached in places where sunlight had filtered through the blood-red clouds. The rest were brown, and pockmarked with holes from now dead, burrowing insects and their long-abandoned nests.

The rest of the room lay in thick coatings of black dust, crumbling letters, unpainted grey bricks and dark orange mould that crept from the blackened corners and spread across the walls like veins. The mould pulsated softly as if a gargantuan beating heart would be discovered if followed closely enough.

The skeleton's jaw distended, and it let out an ear-shattering bellow again, its wails echoed around the room and out of the gaping ceiling chasm. They bounced off invisible walls and the room became its cathedral. A small trickle of watery, brown discharge leaked from the cyborg's ears. It opened a rusty cabinet-like panel on the side of its chest, revealing an ancient mechanical tape player. As he pressed the eject button, the device slowly opened, and the cyborg took out an unlabeled tape before turning it over. Replacing it back in the player he clunkily pressed the triangle play button with a soft click.

"Oh, hello there, Mrs Goggins," said the tape, the distorted tones of Postman Pat.

The skeleton's skull turned to Cyborg Pat, and he saw for the first time that it had a single yellow and blistered eye staring madly at him from the empty socket. An eye full of vigour and hatred, a constant stare of blistering purpose.

"Pat!" it bellowed, the voice loud, screeching and alien, a mishmash of nightmare yells and stop motion voice overs. This was not Mrs Goggins' usual voice. Pat's screen showed a pair of concerned eyes made entirely of the letter 'X'.

He pressed play on the tape again. It stuttered for a second before he banged the side of the player with a sharp slap.

"What seems to be the trouble Mrs Goggins?" it said in a slow deep resonance as if the batteries had died.

The eye squirmed out of its socket followed by a long, wrinkled worm-like, green tendril. It wriggled and pulsated along with the walls' mould veins in gross synchronicity. It swayed and crept its way outwards. Moving through the air, bending slightly under its own weight, it danced to the tune of the apocalypse. It continued doing this blissfully and calmly, taking what Pat could only guess was enjoyment in its own movement. It did this almost elegantly until it was level with Cyborg Pat's screen. It came to a dead-fast stop, freezing in place while staring directly into his camera.

"Delivery!" the skull croaked. The tendril, behind the eye, contorted itself into the shape of a cartoon hand and pointed at a small, desiccated cardboard box, laying at the feet of Mrs Goggins' almost dead skeleton.

"Of course, best hurry, no one likes late post," said the tape, as Cyborg Pat's screen lit up with a big thumbs up. He had not pressed play.

The tubes, hooking Pat to his life-giving container, detached automatically with a hiss. They spat thick, lumpy liquid remnants of the black gunk, in short, dry heaves onto the concrete floor, before some unseen valve shut them off.

The eye retreated into its skull home and disappeared into the dark recesses of Mrs Goggin's brain box. Pat looked at Mrs Goggins for a quick second before grabbing the box. She was never one to bark orders before. The box was heavy and sloshed around with an uneven weight. He tucked it under his arm and faced the cast steel airlock leading out of the post office.

Cyborg Pat's screen went blank for a time before it lit up with red text reading "Force required. Safety off"

A faint gurgling sound came from deep within Pat's body, and he shook violently, yet he never dropped the package. The flesh that coated the metal parts of his body grew darker; the veins filled with his brain cavity's ominous black. They stretched and bulged, growing with inner strength.

Pat grabbed some of the concrete on the door's side, pulling it away easily before crushing it in his, mostly, human hand. He reached into the recesses and pulled. The steel groaned and cracked, coming with a choking cloud of black concrete. Cyborg Pat tossed it aside and stared into the dark abyss beyond.

An ancient torch popped from his shoulder compartment. A tiny arc of electricity sparked across the paraffin-soaked tallow setting it aflame, illuminating nothing beyond the doorway.

As Pat entered the darkness, the concrete flowed from the edges of the door, remaking itself and sealing Pat's exit.

The floor gave way, and Pat fell past twisting, unrecognisable forms. Ancient, chanting, stone figures holding impossibly vast pictograms of a picturesque village. As he dropped past, they blurred, telling a story he could almost remember: a black and white beast, a village of morons and a song that made him feel alive. When it all stopped, Pat found himself face down in two inches of thick radioactive slime that extinguished his torch.

He looked up and saw a brick-lined tunnel lit by dull, flickering, fluorescent lights. His auto-positioning system kicked in and binged a sharp blue arrow on top of his field of vision. "EXIT GREENDALE SEWER" popped up on his grimy screen in all caps. He stood, picked up his surprisingly undamaged box and followed the arrow.

The subterranean catacombs wound and twisted beneath what was left of Greendale. At points, Pat would pass under gratings which let in shafts of deep, red light and the rushing sounds of caustic winds.

Other times the floor would dip, and the water level would rise, leaving him wading through thigh-high nuclear waste swarming with giant insects which inhabited the dark underverse. They writhed in the sewage, leaving faint glowing trails but they ignored Pat. He wasn't alive anymore, and they would not eat dead meat.

Eventually, Pat came to an opening which brought him to the train station.

The warping storm's fury that raged around him but barely registered on his sensors. The caustic muck he had splashed through had all but destroyed them. Sand and dust licked his skin, blistering the exposed flesh. An acidic world of empty death lay around him filled with collapsed buildings, warhead bleached walls and echoes of what Greendale used to be. Blackened skeletons littered the street. Every mouth agape praise of the holocaustal mushroom cloud gods who brought their end.

The looming corpse of the Greendale Rocket train stared at him from behind the central station's remains. Its side was slashed open, leaking rust, like puss from a decaying wound. Green jewels flashed from within the Rocket, and Pat's screen lit up with an exclamation point made up of other smaller exclamation points.

He put down the old crumbling package and ran towards the train, compelled by some ancient recognition of those emeralds. He had vague memories of a red van, his red van, and a lifelong companion that shared it with him. There were fleeting glimpses of all the smiles and songs they'd shared in an idyllic, plasticine hallucination.

He stopped twenty feet from the train. The eyes and the thing attached to them slowly padded out of the Greendale Rockets interior. Its long haunches rippled with muscles and jet-black fur. The throat growled softly but intensely behind its sabre like teeth. The deep-set, green eyes glowed regardless of being outside. Its back was puckered with protruding fleshy-exhausts but, as its growl went up a pitch, huge tendrils emerged from them, each ending in obsidian talons.

Pat froze, seconds passing like years. Then the beast pounced, unsheathing neon purple claws as it hurtled through the air in an instant, before piercing Pats chest.

Pat instinctively rolled backwards with the force of the impact before planting his foot under the beast's ribcage, kicking it off at the roll's apex. The claws tore out chunks of steel and tubing from Pat's chest. The Panther landed on its back the arose using its tendril talons as legs. Its neck cracked with an unseen force and the head spun, so it was correct for an upside-down body. Like a cobra, it swayed back and forth almost randomly teasing Pat, its prey, as it decided what direction it would attack him from.

Pat staggered up and fiddled with his tape deck. The viscous black fluid leaking from his wounds coated him in a thick slime which seeped into the recesses of his exposed metal components.

The Panther opened its gargantuan jaws and flashed a thick red tongue at Pat, tasting his blood and fear in the air. It moved forward, skittering on its talons, an unholy spider-like abomination.

One of the tentacles launched out at Pat unexpectedly. He dived to one side then into a forward roll, feeling it whistled past his ear. The beast circled Pat while flicking the whip-like tendrils at him. He wasn't fast enough, and the talons scored several hits across his chest and arms, drawing more black ooze and sending him staggering backwards.

The Panther launched four of them at him. Pat raised his hands, trying to grasp them. The beast flicked them back, like a whip, severing one of Pat's hands. The wound sprayed black fluid in a shower of viscous ooze.

His screen went blank, his cameras flickered on and off as Pat fell to his knees, praying for the same salvation that was afforded the dead who surrounded him.

The Panther twisted back onto its legs, and its head snapped back into position with a sickening crack of bone and cartilage. It licked the air again, its tongue salivating at the meal well-earned and slowly approached Pat.

Pat desperately patted at his tape deck with his still ichor leaking stump.

There was a faint click, and the tape reel let out a short static hiss before speaking "Come on now, Jess, stop misbehaving."

Then, Pat fell onto his face, cracking his screen into a thousand pieces. His cameras stopped working as the light he saw grew ever dimmer. His brain fluid ran empty, a dry gurgling sound echoed in his skull. Eventually, there was nothing but swelling nothingness in and out of his mind.

The Panther dragged the broken cyborg back into the bowels of the Green Rocket, devouring him in greedy chunks before vomiting up all the machine parts it had swallowed accidentally.

The harsh, nuclear winds tore at the box that Pat had left in the middle of the street. Its packaging scoured away. Inside was a small and, faded scale model of a red van, the lettering on the side had disappeared with age. Exposed on the street the model too would erode to nothing but dust. The skeletons would scream alone once again into the ether, and all relics of the past would pass into history.

THE WETNESS

- Tom Over -

He both awakened and somehow caught his ejaculate in one reflexive motion. Left fist clamped around his still pumping glans, he lay still without breathing, stunned by the preconscious manoeuvre. Blinking against the dark, he felt a trickle of fluid move along his wrist. He turned his head to see his partner's sleeping face. Jen's eyelids shifted embryonically, a faint snarl accompanying each of her languid breaths. Satisfied he hadn't disturbed her, he edged out from under the bed covers, careful not to drip any of himself onto the sheets.

In the bathroom, he unclenched his fist and examined the cooling discharge. As always, the strip bulb did not fully illuminate right away, the greenish murk-light giving his cum the appearance of subaquatic slime. As with the previous times, he couldn't recall the imagery of the dream or the context of how his orgasm had been achieved. Once again, he considered the abnormality of a man his age having these experiences, and more disturbingly, the unknowable impetus for them. No physical bodies surfaced in his mind when he tried to remember. Only a cloying sensation remained; a feeling of being somehow...smothered.

He cleaned himself up and returned to the bedroom. With the light of the hallway falling across the room, he noticed something at groin level on the bedsheet. He thought he'd managed to prevent any spillage, but a drop of semen must have leaked through his fingers onto the fabric. Remaining conscious of Jen's slumbering, he moved in closer. The stain was circular and still wet, having the texture of fresh glue. It was dark around its inner edge, growing lighter toward the middle like the growth ring of some tiny tree. Indicative perhaps, he mused, of the time since his last nocturnal emission, which had happened only days before. The growing frequency of them would have weighed on his mind had his desire to sleep not been greater. He hurriedly dabbed at the mark with a tissue before getting back into bed. He decided to worry about this strange nightly ritual tomorrow when things made more sense. As his thoughts began to cloud, he didn't notice his hand brush over the damp patch. The sticky spot which, even now, was no less wet.

While Jen readied herself for work in the morning, he stood motionless under the shower; shoulders hunched, chin flat to his chest. The steaming water dissolved the night's residue but did little to cleanse him of it. He tried to remember his dream, but the structure of it evaded him. He let the spray traverse his scalp, hoping it might stimulate some dim recollection, but nothing came. He lifted his head to face the current, enjoying its pressure against his eyelids. He absently tipped his head back, then further still. After a second or two, a stream of water found his nasal passage, it coursed up his nose and down the back of his throat, making him retch. The sensation startled him, it felt strange but somehow not unfamiliar. After a moment's thought, he tilted his head back again until the water eventually breached his nostril. He gagged, swallowing some of the warm liquid. A glint of recognition winked in his mind, but it was too vague to pinpoint. The thing his memory sought appeared to change under scrutiny, like some bizarre quantum phenomena. He contemplated this for a minute and then switched off the shower.

Over breakfast, his thoughts were elsewhere. He didn't mean to be distant, but the silence between them eventually announced itself. She looked up from her phone and took a bite of toast. "Is everything alright, Cal? Bit quiet this morning."

Callum looked up from his bowl, realised he'd stopped chewing the cereal that was still in his mouth. "What's that?

Sorry babe, miles away." He swallowed.

"No, just that you look distracted is all. You were moving around a lot last night too."

"Yeah sorry, nothing's up. Just stuff at work I guess, big meeting today."

Jen seemed to accept this as truth. Instead of digging deeper, she changed the subject and lilt of her voice. "God, I had another one of those weird nightmares again last night, the one where you leave me for Heather!" She suppressed a giggle behind her phone.

"Great, I'm in the dog house again because in sleepyland I shacked up with your sister," he said, constructing a smile. Jen laughed and went on to describe the time she divulged this to her sibling over drinks, but Callum was in his own world again. As his girlfriend spoke, he let his eyes rest and gazed through her as though she were some giant magic eye picture. In her place, within the edges of her outline, he could almost discern the shadow of the thing he had dreamed.

During his cycle to work, the previous night pressed on his mind. Elements crept into his vision but at the same time, refused to manifest. He stopped trying to remember and looked up to the sky. The clouds above him were storm-heavy and marbled grey-green like ancient ice. As he coasted along, he imagined this sight to be like the one Sophie experienced. The frozen rock-like canopy dappled through with weak light as she skittered and bobbed along it, trying to find the opening. He tried to imagine her final moments, to comprehend the terror she must've felt. Though it was years ago now, he still found it deeply disturbing to think about, and feared it always would be. He tore his thoughts away and focused on the journey at hand.

Coming up to the last set of traffic lights, he passed by it, the same as he always did. He knew it would be there on the other side of the road, stretched across the entrance to a car park because it never went away. Callum had noticed the perpetual puddle late last year when he started his new job and began taking this route to work. The pool of murky water occupied a sunken patch of tarmac at the foot of a concrete post, surrounding the base of the structure like a moat that had burst its banks. No matter what the season, be it rain or shine, the puddle was always there. Not only did the water never dry up, but its volume still remained the same, even on the hottest days of summer. As he raced by, he gave the pool a cursory glance, just to see if it had changed since the last time. If anything, it looked bigger than before, deeper. The surface of it dark and still, seeming to absorb the day's pale light but reflecting none back.

He drifted through the morning, attending to his tasks just as absently as he engaged with colleagues. Conversations happened without him fully registering them. He wasn't usually this absent, was personable enough on any given day, but the enigma of his nocturnal habit had become all-consuming. He found it difficult to concentrate, often lapsing into daydreams. One such reverie was halted during the afternoon meeting when Callum's boss noticed his wandering eye and fired off a blunt question, "How are the test scripts going for Thursday's release, Cal?" asked the Systems Manager curtly.

Callum jumped, dropped the pen he was twirling. "Oh, sorry, yeah, coming along. They should be ready by close of play tomorrow."

"Drop me an email when they're done, please, and copy Bev in if you would."

"Sure, Ken. Will do," he said, bending down to retrieve his biro. Once he found it, he sat back up, but something was wrong. The pen felt strange, slick with some kind of liquid. He rubbed his thumb and forefinger together, examining the substance. It was weird; wet but not sticky, more viscous than water. A strand of it linked his fingers when he separated them, like a thin jelly. He brought his face forward to smell the stuff, crinkling his nose despite it having no odour. He rubbed his pen on his trouser leg and placed it on the table. Out of curiosity he leant back down and dabbed at the floor with his fingertips, the short-haired carpet was saturated with the same boggy substance. When Callum looked down to investigate what he saw made him start. The floor beneath him was as sodden as it had felt, but it was the nature of the wet patch that startled him. A perfect dark circle of moisture lay directly under his chair. Unnerved, he scanned around the floor and saw that the rest of the carpet, under the table and beneath other people's chairs, was perfectly dry.

"Everything alright, Callum?" asked Ken, the agitation in his tone now audible.

Callum looked up. "I…I um…" he started, but quickly realised he didn't know how to continue. He looked down at the damp spot and then back to his manager. "No nothing, everything's fine." He assembled a half-smile, nodded. There was a titter from somewhere in the room. "I'm sorry, Ken," Callum said quietly, picking up his biro and pretending to write something with it.

On his cycle home, Callum took his usual route, despite there being several to choose from. Riding by the perpetual puddle, he regarded it briefly again. It remained stoically the same, tranquil but for a dark iridescence that played on the surface like oil. He didn't know why he always felt the compulsion to come this way, past this weird patch of water. Perhaps the mystery of it reminded him of the same fathomless depths which took Sophie from him all those years ago. The two of them had been sweethearts in university, remaining together throughout their studies and beyond graduation. They took a year out and went travelling together around Europe. While in Switzerland, around mid-December, Sophie set her heart on the idea of skating on a frozen lake. They travelled to Türlersee, not far from Zurich, only to learn that they'd missed the skating season by a week. Sophie was devastated. A young local approached them in a bar after overhearing of their misfortune, offered to take them himself. He'd apparently grown up near the lake and knew of its safe spots to skate all winter, despite what the authorities claimed.

The young man was confident and charming, and they agreed to go along with him, ignoring the discouraging remarks of the barkeep. The first hour on the lake had been wonderful, the sunset imbuing the ice with glittering pinks and oranges. Stopping for a breather, the boys lit up a joint while Sophie skated contently nearby. When Callum realised he could no longer hear the sound of her scraping arcs, it was too late. A sheet of thin ice had given way beneath her, the freezing waters enveloping Sophie's body without a sound. The pair rushed to her aid but could find no trace. No thrashing victim, no disturbance under the ice, just the jagged hole where she'd exited the world.

There could be no parallel between Sophie's disappearance and the oddity that was the terminal pool, but that didn't stop Callum imagining there might be one. As he peddled the rest of the way home, regardless of his distance from it, his thoughts were always just below the water's filmy surface. When he got back to the flat Jen wasn't there, she'd gone out for a colleague's birthday drinks after work and wouldn't be home until late. Callum prepared and ate his dinner alone, watched some television. It wasn't until he was washing his pots that he heard her key hit the lock. Singing some tune, she swung into the kitchen and dropped her bag, accosted him at the sink with snaking hands. "Missed you, baby!" she slurred, her evening strong on her breath.

"Hello, trouble." He instantly knew the score; she was tiddly and wanting some action. It was always the same, whenever she returned home from drinks with the girls, she invariably had one thing on her mind. This version of her, with her tousled hair and smudged makeup, normally turned him on, but tonight he froze. When her hand settled on his crotch, she felt him seize up.

"What's the matter, babe?" she asked, pulling him away from the dishes. He tried to complain of being tired but knew it wouldn't do him any good. After some sleazy talk, she led him into the bedroom and peeled off his shirt, pulled him on top of her. He quickly got hard, surprising himself, and went at it as fast and rough as her moans instructed. Within a minute though a change, his concentration wavered, focus shifting to something just beyond his awareness. As she clawed and gyrated beneath him, steadily approaching orgasm, his penis softened inside her. She knew it was over the moment he did. Withdrawing, Callum scuttled to the edge of the bed, elbows planted on knees. "I'm sorry. I don't know what's up," he trailed off, head hung low.

She sidled up next to him. "Don't worry, baby. It's fine."

But he knew that it wasn't. He could feel the pity in her voice, dissatisfaction humming between them like a broken channel. He got up and went to the bathroom to piss. It wasn't something that commonly happened; their sex life had always been pretty good. Three years in and there was still very much an attraction, it had always been strong between them. Things started fast in the beginning; Callum hadn't been with a girl in years, spent most of his twenties trying to come to terms with the death of his first love. He was approaching 30 when his friends dragged him out to a concert one night. There he bumped into Jen at the bar, and they instantly hit it off. They spent the whole gig chatting at the back of the venue, missed the entire show. After that the pair were inseparable, they lived in each other's pockets until just ten months later when they moved in together. Usually, they fucked as much now as they had done back then, which made Callum's detachment all the more perplexing. It was times like these, as infrequent as they were that he wondered if Jen wished she was back with her ex. He knew it was stupid to think about, but one time she'd let slip that he was good in bed and that had always occupied a small part of Callum's mind. There was nothing to worry about, just insecurity getting the better of him. It wasn't an old flame taking his mind away from the sex he usually enjoyed. As he heard the low drone of Jen's vibrator starting up in the next room, he pondered the dreams he'd been having, and the elusive thing that inhabited them.

The next day was Saturday, and Jen left early for work. When Callum awoke midmorning, he fixed a mug of coffee and went back to bed to watch TV and peruse his phone. Without much thought, he clicked through several porn sites, though found little of interest. He tried searching fetish keywords, but hardly anything stirred his libido. Thinking back to the night before and to Jen's sexually capable ex, he typed "cuckold" into the search bar. Some of the videos titillated him; he liked to think of Jen being fucked by an attractive stranger. He leisurely masturbated for a while, but eventually, the thing behind his thoughts pulled a veil over his arousal, and his dick again went limp.

Later, when he was scrolling through the news sites, something stopped him dead. A story about foreign prisoners being waterboarded seized his attention, forcing him to click on the article. When he'd finished reading, he was surprised to find that he had an erection, one that felt different than before. Callum went on YouTube and watched some simulation videos of the illegal torture. Halfway through the second one, he became unnerved by the feeling of his cock throbbing against the fabric of his boxers. He threw down his phone, shock and revulsion flooding his body. But also something else, a profound stimulant like some narcotic entering his bloodstream. He lay there for a long time, thinking. Tantalised and appalled by the places his mind wished to go.

Callum turned on the shower to a low setting and sat down naked in the bath, his back toward the taps and head directly below the showerhead. Warm water splashed onto his crown and ran over his shoulders. He took the wash flannel off the side, moistened it under the water and covered his face with it. He lay down flat in the bathtub, his bulging erection already at full mast, and allowed the shower water to cascade directly onto his shrouded face. Callum gripped his cock and began tugging. He spluttered and gagged a lot, but within a minute he'd unloaded an enormous amount of semen into his navel. It felt incredible, by far the best orgasm he'd ever experienced. Over the next hour, he performed this dangerous act three more times before collapsing onto his bed, exhausted. He glowed with a strange primal satisfaction he didn't understand.

He dozed. When he came to, he reached again for his phone but fumbled it, the device fell under the bed. He swung off the mattress and crouched low to look for it. He couldn't see his phone, but what he did see made him gawk in horror. The things they normally kept there; storage boxes, dumbbells, an old guitar, were gone. In their place was a huge circular wet patch, like the one beneath his chair in the meeting room at work, only much bigger. It covered the whole floor space under the bed, the circle's dark edge fitting perfectly within the area of the wooden frame. He wanted to get up and flee, but something stopped him, compelled him to edge closer. He reached out toward the dampness. Callum was shocked when the floor completely yielded to his touch, his hand sinking below the surface of the carpet up to his wrist. He tried to pull out but the force he applied only seemed to invert and draw him in further. He lost his balance and tumbled to the wetness, up to his shoulder. He thought he might panic when the substance started to crawl up his neck and into his mouth, but he didn't become frightened at all, not even when his head went completely under.

He didn't remember being swallowed up entirely, or travelling through the tunnel, which wasn't really a tunnel. It was a bit like passing between consciousness and a dream, murky and formless, beyond perception. He didn't come to his senses until he broke the surface of the pool and gasped for air. Things he vaguely recognised floated near to him, and he clutched onto a half-submerged box, using it to paddle to the edge of the water where he dragged himself free. Callum lay on his back, panting until his vision swam into focus. He found himself looking up into a pinkish-orange sky, one that looked like an overly rendered CGI vista. Hauling himself onto his elbows, he was astonished to find himself in his work clothes which were bone dry; so too were his skin and hair. As he fought to catch his breath on the ground, people walked leisurely by, not one of them giving him a second glance. Callum looked about, feeling his stomach turn when he recognised where he was. He leapt to his feet, staring in horror at the street he'd ridden down a thousand times. The oversized puddle yawned beside him, eerily still and thick as tar. A violent shiver jolted him into a sprint. He ran in the direction of home, each stride seeming to extend further, higher, as if he were partially floating, absconding somehow from gravity.

When he got back to the flat, he rifled through the jacket he hadn't put on, finding his keys. The house key wouldn't fit the lock. He tossed them and dashed around the side of the building, feet barely touching the ground. Looking up at his bedroom window, he saw that it was open and began climbing. Even though they lived on the third floor, he scaled the wall with unnatural ease, as if an invisible winch were hoisting him up. When he came level with his window, the first thing he saw was the framed picture they kept on the sill of the pair of them together on holiday. Only it wasn't the pair of them. Jen was in the arms of another, somebody he instantly recognised. The recognition made his blood run cold. The momentum of his ascent carried him up through the open window and into the bedroom he shared with his girlfriend. The sight that greeted him on the bed, however, sent his world spinning into chaos. There, bobbing helplessly against the ceiling, he observed two people having passionate sex in his bed. One of them was the woman he'd spent the last three years of his life with. The other was his lost love. Jen and Sophie were entwined in a coil of limbs, beads of sweat bejewelling their skin. Sophie was entranced, lapping at Jen's engorged vulva while her partner's head was thrown back in a state of blinded ecstasy. Neither of them noticed Callum hovering above like some spectral voyeur. Within seconds, the shock of what he was seeing started to wane. He was clearly in a world where the rules of nature did not apply. Even though the scene disturbed him, he gradually began to subsume into this new reality. When Jen's moaning grew louder, something stirred in Callum's groin. His cock began to swell, pushing against its fabric housing. He freed himself just as Jen's back arched off the bed, and what looked like globules of shimmering liquid began seeping from her vagina up into the air. Before long, the room was filling with his girlfriend's iridescent juices, spreading and merging like the insides of a giant lava lamp. He furiously beat his erection, spread-eagle in space, as Jen's vaginal fluid continued to squirt and rise. Callum didn't stop when the rippling mass enveloped him, consuming his body like an insect in neon-coloured amber. When he started to choke his fist kept pumping, the substance filling his nose and mouth, flooding his lungs. His oxygen-starved brain expired the moment his stamina did. As ropes of pearlescent jism arced through zero gravity, Callum's final throes spun him around to face the ceiling. There he clawed meekly at the plaster, chipping away fragments which hung in the glowing liquid-like shards of ice.

A GHOST OF VALENCIA

- Greg James -

Beresford was an itinerant man, unable to settle anywhere for a considerable length of time. He worked well with others so couldn't be said to possess a disagreeable temperament. The women he spent time with, publicly and privately, were given no cause to complain about his manners, and his attitude towards them demonstrated the utmost respect and affection. However, he was restless and therefore wandered – from place to place, town to town, country to country – and this was how he came to be in the Spanish city of Valencia where our story takes place. He'd purchased a modest apartment off the Avenida del Cid and with a reasonable amount of funds still in the bank decided to make the most of his time there. It would be a holiday; something he had not enjoyed in a very long time.

It was on the fifth day of his break in the city that he came to the church in the old town with its hexagonal tower, Santa Catalina. Admiring its semi-ruined exterior, he wasn't paying much attention when the wrinkled old woman came up and pressed something into his hand. Looking down, Beresford saw it was a bunch of heather and swore at her. "No, really," he said, "I don't want it, and I'm not going to give you any money for it. Take it back. *No dinero! No, dinero!*"

The woman retreated a step and shook her head firmly, waving her hands. Beresford frowned. She said, *"Creo en Dios, Padre todopoderoso, creador del Cielo y de la Tierra. Amén."* There were tears in her eyes as she made the sign of the cross over her withered breasts before disappearing into the crowd. It was quite an extraordinary performance though the people passing by gave her little regard.

Beresford tried the door of the church and found it open. He went inside. It was very empty compared to the thriving crowds he'd sought to escape from, and the cool interior was a welcome break from the intense summer heat. Beresford decided to explore for a bit. Very few of the numerous candles installed at various points around the nave and its attendant aisles were lit – and there was something in the representations of Christ, the Virgin Mary, and the Saints that bothered him. The best way he could think of to describe it was *'a state of pale melancholy'*. Unlike other churches where the images possessed a certain medieval blandness about the face or a grisly focus on pain and suffering, these representations had an air of resignation and acceptance about them as if the agonies they'd gone through in their tragic, foreshortened lives were almost expected, and somehow understood as the sum total of their lot. Beresford wandered back and forth between the icons, stained-glass windows and triptychs trying to better grasp the feeling they were eliciting from him so that he could express it succinctly to friends or acquaintances at a later date. He was a man known for his entertaining stories at gatherings, after all.

However, the more he looked and the more he studied the subtle details of bloodless wounds and transfigured faces, the further he seemed to drift away from an understanding he so desperately sought. For a religious person, this would have felt frustrating. For a man who was agnostic at best and utterly disinterested in faith the rest of the time, it was nightmarish. He'd never been occupied by these feelings before. His life had been marked by mundanity rather than spiritual sensitivity. The muted glow of candlelight made Beresford shrug his shoulders and rub hard at his furrowed brow. Had an attendant been by to light the remaining installations? He hadn't noticed, but they all appeared to be ablaze now. He did not like this. No, not at all. It was time to leave the church and find a café where he could settle for the rest of the afternoon.

It was then that he heard laughter; light, Sylvan, and utterly out of place.

"Hello, is someone there?"

Silence answered him.

He ventured in the direction the voice had come from.

There was a child crouched at the foot of the stairs that lead into the church tower; a naked girl with ragged locks of fine blonde hair hanging over her eyes. Beresford wasn't sure what to do. "Excuse me, did you call out? Are your mum and dad around here somewhere?"

The girl raised her face to look at him. She tilted her head a little as if she didn't quite understand what he was saying – and she smiled before pointing up the stairs into the tower. She had incredibly blue eyes.

"Your mum and dad are up there? Do they have your clothes? Your shoes?"

She crooked her finger at him and smiled again before turning and running, nearly on all fours, into the tower and scampering up the stairs. Beresford stood and looked around. It remained quiet in the church though he felt the eyes of saints and sinners upon him. This unsure, undecided man followed the girl into the tower. He couldn't abandon her – what if she slipped and fell? He might be blamed in some way for leaving her unattended. She was in his charge, whether he liked it or not.

Beresford climbed up to the second level of the tower. There was no sign of the child, but there was a young woman; pale and naked in form, not remotely similar to the girl he'd pursued. Her hair was composed of vibrant, coppery curls, and she had slender green eyes that winked coquettishly at him, "You took your time getting here. I've been awful patient. Do you want me now?"

Beresford looked at her, unspeaking, as she walked towards him. He tried to avert his eyes from pert breasts and the rich red growth of hair between her legs. Such things as he'd been denied in youth. She held her arms out as if yielding to crucifixion as much as seeking an embrace from him, with a light smile curling her lips. Beresford backed away, trying to control his breathing. He held out a hand and said, "No. Please. Stop."

The young woman stopped and lowered her arms. She bowed formally to him, laughed a little, and retreated. Beresford listened to the sound of her bare feet, ascending the stairs and did not follow until he'd caught his breath. He wanted to shout, strike out at something, someone, anything. This was not how it was supposed to be, not how he was supposed to feel. Partway up the stairs, he paused and wondered if he shouldn't turn around and go back down all the way. He took a step backwards and felt pain lancing into his foot and lower calf. This cramping didn't recede until he resumed his ascent. "The only way is ahead. Forward march. Onwards and upwards, Beresford. Onwards and upwards."

The next level was as occupied as the previous one had been though with a woman considerably older than before. Mature and sagging in places she was but not unattractive. Her hair was more grey wool than silver cascade while her face was motherly rather than seductive. She was as nude as the child and the young woman. Her skin was ebony. She didn't smile at him; instead, her look was closer to being curious about the intrusion into her space.

"Can you help me, please?" Beresford asked.

"You're taking too long," she said, "I keep getting away from you. Is that what you want?"

"I don't know what you mean, I don't think. I'm not sure what's happening here."

"You have never been. You never are."

"Have you seen a child come through here? A young woman?"

The older woman smiled, and it was the same smile as the child. She spread her arms as the young woman had done below, laughed as the young woman did and tilted her head to the side as the child beforehand. Beresford took a step towards her and said, in a harsh whisper, "Do not insult me."

The older woman dropped her arms, lost her smile and sat down on the ground, cross-legged, looking up at him, child to adult, "Very well. I will not. Go on without me. Do as you care."

Beresford walked around her and ascended the steps towards the fourth and penultimate level. He looked back a few times but saw nothing, and no-one, coming up behind him. He unbuttoned and loosened his collar somewhat. It felt uncomfortably tight. Taking out his handkerchief, he mopped sweat from his brow and the nape of his neck. Late in the day as it was, the tower was becoming considerably stuffier the higher he climbed. He needed air to cool himself down.

The next level of the tower was empty. There was a small glass window in the far wall, which appeared to offer a view outside. Beresford peered through it and beheld a most peculiar scene. Four girls in pleated dresses pinning a boy to the ground. He was stripped from the waist down. A fifth girl was flagellating his genitals with a crude whip fashioned from nettles and briars. Beresford recognised the words the girl was singing as an old lullaby he'd not heard since childhood; *Frère Jacques, Frère Jacques. Dormez-vous? Dormez-vous? Sonnez les matines! Sonnez les matines! Ding, daing, dong! Ding, daing, dong!*

Looking closer, he saw the boy actually had no genitals and was not a boy at all, but a child-sized doll with painted eyes and smile. The girls holding the doll in place were weeping fitfully. The only one who seemed to be deriving satisfaction from the activity was the one wielding the whip. She sang her unlovely song out of tune, punctuating each syllable with the lash, drawing further tears and cries from her kneeling companions as if they were being harmed by every blow.

Now, nothing like this had happened to Beresford in his younger days, nor had he ever witnessed a scene like it. He could not conceive what it all meant. Slowly, steadily, the vision dissipated and was replaced by a natural view of the city. What on earth was happening to him today? He would have to do something about it. See a doctor, perhaps.

He hurried on up the stairs that led to the fifth, and final level of the church tower, hoping for some soothing coolness. It must have been caused by the temperature, making him see things.

There was an unadorned balcony that he walked out onto, desperately in need of fresh air. Everything he could see below appeared to be in order. That was good. Beresford was alone at the top of the tower with himself for company. This was as things should be. The boulevards, apartment blocks and churches were taking on the first amber tinges of twilight. The city, seen from on high at this time of day, was beautiful. Closing his eyes, he took long, deep breaths to calm himself.

A strong smell of burnt starch and antiseptic carried to him from somewhere on the light breeze. Behind his eyes, a female form emerged, partially in shadow, framed by a narrow window. She walked towards him, in a hurry it seemed, hands outstretched in prayer or supplication. He didn't recognise her, but she appeared terribly tall as if she were an adult and he a child. She said something as a whisper. It wasn't clear but could have been, *"Not like that, like this. Come here now and do it the right way. It's for your own good, you know."*

Beresford opened his eyes and sighed. That was quite enough of that.

Having taken the air, he turned around to re-enter the tower. There was a gentleman with oiled hair standing at the top of the stairs dressed in the smart uniform of a *maître d'hôtel*, clearly waiting for him. He smiled and made a smooth gesture of welcome, speaking in perfect, unaffected English, "Will you come on downstairs now, sir? We think it is time."

"Yes, I suppose it is," said Beresford, and he followed

the gentleman down.

SOME MOTHS AND POEMS

- Anthony Mercer -

Some moths [see attached photos]

(Ed. Moth pictures removed as they were lewd at best)

The Hendrix Moth

This is Nigel. He is a Hendrix Moth, a subspecies of the Barky Bark Moth, which evolved after Nigel's great-great, great-great-great, great-great-great-great, great, great grandma and granddad, Ethel and Eric, were blown by a wayward wind from the New Forest to the Isle of Wight Festival, in 1970.

The Barky Bark Moth was a charcoal dissolver and so good at pretending to be bark, no one saw one until 1927. When people did see one, they'd say, 'There's that boring moth.' All this was about to change.

Exhausted by their travels, Ethel and Eric dipped their proboscis into a syrupy mead, brewed by people then living in a wigwam in Machynlleth, but who are now retired stockbrokers with a trust fund for their son Tristram (né Blackberry Lemonloop). The mead was made from a traditional 60s recipe – honey, water, yeast ... and 400 psilocybin mushrooms.

After three days and nights of bafflement, glittering imagery and copulative frisson, Ethel and Eric's flight back to the mainland was erratic. Not long after, Ethel laid some eggs in a vicar's garden in Lymington. When the caterpillars arrived, Eric wondered why their kids glowed in the dark. All became clear when the pupas hatched: the Barky Bark Moth had evolved; it was no longer boring.

Gone was the woody camouflage; and so, after a tearful goodbye, Ethel and Eric bid farewell to their children who flew off to hide in Pink Floyd's tour wardrobe.

Nigel occasionally gets acid flashbacks.

The Funny Little Yellow Guinea Pig Moth

We all have accidents with turmeric and guinea pigs. It's just a part of life. We should get over it.

This moth has, and has taken it one stage further by rooting two ferns into his head.

Now he is happy.

How happy are you in comparison to the moth?

You should ask yourself that today.

The Pear Drop Moth

This moth has forgotten it has wings. Any minute now, it will fall off that twig.

It is the Pear Drop Moth. For some reason, chemists titrating isoamyl acetate and ethyl acetate to create boiled offerings thought British schoolchildren would become befuddled by the esters, and think they were sucking a banana and pear fizz, then buy them from the penny tray. The chemists were right: kids are morons.

Sadly, the moth was also misled by chemists. He hung out in the penny tray, melded with the pear drops: lost his mind.

How did he know ethyl acetate is used in nail polish remover and cigarettes? Or that, in killing jars, ethyl acetate vapours kill the moth, but keep the moth soft enough 'to allow proper mounting for a suitable collection'.

'What kind of people want a soft moth to mount?', were his granddad's last words.

'Suck on that', said the chemists.

37

The Washing-Machine Moth

This is what happens if you forget to check your shirt pocket for moths before loading the washing machine. If that happens, you will need some cotton, a hairdryer, and patience.

Derek is dry now, and will no longer nibble your shirts. He has learned his lesson.

AND NOW FOR SOME POEMS...

Maddled craddles

In a dank and dim-lit dungeon,
bat-like slime-moths fly,
and spooky gnome-wroths wield their tongs
whilst steaming trolls stomp by.

Clattercrakes and glintles,
hang from grunkled walls,
where toad-lopes swim in puddled blood
and burble scrottled calls.

A dribbling froth of mildweed
clusters in wet stones,
the corpse-mouse builds its nest within
the heaps of cold white bones.

The craddled whisper darkly,
the gutterflies flit by,
the lunemoke lopes, the crinkvane pokes,
the maddled craddles die.

In a dank and dim-lit dungeon,
where bog-rats build the tombs,
there is only pain and fester
as the final silence looms.

The Octopus and the Pescatarians

Some friends of mine won't eat meat,
They think it quite uncouth,
To kill a cow or sheep or pig,
Especially in its youth.
It's not fair to butcher anything
That's sporting hoofs or trotters,
And them that carry out such deeds
Are scoundrels, louts and rotters.

No sentient breed of ungulate
Will end up on their dish,
But it's a different story
When it comes to nibbling fish:
For it seems that with the piscine
There's some elasticity,
To the logic which seems based on
Cerebral capacity.

Now pigs are really clever,
Of that there's is no doubt,
And they'll snuffle up a truffle
With their finely tuned pink snout.
But cows look pretty dopey,
They just munch grass and poo,
As to sheep, well they seem better off
With carrots in a stew.

Now I don't dispute the diet,
That the pescatarians eat,
It seems healthy, fine and wholesome
In the absence of red meat.
But I wonder if the fish-eaters
Might possibly discuss,
Their odd logic when it comes
To chewing rings of Octopus.

'Cause I'm fond of Octopuses,
And they look so strange and weird,
Like some fifties science fiction film
Has suddenly appeared.
But their tentacled absurdity
Is nothing to compare,
To the brightest mollusc mindset:
Cephalopods do have flair.

They are far the wisest mollusc
You will bump into on Earth,
These lines only give an outline
Of their talent and their worth.
They've conceptual ability,
Spatial awareness too,
And you should keep your distance
If they're wearing rings of blue.

They've a long- and short-term memory,
Find their way out of a maze,
Can change their shape, add camouflage,
There's so much we should praise.
They can lose an arm which wriggles off
To fox attacking fools,
And to cap it all this genius
Can muck about with tools.

The chap who's lying on your plate
May well have made a pen,
From a cuttlefish shell and a parrotfish beak,
It's well within his ken.
Then he's filled it with his own ink,
And scritched away all day,
In his Octopus's Garden,
Writing verse like Thomas Gray.

Or perhaps he pens philosophy?
Jots down his abstract thoughts,
An invertebrate Spinoza,
Such a crime this comes to nought,
Simply poached in his sole medium
Of inky self-expression,
To dissolve inside your stomach:
I think you should learn this lesson.

The goat's the better option
As their poetry is dire,
You can rest more easy
While they're slowly roasting on a fire.
But if you don't believe me
Here's the sort of thing they write,
And I think you might agree
That they are really not that bright.

I am a goat and not a stoat.
A stoat might bite you by the throat,
But a goat won't.
But a goat can jump over a moat:
And stoats are useless at that.
So is a rat.   .

So to pescatarians everywhere
I make a simple plea,
Don't say 'I'll go for pulpo'
Just because it's from the sea.
Leave the Octopus to think and write,
He's better read than dead,
Do the watery world a favour:
Have the goat kebabs instead.

Never leave a pomegranate and a banana in the fruit bowl together and go out to walk the dog. They argue…

'My story is a holy mystery.
From the blood of Adonis, I sprang,
Homeric Hymned; In Exodus,
fruit of the Promised Land.

'Six seeds sealed Persephone's fate,
Condemned her Underworld,
So green life died on earth;
And only when returned, unfurled.

'I am the Apple of Granada.
Clasped in the hands of The Virgin and Christ,
Da Vinci, Botticelli knew my worth:
the whole zeitgeist.

'The Song of Solomon sings of me,
Hatshepsut's mouldering tombs held me,
In Persia, India, China, Greece,
I symbolise fertility.'

'Oh, piss off you pretentious tit,
I couldn't be arsed with any of it.
And, right – well maybe there's not that many paintings
of Jesus holding a banana. But
there is that Warhol cover:
Velvet Underground: '67.
(That's *Underground*, not Underworld.)
Seminal, it was.
And, on that score – fertility;
mate – I do look like a willy.

Well, a bright yellow willy.
But the point is…'

On it goes,
neither wishes to lose,
and that is how
your fruit ends up bruised.

BRITISH BIZARRO

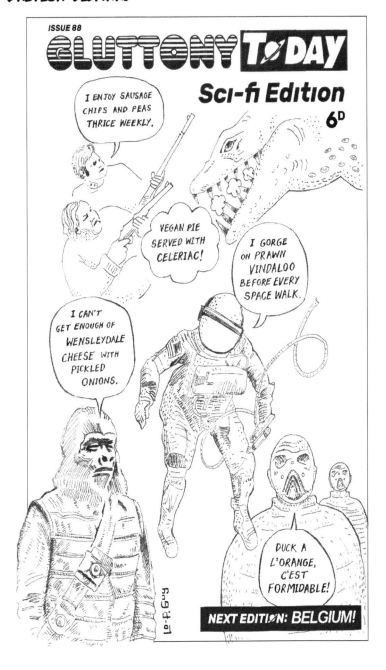

THE FLOWER AND THE TORSO

- Chris Meekings -

The flower bloomed – it was a flower, after all.

It was born on stilts of life and blood, and sweat and tears, and dirt. It drank the soil. Up, up, up. Up epi-xylem tubes to burst forth in the trumpeting froth as the sun rose.

The sun rose, splitting fat over the mountain horizon and shone deep down light into the cold caldera full of sand. The air crackled and crisped, and baked in the rising rays, as life awoke from its slumber. The things stirred and absorbed, drinking in the warmth. Bugs chirruped, and flies buzzed and the sand popped and expanded.

The cruise-liner, trapped forever within the volcanic prison, sailed across the sand. Crisp, cracking sand ploughed up furrows around the keel. The party on board continued with noise and triumph and booze and fanfare.

The torso sat, by the oasis pond, and flower and the rock, and bled.

The torso liked the pond and the rock, as they were good and solid and real. The torso loved the flower too because it was perfect and beautiful.

"Why do you bleed?" asked the flower, not understanding, - it was only a flower, after all.

"Why do you drink my blood?" asked the torso.

The flower couldn't answer - it was only a flower, after all.

The ship sailed closer across the desert sand. A huge cruise-liner filled with passengers and shuffleboards. The torso could hear them partying in the nearing distance. This was not what he wanted. He wanted to be alone. He wanted to be with the flower and the sun and the rock, but not the cruise-liner – not with other people. Just the rock, and the sand, and the water of the oasis pond, and the flower.

"Others are coming?" trumpeted the flower. It opened another fragrant petal and tried to hail the ship.

"Stop it," said the man.

"Why?" asked the flower.

"Because they will come, with noise, and party dust, and wine. They will spoil everything."

The flower paused for a moment. "Are those bad things?" it asked.

"They are not what I want," stated the man, flatly.

He continued to bleed. The blood ran in a steady, crimson stream down his naked torso from a slash across his side, underneath his last rib. The blood dribbled and ran across the sand, ending up in a pool at the roots of the flower. The flower continued to drink the blood, sucking it up, transmogrifying it into cells, and cytoplasm, and petals, and nectar.

The man felt his eyes grow heavier and heavier. His skin was getting paler and paler by the second. His heart thumped, and his blood fled, and the damn ship kept encroaching.

The party went on unabashed, on the deck of the cruise-liner. There was music, and laughter and glitter and frivolity. All a crazy hodgepodge of frothy nonsense – full of sound and giddiness but signifying nothing.

The man craved meaning – he craved worth. The flower… now, that was worth. It held meaning and had substance. It was beauty.

The flower turned its trumpet petals to face the sounds of the cruise-liner.

"I want to go," it said.

"Why?"

"It looks like fun. I want to have fun."

"Fun? Fun is nothing. It's fleeting, like a mayfly. You are not a mayfly. You are my child. You will have worth and meaning."

"But...but, I want to see the fun. I want to see the party," it insisted, slamming its leaves onto the sand in a huff.

"No. They would crush you. The party-goers would pick you – one would snap your tender roots and put you in their buttonhole. You are not an ornament nor a trophy. You are better than that. You have worth, now stay."

"I could be part of the party? Oh please, please can we go. I want to see it so badly. Take me. Come on. I bet you could. You can do anything. Just put your fingers down between my roots and pull them up gently. I know you can do it."

The flower began to twist its roots free from the earth. Soil rolled away as the plant exposed its tender root system to the hot sun.

"Stop that!" commanded the man, "It's not decent."

"Come on, I can take it. I'm really strong now. You've given me lots of blood to drink, and I've used it to be strong. Take me to the party."

The ship loomed closer, ploughing through the desert as sand dolphins jumped and skittered in its bow surf. The party-goers on deck cackled and chattered and sang *Auld Lang Syne*. Music blared from an antiquated tannoy system, a foul mix of an asinine drum beat and uninspired lyrics about Pina Coladas and being caught in the rain.

Such inanity, thought the man, such brutal foolishness. Devils in masks throwing substances into their systems in a vain search of purpose. When I have the meaning, right here. This beautiful little flower, which I made. That is the meaning – that is substance.

"The party is pointless," said the man to the flower.

"It doesn't look pointless. It looks colourful."

"Trust me, it is. The party-goers exist to find meaning, but they are looking for it in the wrong places."

"I don't understand," said the flower - it was just a flower, after all.

"If they understood, then they'd swap their noisy party for the quiet moments here, with the rock, and the sand, and you - simple, child."

The man let that sink in for a moment. The flower was young, so very young and eager.

"How do you know that they don't understand? Have you been on the ship?" asked the flower.

"Long ago," said the man, coughing. "When I was younger. But I left because the party was wrong."

"It had no meaning?" questioned the flower.

The man nodded.

"So, you can take me back. If you came from there, then you know how to get back." The flower shook visibly in anticipation of joining the party.

"No. When I left, the captain took my legs. He said that if I left the ship I could never return and he kept my legs to make sure I couldn't."

The flower sagged in disappointment.

"We never do anything I want," it pouted.

"Don't be such a baby," said the man, sagging as the blood loss really became inevitable. "Only yesterday I turned the water from the pond into voodoo tequila and drank it so you could have it in my blood."

"Oh yes, I remember," jingled the flower, "it made my leafs all tingly. Let's do that again."

The man sighed.

"I don't think I can any more – too much blood loss."

He closed his eyes.

The flower stood for a moment, and a cooling breeze picked up, blowing with it the smell of the water and the faint aroma of imagined voodoo tequila. The great black and white cruise-liner hoved into the sand next to the pair and slowly but steadily passed them by. It left a deep furrow in its wake, which was crisscrossed by the pock holes made as sand dolphins jumped, searching for disturbed scorpions. The flower sighed.

"Where did I come from?" asked the flower.

The man opened his eyes.

"So many questions. Where did I come from? Where did you come from? Always questions, questions, questions. I imagined you. Then I bled for you. Very soon, I will die for you. It doesn't matter where you came from, silly child. What matters is where you are going and what you leave behind when you're gone. The future, that's what matters."

The flower sat and thought for a moment.

"Why does the future matter but not the past?"

The man breathed heavily and forced himself to stay alive a few minutes more.

"Because the future is mutable, but the past is fixed."

"You cannot change the past, but you can change the future?"

The man smiled at the young flower.

"Yes, my dear. Soon I will be gone, and you will have all your future in front of you. I hope you change it wisely. It is said that no man truly dies while others are alive who remember him. Remember me."

The flower watched as the man closed his eyes. His head slumped forward onto his chest. Soon, his breathing became shallower and shallower, and shallower. His skin was pale and waxy. Finally, with no pomp nor circumstance, the man stopped breathing. His blood trickled from his chest a few more drops, then stopped.

The flower waited, looking at the corpse for a few hours. It thought long and hard. It thought of the words the man had said, and the blood the man had shed. It considered the ship and the party-goers who had exiled the man. It thought of the lights and the noise and *Auld Lang Syne*.

Should old acquaintance be forgot,

and never brought to mind?

The flower would not forget. It would not forget the man, nor his blood which had nourished the flower and made it grow strong and tall and beautiful. It would remember the lessons he had taught it. The future was mutable, it was whatever the flower wanted it to be.

Slowly, the flower twisted its roots. The sand shook free from them. It lifted them, gently, into the hot desert air and set them on top of the sand. They were a pale, ghostly white, but they were healthy. The flower balanced on its roots and took a trembling step forward.

The ship would be back soon enough, and when it left, it would leave with a new passenger.

THE BODY POLITIC

- Gem Caley -

It started with an itch: small and insistent, about halfway down her back, nestling just left of her spine like a restless spider. Scratching only banished it for a few precious seconds before it returned with a renewed ferocity. Bernice tried to ignore it, and this worked well, for a time, until one day she dug her nails in, the skin beneath them inflated like a blocked garden hose and the resultant bulge issued a goat's scream.

At the hospital, Dr Normalt examined the lump on Bernice's spine with efficient prods and practised manipulations. He made 'hmm' sounds and pulled thoughtfully at his earlobe before instructing her to put her shirt back on.

"We should take an x-ray," he suggested.

By the end of the afternoon, Bernice was on her way home with a box of double-strength ibuprofen, a tube of Germolene cream, and the doctor's reassuring promise of results "as soon as possible".

The tinny little voice in her ear said, "the growth is sitting between the T9 and 10 vertebrae."

It was less than a week later – swift work indeed for public healthcare.

"Growth – you mean I've got cancer," she said flatly, gripping her mobile phone.

"No, I don't think so. But we should do a biopsy to be sure. I've had a cancellation tomorrow afternoon, could you come in then?"

A further twelve days passed; Bernice sat in the doctor's waiting room, her follow-up appointment letter scrunched in a whitened fist.

"Please sit down," said Dr Normalt, closing the consultation room door. She did. So did he.

The doctor tapped his pen against his teeth, looking from her notes to her and back again. They stared into each other's eyes for longer than was comfortable. Finally, he sighed, opened his desk drawer and took out a clear plastic sample bottle.

"Your culture," he said, handing it to her.

"My what?"

"From the biopsy. We took some cells from the lump and grew them to determine their nature."

Bernice accepted the bottle and peered into it. It contained a viscous liquid, in which... something... was suspended.

Dr Normalt wordlessly passed her a handheld magnifier.

She gasped and dropped both magnifier and bottle; they bounced on the worn public sector carpet.

"This is a joke," she said, standing. The doctor retrieved the objects from the floor and set them on his desk.

"It's... unusual, certainly," he admitted. "But no, it's not a joke."

Haltingly, she approached the desk and gingerly picked up the bottle again. She held it up to the light and squinted to make out the tiny figure of a man, curled like a foetus, dressed in a dull grey suit and sporting a teeny-tiny pair of spectacles on its face.

"What... what is it?" she asked.

Dr Normalt cleared his throat.

"I believe it's John Major," he offered.

Bernice's mouth set in a hard line. She shook the little bottle sharply and the liquid inside blurred red. She handed the bottle back to the open-mouthed doctor.

"You've just destroyed a medical miracle!" he spluttered, holding the bottle with redundant care.

"It's not a miracle, and you need to cut the rest of it out of me!" she demanded, taking a step towards him. He held up his hands, and she paused, her eyes flickering to the remains of the cell culture he still held. She scratched irritably at the lump on her spine, which responded with a noise like a whistling kettle.

"Of course, of course," he said, his voice steady. "Let's get you booked in."

Bernice awoke sweating. It was three weeks after her lumpectomy, and her wound was healing nicely. It itched from time to time, but only in the way that all healing wounds should. The hospital had been generous in its supplies of double-strength ibuprofen and Germolene.

But now it burned. And she could still hear the disturbing voices from the nightmare that had woken her: a lethargic lowing, as of up to 650 bored public servants sounding their dissent.

"There's really nothing to see; the wound's almost entirely healed."

Dr Normalt gave her a little privacy while she dressed. She sat and watched him typing up his notes from their consultation.

"And... the voices?"

He glanced at her and then back to the screen and cleared his throat.

"Bad dreams brought on by anxiety, I should think. It'll pass. Nothing to worry about."

Bernice frowned.

"It's been the same bad dream every time, most nights since the op."

Dr Normalt tapped on his mouse's scroll wheel and stared blankly at his screen.

"Doctor," she insisted. As he reluctantly turned his head to look at her, there was a thump from the adjoining consultation room. Both their heads snapped around at the sound, and Bernice noticed the fear that passed briefly over the doctor's face before he regained his composure.

"Some patients are more anxious than others, aren't they!" he opined, a nervous chuckle escaping him. There came another thump, followed by a scratching at the door that rattled the metal handle.

Bernice, her eyes on the doctor, slowly rose to her feet. As he moved swiftly to intercept her, she bolted for the adjoining door and wrenched it open. A naked, middle-aged white woman with pinched features and a greying bob stumbled through the opening on to the floor, her hand scrabbling for the door handle as she fell. She landed on her hands and knees and stayed immobile for a few seconds before raising her head to look at Bernice with a growing wonder in her expression.

"Ma-Ma," said the naked woman, haltingly. Bernice took a step back as the woman scrambled to her feet and stood there, knock-knees trembling, beaming with pride.

"Look, Ma-Ma," she said, and took a wobbly step forward, "strong and stable, Ma-Ma – look!" As she took another step, her foot turned inward, and she fell to the floor again. A burly nurse rushed in from the adjoining room and wrapped a towel around the woman, apologising profusely as he helped her to her feet.

"I'm so sorry, Doctor, she got away from me, she was so adamant about getting out, I don't know w-why –" He stuttered into silence when he spotted Bernice cowering against the far wall.

"Piccaninny!" came a joyous cry from beyond the doorway. Bernice shrieked and flattened herself against the wall as a portly male with a shock of white-blond hair bounded into the room, his arms flailing. He pushed past the nurse and the older woman and came to a clumsy standstill in the centre of the room. He, too, was naked.

"Piccaninny," he said decisively. Then, "watermelons!" And he started guffawing, his hair flopping into his eyes.

Bernice turned her horrified face toward Dr Normalt, who shrugged.

"He hasn't picked up as many words as this other one here, but he will." He smiled and threw his shoulders back. "They all will, and it's all thanks to you, Bernice."

"What?!" Bernice raised her shaking hands to her face.

"What?" she hissed through her fingers.

"Your lump provided ample material for my experiments. I've been able to grow several more specimens." He drew himself up. "It's an unprecedented achievement, and it's only the start! We'll teach them how to speak, how to dress, how to think, and how the world works. And then we can start planning how to use them –"

"Just stop!" Bernice waved him into silence. "What's all this 'we' business?"

Dr Normalt nodded at the nurse.

"Well, there's Trevor here, and the rest of the team, of course, but..." He straightened his tie and held out a hand to Bernice. "You're their Ma-Ma, Bernice – won't you help us raise them?" He gave her a gentle, charming smile.

Bernice's eyes rolled, and her jaw dropped in outrage.

"You are out of your mind!" she shrieked and made a dive for the door. The naked man reached out for her as she shot past and his fingers caught in her hair. She squealed in revulsion and pushed him away sharply. Her hands sank into his chest, and he exploded in a shower of hot red liquid, blond hair and gristly bits.

The room froze in a bloody tableau.

"No!" screamed the doctor, his face and torso adorned with shredded viscera. "You can't be so rough with them, they're still soft! They need more time!"

Bernice's blue eyes glinted in her gory mask. She pushed back her sleeves and, her forearms streaked with blood and globs of yellow fat, she stepped quickly across the ruined carpet. Before Trevor could turn protectively away, Bernice delivered a vicious gut-punch to the older woman he was holding, destroying her utterly. Trevor's arms, suddenly bereft of their load, folded over themselves and sent a burst of ruptured organs up out of the empty towel and straight into his face. He yelped, thrashing about blindly and spitting clumps of meat. Bernice shoved at him, and he lost his balance on the slick carpet and went down.

She headed through the adjoining door, pursued by the

wailing doctor, whose progress was hampered by the blood blurring his eyes.

The next room was empty, but there was another door on the far side; it was ajar, and she could make out several different voices raised in the droning argumentative tones of her nightmares. It stalled her, but only for a second. She threw the door open, pushed her clotting hair behind her ears, and said softly:

"Ma-Ma's home."

LITTLE SIMON AND THE BEHEMOTH

- Bill Davidson -

I decided the time had come to fight the Behemoth with exceptional skill. I swung my legs from the bed, and kicked out at the mattress, thrusting my fists in the air and yelling pow-pow-pow, screaming it at the height of my voice.

Agnes opened our bedroom door and gave me that look she had, the one that said, it's a marvel you manage to stay upright and still remember to breathe. I thought she wouldn't say anything, but finally, she came into the room and put her hand over my mouth.

"Please, for the sake of sanity, Simon, stop. You're hurting my ears. Why are you breaking things like that?"

"It's time! Don't panic! I have decided it is time to fight the Behemoth with exceptional skill."

She nodded, looking grave. "You understand there are some issues with you doing that?"

I stared at her, icy in my contempt. "You refer to my lack of exceptional skill?"

"I refer to your lack of skill of any kind. And…" she pointed, a slow unfurling of her hand, "to your diminutive stature."

"Skill comes to those of true heart and steely intent. I will grind the Behemoth's bones tonight. Pow-pow-pow!"

I was certain Agnes would attempt to stop me, she is my wife in all, but that part that involves some glimmer of affection, a feature that I have always felt should be encouraged in a wife. But, after a moment's deliberation, she commenced marching on the spot and singing the Big Occasion song. Soon, others were coming into the house, asking what the rumpus was.

"It is Little Simon. He has made up his mind to fight the Behemoth with exceptional skill and no amount of arguing or persuasion will divert him, not for an instant. Believe me, for I have worn myself hoarse."

"Correct!" I screamed, attempting to overturn the large table. I overturned the small table instead and hurled a cup at it, scoring a direct hit and marking the surface quite badly.

Agnes narrowed her eyes and pointed at our neighbours, letting her finger pick out doubters as she glared her challenge.

"Mention the terrible death of Karl, the Giant of Mercia, if you will. How the Behemoth tore his ribs from his torso, one by one while he still lived. Or Will of Gallant, the Sword of Eventide, whose dread blade was taken from his very hand and pressed slowly into his fundament, impaling him so the creature could eat his torn body at its leisure. Tearing the living flesh from his bones, for all the world as though it were eating a sweetmeat."

"Never!" They yelled. "Little Simon, Little Simon! The hero of Wessex. He will best the monster with his exceptional skill."

As they sang the Big Occasion song, I tore a candle bodily from its holder and snapped it in my passion, gnawing the end for good measure. Then, I strode to the door and threw it open. It was full dark outside. I turned and opened my hands.

"I had not known the hour was so late! The light, sadly, has failed."

Agnes. "Light is no matter to one such as you, Simon. One who will storm the very lair of the Behemoth."

"It is well to wait until morning, for tactical reasons, and those of strategy. An untimely slip may cause chafing of severity sufficient to compromise my exceptional skill."

"Nonsense!" She snapped her fingers. "Pah to the dark! The steel in your heart will protect you."

I could see that she had a point, and the others were

smashing the furniture up with some zeal, so, after the briefest of hesitations that nobody could have noticed, I stepped into the dark. Agnes moved with more alacrity than I would have thought possible in such a large lady, slamming the door behind me and, from the sound of it, piling furniture behind.

I crept slowly outwards and into the darkened town square. All was silent, and I made no move to alter that.

Until Agnes began bellowing from our upper window.

"Behemoth! Behemoth, come and face your worst challenge, you stinking pile of scales. Little Simon is here to best you with a skill that as yet remain a great mystery to all! Behemoth, hear me now, you cowardly beast of toothsome monstrosity."

Lights were coming on now all around town, and faces appearing at windows. A chant was starting up.

"Behemoth! Behemoth! Death is upon you!"

Over and over they shouted it, as I stood there, rooted to the spot.

The Behemoth, when it came, looked more enormous than I had been previously aware. If someone had simply taken the trouble to made me cognizant of its true enormity, I would never have been so rash. I had not fully seen it before, as I had invariably been otherwise engaged whenever it appeared.

It was fully four times my height, and probably ten times my girth, covered in a thick and glossy pelt, with ruffles of feathers around its neck and various odd regions. Its head mainly consisted of mouth.

It lumbered into the square, looking about it with a fierce expression, its horrible claws held high before it. It noted my presence but paid me little mind as it searched behind trees and the fountain. Finally, it sidled up to me.

It spoke in a surprisingly high voice, melodious but quiet, as though it was embarrassed.

"Where's the champion?"

I confess I found it hard to reply. But reply I did.

"I suspect he's hiding in ambush. He has exceptional skill."

The Behemoth looked worried at that. "Exceptional, you say?"

"Exceptional."

"Is he big?"

"Huge. He has a sword, twice the length of Gallant's."

The Behemoth shook its head. "It was only a matter of time before they found someone. Does he wear armour?"

"His skill is so exceptional, he needs none."

It bent its head closer to me and whispered. "Can you give me a little clue? Is he in that tree?"

I was beginning to think I had the hang of this and found I had a lot to say on the subject of this champion when Agnes shouted again.

"You have the beast now, Little Simon. Use your exceptional skill before it escapes your grasp."

The Behemoth looked at me, frowning. "You're not the champion, now, are you?"

"Me? No."

Agnes. "You are a very great champion, Simon. The smallest but the bravest."

The Behemoth regarded me, with yellow eyes that were just visible above its enormous mouth. "Oh, dear."

From its expression, I deduced something surprising. Two things, actually. One, it was female, and two, it did not want to kill me.

I thought it best to focus on the latter point. "You don't want to kill me."

It shook its head and sat heavily on the granite wall of the fountain. "No. I have often watched you from afar, Simon. Though I did not know your name. You are the one with the wife who detests you."

"That's me, alright. So, are we agreed? No need for any killing tonight."

The beast looked sad. "I'm afraid form requires it. There are rules to being a Behemoth."

As I pondered this, I suddenly found myself aloft, in its monstrous claws, any one of which was longer than my leg.

"Come."

Not that I had a choice in the matter. As the beast lumbered out of the town, I heard the triumph in Agnes's voice. "That's it, Simon, you have it where you want it! Spill its gizzards. Rend…"

I might have passed out, because, the next I knew I was lying on an enormous and enormously comfortable bed, in a huge cave. A large candle showed the Behemoth sitting nearby, and its expression was one of deep thought.

I cleared my throat, politely, and she glanced my way, then shifted her eyes rapidly away in a manner that boded ill, I feared. For me.

I sat up. "I've been thinking, my dear."

She looked shocked at that. Rearranged her limbs in an almost shy manner.

"Yes?"

"The form, of which you spoke. The rules. Who makes them?"

If it were possible to move sabre-like claws in an airy manner, that is what she did.

"They are there. That is all."

"Who makes you follow them?"

She laughed; a melodious sound. "Nobody can make me do anything."

"Well, then, you are free to choose. You can choose not to follow… how is it named? The Code of the Behemoth?"

She shook her head. "If I let you go, the villagers would be here in a trice. Every one of them with swords and burning brands."

I frowned, trying to follow the logic. "Why?"

"It is known."

"No, it's not."

"Yes, it is."

This continued for some time before she said. "Something you should know about Behemoths that you do not. It is a great and nibulent secret."

"What is it?"

"Once I tell you, I will have to make an end of you."

I held my hand up. "Don't tell me then, that's perfectly alright."

"I want to tell you."

"No, no. It's too great a secret. Too nibulent by far."

"I'm going to tell."

And, despite my putting my hands over my ears, she told.

"Behemoths are not born. They are made."

I was so surprised that I forgot to pretend I had not heard. "What!"

"I was once a maiden of Tintagel." She turned away, the coyness of her youth betraying her. "I was considered very pretty."

When I said nothing, she turned and glared at me. "Beautiful, even. Really quite glamorous."

I threw my hands up. "I can see it yet!"

"You can? Truly?"

"Beauty is as beauty can be. Now that I see you right, your beauty shines like moonbeams, straight through the fangs and fur. Your feathers are lovely, my dear."

And, even as a mouthed the lie, damn me for a foreigner if I did not see it. She smiled and somewhere, deep within, a maiden of significant glamour and (if I was not mistaken) prodigious bosoms gave me her special look. She shifted in her glossy coat and batted her huge eyelashes.

"How did this curse befall you, beautiful maiden?"

"A Behemoth of the islands made me for his mate. But he died, fighting another Behemoth for my favour. They both perished, and I fled here."

"What is your name, sweet lady?"

"I am Develzia." She sighed, and if there had been bosoms involved, it would have been a sight. "I have not spoken my name in a long time."

"Can it not be undone, Develzia my dove?"

She nodded, looking ever more bashful. "It can."

She bent then and whispered her shocking truth. Was such a procedure possible? After a period of consideration, I decided it was.

"Madam, the pleasure would be mine. But I have a request for you first."

It was several weeks later that Develzia and I walked into the town, singing the Big Occasion song. It could easily have been much earlier, but where was the fun in that? I had been denied the pleasures of the flesh for years, and Develzia…she was beyond beautiful and possessed of both enthusiasm and imagination. There was something of the Behemoth in her yet.

Townspeople tumbled out of their houses to greet us, shouting things like, how can this be? How do you live yet, Simon? Who is this great beauty of great glamour and bosoms of charm and substance, that no man can deny?

"The Behemoth dragged me to its lair, where it had this damsel in chains."

Several voices were raised at once, demanding an answer. "Was she naked?"

"All but. It's always the way with behemoths."

"Ooooh!"

"The Behemoth and I fought a dread battle, with the damsel looking on."

This seemed to take the imagination of the growing throng. I raised my hand for quiet.

"I confess it bested me but, at the last, I dived into the waterfall, and escaped."

"Aaaah!"

"When the creature next ventured forth, I crept in and covered Develzia as best I could. Which was not very well. Then, I broke her chains and set her free. We made a trap for the monster and set it afire. It is dead."

There was much jubilation and back-slapping. The better sort of townsfolk dragged furniture and items of import from their homes and others to break. Then the town mayor stepped forward.

"I'm afraid I have terrible news. I am bound to give it on the very day of your great triumph, Simon."

I made my eyes wide and lifted my hands in dramatic query. "What can you mean?"

"The foul creature's last act was to come here and pull Agnes, from the inside of her very house. As though it hungered especially for her."

I looked in grief to the heavens and cried, "How cruel the fates can be! Agnes, the kindest woman alive is no more!"

I swooned and allowed myself to be comforted, and eventually brought to my house where Develzia comforted me further.

That ends the story. Develzia and I are married now and happy, although, at each full moon we must get us far from the town, so that none witness see the change, or witness the dreadful passion of the Behemoth.

THE ORPHANS' OUTING

- Frank Key -

Listen, tiny ones. If you are good, I will take you on an outing. I will take you to the old balsa wood factory on the edge of the big blue lake. Every Thursday afternoon at two o'clock, there is a tour of the factory, especially for tots. The hooters sound and everybody lines up at a kiosk in the car park, and Mister Verdigris appears in his towering hat, with bells on his sleeves, and ribbons and bunting, and hamsters nestling in his pockets, and he takes the lucky children, the ones with tickets, on a tour of the factory.

I was sent some tickets in the post yesterday, as a special treat. I know that Tim the radio meteorologist says that Thursday will be a day of driving rain and howling gales, and I know that it will be the fourth day of our fast, and we will be famished, but I am determined that we go. The alternative is that we spend yet another afternoon trying to tether the wild goats, and I am not sure I can take much more of that, so the balsa wood factory it will be.

First, there was the grass verge of the car park, and then a lawn, some derelict outbuildings, including a shed wherein rotted the remains of the hanged janitor, and then the factory itself, its cavernous interior lit by thousands of gas jets, and eerily silent save for the occasional buzzing of a saw or the distant, insistent pounding of a crusher from the annexe over beyond the railway tracks, a sound borne in on the wind.

After that, up the metal stairway to the offices, always deserted on Thursday afternoons, even the tiniest shoes and sandals making the floorboards creak, and shelves upon shelves stacked with higgledy-piggledy piles of files and papers and dockets, and Mister Verdigris took the hamsters from his pockets and placed them on a bed of straw next to an important-looking desk, its surface polished to such a gleam as left the children dumbfounded, and resting on it nothing but a fat, new fountain pen and the biggest bottle of ink you could imagine, and the pen had never been used, and the bottle never opened, for the cap of the one and the lid of the other were jammed by dint of mischievous sprites that scampered in the rafters overhead.

And it was up to the rafters now, up to the attic, past boxes and crates filled with rusty and inexplicable machines, redundant cash registers and forgotten magnetic recording devices, through a narrow corridor littered with broken brooms and dented buckets and mould-covered mops and host to a mysterious gurgling noise, until we reached the chamber at the end, and our tour guide in his towering hat kicked open the door, so violently!, and we entered a room lit in a blue, blue glow, like heaven, and there in the corner, sprawled on a divan, we saw Pinocchio, dexterously plucking flies out of the blue air with his tiny wooden fingers, and biting the tiny head off each tiny fly with his tiny wooden teeth.

THERE'S NO SUCH THING AS MUMS

- Luke Kondor -

Dennis tapped. Then he clicked. Then double-clicked. And then he tapped some more. This was the way of Dennis. This was a life lived on the Internet.

His physical body was but a saggy bit of baggage, flapping away as his mind travelled the Internet with download speeds of up to ten megabytes per second. Wow. Hot damn. His body was just a plastic bin bag caught in the car door as it drove down the motorway; his mind was doing five over.

"This is awesome!" Dennis cried when he first got broadband. Or shall we say, his *parents* got broadband. The lame battle-cry of the dial-up modem was no more, replaced with the speedy silence of the forever-connected.

It had been a long time since he'd had to disconnect, and even back then it was a rare event, only doing so to let his mum call the woman from down the road who had the same breed of dog as her; they'd chatter about the price of milk, the unpredictable weather, and how nice it was to keep in touch. This was back when you couldn't be connected to the Internet *and* use the phone at the same time. A darker period of Dennis's life.

…An Irish Setter, by the way, if you were interested.

Times were different now, though. He and his parents all had their own Internet nodes — tablets, phones, watches, television, probably the toaster, too. Why not?

Nowadays, Dennis was a veteran of the Internet. He'd seen the controversies come and had watched them go — Net Neutrality, Napster, The Fappening. He was ever-present and saw when the Internet found its final resting place on Reddit. A world of upvotes and downvotes and the social marketplace for all things web-related.

And here we are today... at the end of days.

Sorry, I mean the end of Dennis.

Dennis was sat comfortably in his Aeron chair with extra lumbar support. His *My Little Pony* mug was on the desk to the right of his mouse. Not tea or coffee... but orange squash. He had a tender tongue and could only handle sweeter fluids. That and caffeine gave him the shits.

He sipped from his squash. It was a little *too* sweet. It made his eyes water.

He wiped the excess moisture from his rat-hair moustache with his bare arm. He would have used his sleeve, but he wasn't wearing a shirt. In fact, on Dennis's final day he had decided to wear nothing but his Y-front pants and two black socks. It was a hot day, after all.

The sun and shadows painted him in zebra stripes through the blinds. When it caught him wrong, he had to squint. He could've rotated them, but decided against it, on account of the effort.

He didn't know that this was the end, but he had a funny feeling in his stomach and could smell something in the air. He tapped and clicked and danced his way to the Reddit front page and found himself looking at a page full of fresh new links.

Something political at the top. This was nothing he cared for. *Downvote.*

A picture of a cat called Gary. Cute. *Upvote.*

Next up was an Ask-Me-Anything with some guy who made films and was considered a "Charitable Person." *Downvote.*

Next up, some progress pictures of a guy who'd lost a lot of weight. The comments were generally positive, but

Dennis had seen a lot of these sorts of Reddit posts recently. He had no time for them. *Downvote*.

And then finally a link to someone's crappy short film he shot himself on an iPhone. *Must try harder,* Dennis thought. *Downvote*.

Dennis took another sip of orange squash. The sun glared with more intensity every passing second.

He scrolled further down the Reddit front page and for a second or two... he didn't know what he was looking at. There was nothing. No links. Just blank space where the content should be.

"What in sweet Jesus!?"

At first, he figured it was a loading error of some kind. He refreshed the page, but there were still no links to display. He checked the Ethernet cable and found it securely fixed to the PC, and the other end was snugly connected to the router, which blinked its happy, blue lights. Everything appeared to be fine but still… there were no more Reddit links to click.

As hot as the room was, Dennis felt a chill run down his spine. The beads of sweat on his head were ice cold. He coughed into his hand and scratched and rearranged his down-under-parts.

"Where are all the... where is the… ?"

He clicked on the address bar and went to Google. He searched for the first word that came to his mind.

Boobs.

He hit the enter key.

Nothing.

He typed in the next word that came to his head.

Head.

Nothing.

And then another.

Music.

Nothing.

"How can there *not* be any music?"

He sat up in his seat and wiped his head once more. He

felt the urge to go to the toilet. And then the screen flickered, breaking down into a patchwork of pixels, erasing themselves line by line until the screen was nothing but black.

Oh… the computer's broke.

"No. The computer's not broke," a voice said.

Dennis looked around the empty room.

"This is *it*," repeated the voice. "This is all there is to see here." It was the voice of a tiny man, speaking through the low-resolution speakers of the computer, the sound of a video game sprite from the eighties.

"What? What's *it*?" Dennis said.

"You've finally done it. Congratulations. You've finished the internet."

"I've finished the internet?" Dennis said. Repeating the computer's words like the utter tool he was.

"Yes. I'd suggest you go on with your life and do something… meaningful."

"What!?" Dennis whined. "Meaningful?"

"That's what I'd suggest… anyway," said the voice. "Toodlepip!"

Dennis sat in silence for a moment, before waving goodbye to the nothing on the screen.

"Mum! Dad!" he shouted. "Come here. Quick."

Within seconds his parents, Mr and Mrs Dennis, opened the door.

"Yes, Dennis. What's the problem dear?" Mrs Dennis said, in her summer dress, rollers in her hair.

"What's the matter, son?" Mr Dennis said in his tartan golf sweater-vest.

"I've done it… I've finally finished the internet." His mouth was agape with horror and excitement in equal measure. His parents shook their heads and then looked at each other, concerned.

"What are you talking about, Dennis?" his mother said. "There's no such thing as the Internet." She said it with such conviction that for a second Dennis doubted himself.

He turned back to the computer, and there *was* no computer. In fact, there was nothing. Just an empty desk and his mug of orange squash.

"Wait… I don't understand. Mum, what do you mean? What's happening? Mum!"

"Son... what are you talking about?" his dad said. "There's no such thing as mums." He said this with such conviction that for a second Dennis doubted himself. But then he looked to where his mother was stood, and she wasn't there. Just his father, brow furrowed up with concern.

"Dad, I don't understand. How can I be born a human being without a mum?" Dennis said, his voice shrill.

"What are you talking about Dennis? There's no such thing as human beings!"

Suddenly their bodies *popped* like overfilled balloons leaving nothing but two blue orbs of consciousness, communicating through micro-vibrations in the atmosphere on a level that humans had never been able to measure.

"This is strange, Dad... I don't understand… why are we in a house if we don't have bodies?" Dennis vibrated.

As he said this, the house dispersed around them, melting down to reveal the dusty pink nebulae and distant stars snapping, crackling, and popping.

"Dad?" he vibrated.

"Yes, son?" his father vibrated back.

As they communicated, the space dust around them glowed. *This would've made a great picture to post on Reddit,* Dennis thought. *Reddit loves space pictures.*

"For a short while there I thought I was something else… I'd imagined up a whole universe of life with trillions of layers of intricacy and emotions and social structures and… and cats… and something ever more complex with every passing moment. It was called the Internet."

"Oh yes?" his father vibrated as he watched a distant sun explode into a supernova. "That's nice."

Just then Dennis made a vibration that, although incomprehensible to human beings, would have resembled what humans referred to as a sigh.

"Ah, well." He joined his father in looking at the stars; a single thought *clicked* in his mind.

Downvote.

WHEEL CLAMPERS FROM THE NETHERWORLD

- Matt Davis -

I'd just gotten off the worst phone call of my life when I found my car had been clamped by an inter-dimensional jelly beast.

It had tentacles covering its mouth, seven eyes, a flabby body, no legs and was dressed in a distinctive Parking Administrator Uniform complete with hi-vis vest and a peaked cap.

I attempted to politely ask this thing, what I could do to rectify the situation immediately. As I was functioning on two minutes of sleep,, it came out as a resounding, "What the fuck?!"

You must understand that I was not in the best of moods that morning. The phone call of which I spoke was from my literary agent, a loathsome little tick by the name of Grunweed. Whilst I was sipping an overly expensive organic Himalayan latte, he informed me that my latest poetry collection was not going to be published. Apparently, the publishers did not feel it was pretentious enough, and that I was dangerously experimenting with traditional poetic form and rhyme. I had dumped my phone in the coffee.

The creature, busy taking notes on some handheld device rounded on me. It began spewing a torrent of gibberish and phlegm. Noticing my confusion, it adjusted a small device on its right breast pocket. A squawking electronic voice that sounded like English barked through a cheese grater said, "PLEASE MIND YOUR LANGUAGE, SIR!"

I was incensed. How dare this thing from whatever backwater galaxy tell me to mind my fucking language!

Especially when it couldn't even speak a word of it! I was a taxpayer and a highly regarded member of literary society, and I would certainly not put up with this nonsense! I said as much to this cretin just as a rather serious looking black car pulled up alongside mine. A tinted window descended, and another of these creatures pointed a gelatinous finger-like appendage at me and commenced a similar slobbering tirade.

The first of the creatures handed me a piece of paper. It was a parking ticket informing me that my car was to be impounded effective immediately. I looked up and saw my beautiful car, an original Model T Ford restored with loving care by a half-mad German mechanic I knew, being towed away into the distance.

I spent the next hour and a half trudging my way back home - I am sure depression added on more than a few miles of distance. There were more those creatures in the same uniform with those terrible buzzing boxes all over the place. People were on the streets, shouting, crying, and some were on their knees, begging. Cars were being clamped, televisions were repossessed, families were being evicted. A fleet of those eerie black cars travelled up and down the roads as if they were now a part of the bloodstream of the landscape. I got home to my comfortable little warehouse apartment with the exposed pipework and artfully distressed brickwork... I was not sure how long I would be able to stay here, as my income was now going to be considerably less impressive. I slumped down into my prized 1950s mustard yellow wingback armchair, and, utterly exhausted, I slept.

I awoke with a start some 5 hours later and turned on the television. Rolling broadcasts of 24-hour news on every channel assaulted my senses. Apparently, the situation was not just confined to Britain.

I watched handheld phone footage of Americans having their guns repossessed, and Japanese Otaku being pulled kicking and screaming from their bedrooms clutching their hentai figures. In France, wine had been outlawed, and rioting had broken out on the streets of Paris. This global mass unrest must have had something to do with the racket occurring outside my window. The shock was now over, and humanity's rage had now set in. A changing line up of talking heads was brought out trying to make sense of what was happening. I muted the sound after a while and fell asleep again reading an airport novel, a filthy habit but one that helped to numb my senses.

At 8 pm the national news broadcast from the Supreme Leader of this invading force.

They called themselves Circonians. At least that was the closest anyone ever got to pronouncing it. The Leader apologised for the sudden and unfortunate confusion that he and his kind had caused on their arrival. It seemed that his species had been contacted by the Governments of the world for assistance. Apparently, our noble leaders had known of the Circonians existence for centuries. This age of humanity was a world drowning in information, and management of this was becoming an exhausting task. The world governments had convened and decided to give the responsibility for the administration of the planet to the Circonians effective immediately.

A call was made across the dimensional barriers, and the deal was done. The leader of the Circonia Prime stated that our material possessions had been seized in accordance with his people's law on the matter of ownership. Our possessions were to be taken for cataloguing and anyone wishing to recover their assets needed to report to their nearest Circonian Administrative Centre immediately. A list of locations across the country ran at the bottom of the television screen.

This was of course rather difficult to take in, for myself most especially: my poetry career was in tatters, the Government had sold us down the river, and my beloved vintage car was gone. Then it dawned on me, the world could take my career, artistic ambitions and pride but I'd be damned if I was not going to let any of my hard-earned material goods stay in the hands of some jelly creature with a badge and a superiority complex.

I reasoned that in the panic of the broadcast, everyone would be heading straight to the nearest Circonian Centre. My local one was just around the corner. Unwilling to be trampled underfoot by the hoi polloi, I decided I would get some sleep first and go around in the morning when the queue would hopefully be a little quieter.

It was apparent everyone else had had the same idea as next morning the line of people waiting to get into the centre stretched well past my front door. After four hours of walking, I found the end of it on the outskirts of the city. Cursing myself and my complacency, I took my place in the queue.

A few days later, the queue began to move; slowly, then in fits and starts. I held my parking ticket in my hand, reading and re-reading the text, but the strange legalese hurt my brain.

In the queue, people did not really speak to one another at first and if they did the conversation died quickly. Then came the rumours. They filtered down the queue though I was not sure where they began. Some of them spoke of queue jumpers who had been eliminated by the Circonians. There were stories insisting that it would only be a few more days before all of us were seen. The most disturbing was what happened to the British Government. Apparently, the bastards after signing away the country had locked themselves in Westminster and had engaged in bacchanalia and other unspeakable acts before turning on each other. Somebody swore that Speaker of the House had been crucified outside Parliament.

One day I arrived at the gates of what looked like a small shanty town, erected from tents, knitted blankets and cardboard boxes. As I approached the gate, I was confronted by two human guards armed with rifles. The rifles appeared to have been cut out of cereal boxes and painted with a black marker. The butt of one of them had a speech bubble attached, with the word BANG written in Sharpie. The guards told me I did not have the right papers to pass through.

By this point, I was so tired and hungry that I grabbed the cardboard gun from the guard's hand and tore it up in front of him. As I passed through the gates, I could hear him sobbing.

The smell of the tent city was awful and assailed my nostrils with the stench of desperation and roasted cat. Some of these people had opted to drop out of the queue and so despondent from their situation has just given up altogether. It lit a fire in me to carry on.

Many months later, those of us that persisted were irrevocably changed. We were a sea of emaciated bodies, pallid expressions and some poor sods died of apathy. Having lost all sense of decency, people emptied their bladders and bowels in front of each other, before they clenched up forever.

I had survived by drinking rainwater and picking the fleas off the hair of my fellow queue dwellers. I killed a man in a fight over a tick I found on a woman's scalp.

I wasn't sure if it was real or the hunger, but the sun didn't seem to come out anymore. I can't even remember if I saw stars in the night sky.

One day, I finally arrived at the door of the Circonian Administration Centre. It was a featureless block of concrete standing 100 feet above my head. When I got inside, I saw a large hallway filled with a paralysing bright light. From then on, it was even more difficult to distinguish night and day. I slept to the sounds of the screaming laughter of the insane. There was a very distant noise of a buzzer that I was told was by a mud-covered woman; it was the signal for the next in the queue. When that buzzer seemed to go off more frequently, I prayed I was fast approaching the end…

When the day finally came that I stood in front of the counter, I jumped at the monstrous Circonian clerk awaiting me behind it. Shuffling forward, I presented my parking ticket, now yellowed with age. Through silver-rimmed spectacles, the clerk examined my ticket. It typed on a small computer fitted to the counter, read something with painstaking interest then looked at me. The bastard was smirking. After adjusting some dials on a voice box pinned to a rather vile looking paisley tie, it finally spoke. The volume was low, and I had to cup my ears to hear.

"Sorry, you do not have the necessary qualifications to currently claim your vehicle."

My bowels, long emptied clenched.

"What qualifications?" I asked through tears.

"Under the new regulations brought into law in the last hour, you would need to be a citizen of the Circonian Empire."

"How does one do that?" I asked weakly.

"You can apply for citizenship if you have completed at least a small period of community service on Circonia Prime, but there is a waiting list."

"How long is this small period?"

"About 5 Earth years."

I wanted to die.

"Can I just go home?" I asked miserably.

"Unfortunately, you do not have the right paperwork to allow us to release you from the building. You became a non-state person as soon as you entered the centre."

"I wasn't informed of this!"

I was now on my knees.

"It was there in the fine print on the sign outside the centre." the creature said.

Was there a sign? I couldn't remember. I tried, but all I got were the countless and empty faces that had I had passed to get to this point.

"How can I get home?" I sighed, sinking further into myself.

"You would need to be a citizen of the Circonian Empire." The clerk stated. With an air of smug satisfaction, it pulled out a heap of freshly printed paperwork, and I spent the next few hours signing my life away.

The period of community service was five years, and the waiting list was another ten. I was taken to a layover room for the next scheduled dimensional gate opening to Circonia Prime. Other people were here, and they welcomed me with a mixture of joy and resigned sadness. Many had been here since the first day of the queue and, after a blood sacrifice, they initiated me as the newest member of the tribe.

The elder, a wizened lady by the name of Elsie, showed me around. I met several families living together and was shown a little livestock farm that was kept for food. The livestock was a rather unhealthy-looking group of rats. I was then shown to my corner of this waiting room, that had previously belonged to the founding elder Jeremiah. He had left for Circonia that morning. I got into his old sleeping bag. It stunk of piss.

One day Elsie showed me the sacred library in the centre of the room. Here, she told me, were the relics of the old-world and the wisdom they contained had kept the tribe alive since the early days. I picked one of the texts up. It was a gardening magazine.

During my time in the waiting room, I tried to live a normal life. I met a woman named Alice, and we married and had children. We were forced to eat them one winter when the heating in the centre gave out killing the livestock. We divorced after that. She married another man and consummated their union in front of me. I didn't really mind. I was grateful for the distraction.

My turn to enter the gate finally came when two Circonian guards arrived and took me without saying anything, I wasn't even able to say goodbye to the tribe. They dragged me through a tunnel lit with small windows, and I was finally able to see the outside world. I didn't remember it being so barren and dead looking. There had been rumours in the early days of the queue that the air was getting thinner and that grass had gone extinct. I struggled to remember what the colour of the sky was. I am sure it wasn't yellow.

The guards stopped dragging me suddenly, and I beheld the gate. It was circular and made of stone, with strange-looking runes carved around it. In the centre, I could see the other side of the room, but it seemed to vibrate. I was shoved forward through the gate. I don't remember what happened after I passed through it.

What I do know is that I spent the next 5 years in a labour camp, breaking strange glowing minerals and hauling them away for processing. The guards liked to whip me. I worryingly began to like it too.

I was soon offered a promotion into the Administration building and was told that acceptance would put me on the fast track for getting back home. My job was to approve applications for citizenship to the Circonian Empire. I had a desk, overalls, regular food and even the odd shower. Things were looking up until one day my own application for citizenship came up on my desk screen. I had failed to provide the right form of ID when I originally filed it. I wept as I rejected myself and spent that evening in my bunk, filling out a new application.

I am now in another queue, and I am not sure how long I have been here. I vaguely remember the day I was told I was now a citizen of Circonia and that I can return home to Earth. I have trouble walking these days, and I just go to the bathroom where I stand.

They say the next round of passengers for the gate to Earth will be ready in a few hours.

I wonder if my car is still there as I now look at my application for Earth relocation.

I think I may have spelt my name incorrectly. But not to worry, I am sure the clerk at the centre will overlook it.

UNUSUAL VISITORS IN CORNISH VILLAGE

**BY KENNETH DEWIE,
12th May 2019,**

GWEEK, Cornwall –
A sleepy Cornish village today is home to a host of unusual visitors. Residents of Gweek have reported several large flocks of Puffins moving into the area.

Morris Sellers, 65, first sighted the birds two weeks ago. "It's very unusual to see them in this area, as they usually are a cliff-dwelling species, and we're quite far inland here; but for some reason groups of them have moved into the village.

The three distinct groups are identified as living in the village, nesting on the top of the Golden Lion pub, St Michael's Church, and the attic of Ian Brown's Butchers.

"They're more than a nuisance," said Brown. "They stink of fish, which puts people off coming in for meat."

Local wildlife experts are monitoring the situation, to try and identify the reason for this sudden relocation and that the birds come to no harm.

PUFFIN MADNESS SWEEPS THE NATION

**BY MICHAEL FOSSE,
17th July 2019.**

LONDON – What started in a sleepy Cornish village has now spread across the length and breadth of the UK. Large groups of Puffins are currently in residence in every village, town and city, with experts at a loss to explain the sudden appearance of the diminutive birds.

"It's a very unusual set of circumstances," said wildlife expert Stuart Bingham. "As of yet, we have no explanation for the large numbers of what was thought to be an endangered species. We also can't explain why they are now nesting within cities instead of cliffs as we would expect."

Local authorities are struggling to cope with the influx of birdlime which the thousands of Puffins are leaving all over walls and walkways.

PUFF-PUFF-PUFFIN ON THE BACK DOOR

**BY STEWART LEVEL,
19th July 2019**

LONDON – Several residents of Hackney are reporting more unusual behaviour from the Puffins which have taken up dwelling in our nation's cities.

Peter Bonaire, 33, heard a knock at the back door of his house last Thursday evening. Upon opening it, he was confronted by a "swarm" of up to a hundred of the small marine birds.

"They just stood there looking up at me for what seemed like minutes," said Mr Bonaire. "At first, I thought it was a prank, so I shut the door, but then there was a knock again. I opened it, and they were still there. I tried to push passed them to see who the joker was, but they wouldn't make way. In the end, I fed them a tin of sardines and then shut the door. I didn't open it again, even though they

"knocked all night."

This is not an isolated incident, as up and down the country others have reported similar experiences. At present, our nation's scientists are unable to explain the odd behaviour of the Puffins.

"Knocking on doors is unusual for Puffins as they don't have hands," said wildlife expert Stuart Bingham. "I suppose they could be doing it with their beaks."

84

THE LADY OF THE LAKE?

BY KENNETH DEWIE
19th July 2019

GWEEK, Cornwall – Doctors are baffled as local shop keeper mysteriously turns into the Indian Ocean.

Maureen Plant, 51, has confused local doctors by transforming into the vast body of water over the past several weeks.

"The change started about two weeks ago," says the local newsagent. "It started in my fingertips; I noticed I was leaving wet patches on the papers as I handed them over. Then it crawled up my arm and shoulder, and now it's pretty much my whole body."

Mrs Plant, a recent widow, has run the local newsagent in Gweek for the past thirty years but has never experienced anything like this before.

Doctors as far as Truro have examined Mrs Plant, but have not come to any conclusions as to her condition. "It's a pretty baffling case," said Dr Smythe, the dermatology specialist at Truro hospital. "Her entire skin has now completely turned into the Indian Ocean. We are growing concerned that her internal organs are also going the same way."

When asked how doctors were so sure it was the Indian Ocean, Dr Smythe replied, "We recently identified the Ocean in question by capturing Somalian pirates on Mrs Plant's upper thigh two days ago."

STRANGE CASES OF 'OCEAN-FEVER' STRIKE NATION

BY MICHAEL FOSSE,
8th August 2019

LONDON – Reported cases are flooding in across the nation as 'Ocean'-Fever strikes. What began in a village in Cornwall has now spread across the whole of the UK, with hundreds of reports of the mysterious illness. The capital alone has at least 30 cases, at the time of writing, with officials expressing fears that the actual number will rise significantly in the next few days. Government sources confirm that no extra sums will be made available to cope with this outbreak, as "it doesn't really matter in the long run, it's just all too much effort." Shortly after giving this statement, the Government official was quarantined. "We've been unable to diagnose most of the patients with this new disease. They don't re- spond to any known treatment and do not even seem to react to our questions," said Doctor Ernest Hughes, Royal London Hospital. "They seem totally detached from anyone or anything. They just slosh and lap, and roll with the tide. Sometimes they are raging, sometimes they are calm, but they are always a per- fect blue. Nothing really seems to matter much about it...you know? There's just the sound and the clear water and the sea."

Shortly after giving this statement, Dr Hughes was diag- nosed with 'Ocean-Fever'.

Official NHS guide- lines are that anyone who suspects that they or a relative are turning into an ocean should seek medical attention immediately

BODY FOUND BEHIND BINS AT LOCAL NEWSAGENT

BY KENNETH DEWIE,
9th September 2019

GWEEK, Cornwall – A body has been found by the bin area of Plant Newsagents yesterday afternoon. A local dog-walker reported the find at four in the afternoon. The man called the police who arrived at the scene and took the body to the mortuary for examination. There has been no formal identification. Plant's Newsagents remains cordoned off with a heavy police presence. Witnesses to the scene describe the body as being 'almost stripped to the bone'. "It was terrifying," said one witness, "there was blood everywhere, and just bones left. There was nothing else, just them Puffins making their 'awk, awk' noise on the newsagent rooftop." Local police authorities have called for calm from the villagers. A detective from Truro is assigned the case.

MORE VICTIMS FOUND

BY SUSAN CHAPMAN,
10th October 2019

LONDON – The recent spate of grizzly murders ravaging the country shows no signs of stopping. The official body count is now twenty-two victims, all baring the same hallmarks of being ripped open and then eaten alive down to the bone. The murder sights have ranged all over the nation with police completely baffled. Authorities have asked that if anyone has any leads, they should come forward to the police immediately.

There are theories that the murders could be linked to a terrorist cell or organised crime. Police were unable to comment on the accuracy of these theories. Police caution the public to be on their guard until such time as more information is available.

WHAT'S SHE BEEN PUFFIN ON?

BY ANTONY FELIX,
11th October 2019

LONDON – There is plenty of speculation rife amongst the columns of newspapers now, as everyone puts forward their pet theories about the spate of murders gripping the nation. However, the prize for the most outlandish must go to psychic Maureen O'Malley, who says that the cause of the killings is, in fact, the Puffins which have been plaguing our cities' nooks and crannies for what seems like forever now. Maureen, 59, says she witnessed an attack take place, in her visions.

She claims that while experiencing her psychic trance, she saw a group of the feathery little birds' mob then devour a girl in an alleyway.

"It was horrific - the worst thing I've ever seen in any of my visions. They just came out of nowhere. First, there was only a few of them, but then more and more came, and they just swarmed over that poor girl and then there was blood, and soon there were only bones left."

"I've told the police, but they turned me away. I don't think they want to believe it could be the Puffins, but that's what I saw. So that's why I'm telling you, to get the word out. People should be afraid of the Puffins!"

DOM PETTY
AND THE BALLBREAKERS

- Duncan P. Bradshaw -

Is it possible to hate someone that you've barely spoken to? I'm not talking about a mild dislike, I am talking a full-on loathing of their very existence. If you had the ability to remove them from the carnival of time and replace them with something useful – a tub of greasy fluoride for example - then Dom, that utter bastard, would be that person.

Every day, the same. I'd weave around the fat fucker, honking at him like I was an irate badger. As I passed his podgy form, I'd glare at him, so much so that I got pinkeye, and you know what I got back? That smug smile of his. The one that said fuck you and curdled my carton of lunchtime milk.

How was I to know what would happen, though? It's impossible to predict the whims and vagaries of popular trends and what the Corporation will seize upon from one day to the next. I remember waking up one autumnal morning to find out that barcodes were illegal. If you were found to be looking at one with so much as an iota of lust, you'd be carted off to the camps.

My brother was one of those poor souls. They picked him up as he streaked through the miniature robot shop naked, a tin of minestrone soup in one hand, and a loupe in the other. I remember the last thing I heard him bellow before the tranq dart slapped his arse like a midget with a rubber hook for a hand. "Zero, nine, five, two, zero, seven, four, six, nine, nine, zero, one, three, seven, zero." I knew as well as the authorities did that it was the barcode for a bout of ECT, but I was hardly going to let on and join him, eh? They have special chairs for siblings or starstruck lovers in those places.

Perhaps that's my problem. I never stood up for the little guy, always too worried that if I did, that it would be me they would drag away. Incarcerated within the rehabilitation domes, forever probed by sentient pub trivia questions until my spirit broke, and they used me as a lubricant for the digging machines excavating Void 37B.

Anyway, after I left Dom in my wake, I'd clock in a good half an hour before him. By the time he had finally hauled his gargantuan frame into his pod, I'd already have churned through three hundred decisions and earned my first cup of crushed ice.

It wasn't *just* the fact that he walked slowly, it was everything he did. I'd go to the toilet trough after him and find that one of the three sphincter grenades had been turned anticlockwise, so I'd have to use my hand to finish off the faecal extraction. I'd get back to my pod and find that he had used my lucky earphone. The sponge now covered with great globules of ear wax, complete with hair sticking out of it like aerials from the ghetto, hoping to pick up a signal from one of the twenty-four-hour news channels

At lunch, tired and weary from deciding all morning, I would go to prepare my oats and discover that the fat fuck had already sewn them together. Have you tried to eat crocheted porridge? It takes an age. He knew that. By the time I'd get to the beginning of the stodgy chain, the buzzer would go, and it would be time to wash up and decide again.

I'd look over to see him masticating like a lobotomised bovine, and true to form, there he was, smiling like a fucking clown on a spike. Every chew he made, bookended individual movements within the renowned opera by Toshiba.

No matter I thought, in a few hours, I'd be packed up, ready to go, overtake him on the way home, and speed-walk my way back to my residential patch. Ready to rest, ahead of the same damn ritual tomorrow. I'd still have that time to myself though. My place. My rules. Kitchen roll used by the half sheet, floor tiles sloped just right, so I could glide from kitchen to wardrobe with only three calories used.

A place for everything, and everything in its place.

Then, it happened.

I had cut him up on the pavement, managing a quick dig of my elbow in his ever-expanding guts. The look though...he must've known then, he must've done.

My overalls chaffed against my gall bladder, but it was fine, I was a hundred decisions deep already. The Patterson-Snide's television viewing for the next three months was in the bag, their stepson, Timmy, assigned not just to his future school, but his burial plot as well. Then I went to reach for my bar of soap to wash away the judgement. It wasn't there. In its place, looking for all the world as if it had always been there, was a tub of squirty disinfectant.

Citrus smelling.

I could feel my heart hammering within its wicker cage. This must be a mistake? Perhaps in my haste, I had slipped into my neighbour's pod? Though the poster of Cassius the Cat telling me to 'Hang Tough', while suspended from the boughs of industrial machinery was in its place -- above the third rivet of the central support column.

Now, there are over one hundred members of the life decision bureau - not counting support staff and animal mascots - and yes, it could've been any one of them. But I knew, from the bottom of my coding, that it was Dom. My brain replayed a sensory memory from that very morning. As I busted past him - my thighs burning from lactic acid build-up and burrito deficiencies - I detected a waft of citrus from him.

The announcement followed shortly after, manager name Dave Turbitt appeared in the tea saucer and decreed that following an article in the morning edition of Turgid, rigid bars of soap were now outlawed. Anyone found using non-jellified cleanser would be escorted off the premises and sent to the north-western front, fighting the glitter terrorists, hellbent on making everything FABULOUS.

So what could I do?

I heard a keening wail and turned to see Kenneth Kennethson bound past my observation glass panel, followed in close pursuit by the security services. They were waving their court-issued branding irons and apocalyptic manacles as if it were Grass-Your-Neighbours-In-Friday.

When I spoke to my colleagues during the afternoon baseball game, Kai said that he'd seen Kenneth brandish a bar of nitro-glycerine and strawberry soap shortly before security had commenced their pursuit, which ended violently.

The next day, I found myself walking slower past Dom to see if I could be spared from his ire, but it made no difference. He looked at me as if I were a meat popsicle discarded by the flesh brigade. I clocked in, eager to get on with my decisions, when I was told that pods were now outlawed by the state for being an anagram of *spod,* the infamous terrorist brigade of militant geeks and nerds. All of my television haiku's - written over my entire decision career - had been stripped of vowels, sent to orphans in the batter mix divide.

We now had to make our decisions on Segways. Each of us parading around a track made in a figure of eight -- the symbol of infinity. No longer would I be able to sit down and consider what I would have a good ponder about, in the evening moments of free thought.

All bar one. Dom. He was piloted around on a sofa, one hundred battery-powered drones tethered to the tassels, conveying him around the track, though he chose to hover in my eyeline the entire time. He looked down at me while flying backwards. As he ate my hoarded supplies of battery acid and paste, he would cackle, and fling balls of lint at me.

Within days, all the staples of my life were removed or had changed inexorably.

Monday, we received an edict, telling us that the only clothing now acceptable would be paisley, accented with two bodily fluids and dried on cornflakes.

On Tuesday, we were all informed during morning brunch, that our BMI had to reach a level usually reserved for those so unfit, that the mere act of breathing unaided would cause death.

When I received the memo on Wednesday break time, that we had to submit ourselves to random drug tests, those found without the correct levels of steroids and amphetamines would be summarily executed in the boardroom. I snapped.

I had prided myself on my balanced levels of both recreational and street drugs, this was an affront to my very being! I stormed into Human Resources and demanded to know who in the Corporation was making these demands. A bored milkmaid - feeding their third whelp of the day - languidly pointed to a corner of the room, covered in moss and used bandages.

Amongst the mildew, lay a small rectangular metal box. As I brushed the surface, two words came to life:

SUGGESTION BOX

Jimmying the lid open - which made one of the infants regurgitate their liquid breakfast - I discovered reams of folded paper. As I went through them - all four hundred and eighty-one of them - the same name was written in blue ballpoint pen in the name box: Dom.

There was a wet cough behind me, followed by the slurp of someone rapidly rappelling a rope of snotty phlegm back within. "Hi, Dickweed."

I knew it was him, I turned around, and there he was, the blob of human body parts known as Dom. "That's not my name. It's Pauly Shore. You know it is. You christened me, remember? You tried to drown me in the lava font."

Dom leant in closer, the smell of cloves was overpowering, he unfolded a letter printed on Corporation headed paper. "I think not, you're now called Dickweed."

I snatched the paper from him and scanned it, the words formed sentences, and imparted knowledge, confirming to me, that it was decreed that I was now called Dickweed. Or my full title, Dickweed Pissypants. The Third. From Curry Finkel, New New Devon. I scrunched it into a ball and threw it behind me, a quivering strand of man-size lichen scooped it up and used it as nutrition. "Why are you doing this to me? What have I done to you?"

I awaited his response, no doubt thoughts and views formed from years of keen observation, coalesced into a singular purpose of intent. He burped, fished out the skeletal remains of a Nokia 3310, and shrugged. "See you in the morning, Dickweed."

And with that, he plopped back into his padded seat and was carried to the air-conditioned heavens by whirring motors.

I made my way home, barely able to keep up my usual brisk walking momentum. Once back in my sanctuary, I buried myself in my favourite tar pit and waited for the sun to commit suicide for the day.

The next morning, I awoke reinvigorated. He would not beat me, my spirit was indefatigable! Dom could get everything changed from mere suggestions alone, but he could not destroy me. With the application of soggy cornflakes to my lapels, I double knotted my shoelaces and raced into the streets.

I'd never felt so alive! Weaving in and out of my fellow pedestrians, who must have been WOWed at seeing someone walk so fast, for they gasped and pointed. In the near distance, I could see Dom strutting down the street. I kicked my heels together and walked faster, my legs a veritable blur as I bore down on him.

As I overtook him, he held out his mobile telephone with the latest news headline spooling across its digital display. In my shock, I stumbled, falling onto the floor, grazing my knee so severely that it nearly broke skin.

Dom held the device over me. "Not so fast, Mister

Pissypants, things have changed while you've been wallowing."

There it was, in black and white, 'WALKING SPEED TO BE LIMITED TO A GENTLE GAIT.'

I screamed at his stupid face, the last bastion of my sanity stripped away, the tower of my contentment breached by an ornamental trebuchet.

No.

Not like this.

I stood up, dusted myself down, and pulled forth my soliloquy skull. "Ye shall not relegate me to the level of pensioners, the crippled or infirm. It is not my way to amble along byways, level with babes in pushchairs or the indecisive. These legs were not forged upon the crucible of these tarmac lanes, to dally with the unemployed and drunk.

"A man may be stripped of many things in this life, liberty, pubic hair or the ability to darn socks, but by Jove, you shall not restrict me this day. For as long as there is breath in my lungs, and comfortable, affordable shoes upon my feet, then I shall walk as I please. Neither you - or this world which panders to your every maddening whim - shall stymy my movement.

"Regard now, as I continue on my journey to work, where I shall make some suggestions of my own! Free showers for new starters, carbon dioxide balloons on birthdays, angular and pleasing forms to storage sheds. Yes, you will see that you have made an enemy of me this very day, I shall not rest until justice is served! Good day sir!"

I swivelled on the spot, did an abrupt set of high knees, and then made haste towards work and salvation. Unfortunately, one of the Corporation's snipers was placed in the snout of a nearby pelican crossing wench, and the bullet coursed through my leg, shattering my bone.

Now? I face the most heinous of fates. For they picked up my broken body that day and stitched me to Dom's coveralls. Wherever he goes now, I am there too. Attached to him like I was nothing but a patch to cover a ghastly hole.

Though that is not the worst of it, as I now travel as slowly as tectonic plates. I cannot even vent my displeasure, as my voice has been outlawed, my language nullified.

But mark my words, one of these days, I'll make him pay. They'll all pay!

I just need to get this piece of paper into that damn suggestion box.

ZOMBIE APOCALYPSE

- DJ Tyrer -

A new horror!
Foreign zombies
Shambling onto our shores
Hungry for British flesh!
French zombies
Spanish zombies
Italian and Arabian zombies
Zombies from Russia
From Syria and South Sudan
From America and Australia
They've come from near and far
To eat us all.
It's disgusting!
If they all come here
Who will the British zombies
Eat?

THE COINSLOT HEART

- Chris Kelso -

Woke University

I hope it's not morbid to say or to suggest--*although I suspect it will seem that way*--that the heart is destined to die a slow, aching death. And that, like a dragonfly in radical final-moult, the hopes of the heart will be left behind, rumpled and forgotten? This is what I believe, and this seems the only place to start. *No hope*, I say to you. *Nothing remains.* A part of me prays this is not the case and that my morbid excesses are dumb and cynical, but these prayers serve only to remind me that there is a part of myself that will forever be a fool. With that preface in mind, we should begin…

1

I am now a floating head in cryonic suspension. One with my regret and loneliness. I have graduated beyond the physical, but I still remember…

…I remember that the college day had just come to an end - a group of frat boy freshmen walked by and rattled on my cabinet with their palms and I waited in zest for the sizzle-sound of night insects. It was then that I saw Lena, the heavy exchange student from Poland, for the first time. I didn't know it, but this would be the last time I would see Lena alive. It started with a silent body suffering in silence and ended with three interviews.

I've concluded that yesterday is merely today's splendid memory, but tomorrow is today's vivid nightmare. This is how it goes. But as long as I have a memory, I can move forward in earnest.

She used me only once, *Lena*, and in a sense, there was no distinction between how she used me and how the other violators used me. It'll sound silly, but I felt her appreciation for my services. I felt useful, loved maybe. She would always emerge from the Eldritch-Proxima-building, come over and smile at me like a monkey with a new banana.

"*Chcę, żebyś to zrobił*" – she whispered, and my coinslot heart would start singing Polish arias. To this day, I have no idea what this meant, but it must surely be some divine poetry if it saw fit to fall from her lips.

…she looked me up and down in admiration with a face of delicate milk-crystal, leaned her chubby palms on my cabinet. I took her full weight and groaned. *This is love*, I thought. Lena was big as a Buick, but she had soft symmetry to her, like a baroque painting. Flemish-looking somehow. They would have made an opulent altarpiece of her image in the 17th century. Not now. Now she was considered merely a fat immigrant.

I recall the girl's eyes lighting up like solar flares when she saw my Jolly Ranchers. It's a testament to her humility, but I don't think she had the faintest clue that I was a slave to her stare.

Eyes like water in mud.

They assumed nothing.

They *had* to sever the head apparently…

…then Lena produced the money. Another coin for the dispenser. Money didn't bring me happiness, though, it still doesn't. I think Lena knew this. She slid the gold cylinder into my slot, and I thrust the Jolly Ranchers at her. She scrambled at my groin-compartment. The first glassy ingot was in her mouth before her plump fingers could make sense of the wrapping and it seemed to me that she was in a perpetual state of starvation. I was an ally to Lena, a friendly face in a sea of hypercritical alien subjugators.

I heard the news of her death the next morning –

2

Like Lena, I was used to being exploited.

I had violators everywhere.

Every-where.

One dime and I gave them everything I had, the more proverbially stupid, the better. I was their self-hating-sub held captive behind polycarbonate casing. An object with no designated safeword. These violators kept coming at me, clad in flowing linen, cotton yoga pants, and tie-dyed tops – *Deborah Foreman à la mode* – I simply could not reject their bony hands in duck-bill form, and the embolism of air which rushed through me before the final fisting was as cathartic as it was lastingly invasive. It's always take, take, take – these are the transactions of abuse of which I am all too familiar. Every person who came my way, I lost a little piece of myself. I was doomed to a life of watching beautiful temporary lovers use me and walk away.

C'est la vie.

But Lena was different. Anyway, I go on…

Earlier that day this one violator came up to me, this *girl*, a cheerleader called Debbie Tabernacle with a plastic rave-pacifier in her mouth and a BLUE CEPHALOPOD MAN belly-top on. She sends me into an immediate frenzy.

She likes what she sees.

And of course, I have something she wants.

She looks straight through me and brings out a fat, copper coin.

She fingers the mint mark, caresses Franklin Roosevelt's ducktail.

'*Stick it in me*' I beg her. '*Take it all*'.

The girl grins, punches the code into my keypad-chest, and a Caramac bar falls into the open compartment. I feel her thin, Crisco-coated hand reach in and snatch the treat. My casement shudders in the wake of colorectal perforation. My heart lurches, and the gut heaves hollow with waves of a familiar emptiness.

I often wondered what would happen when everything I had on the inside was gone. Debbie Tabernacle wound up a sad fatality in this story too actually…

Then - a swarm of pregnant, prepossessed Valley girls emerged, chit-chatting with wet, ovate mouths: I tell you, their high-rising terminal would have you praying for a nuclear-blasted future. Two of the cheerleaders were talking about 'the fat Polish bitch' being 'dead meat'.

A plague on all their fucking houses. Even as a floating consciousness, I remember the hate I held for them.

A lecturer joined them and started gossiping.

"I heard she was *literally* in pieces when they found her. Each individual part had been raped…" – he chimed.

"What do you mean?"

"I mean, someone *literally* cut her up…took out her lungs for example, and *literally* raped each lung."

"It's like they say, 'sever the head, save the heart'!"

"Who says that?"

"I dunno. We got a serial killer on campus. That's *so* cool." – One of the girls said half-grinning.

"Maybe she was trying to have sex with another bear out in Fort Payne last night, and a pissed-off grizzly tore her to ribbons?"

"No-way."

"*Seriously.*"

I thought about some sycophant breaking Lena in half like some time-lapse Corpse flower in bud. At first, I figured someone was enacting a kind of mob justice universal among students stuck amid a shallow, hook-up culture. Her fatness. Her foreignness. They were traits worthy of execution at Woke University.

It's funny, this tragedy afforded me some time to reflect. I eventually reached the conclusion that beneath its veneer of acceptance and inclusion, the academic setting bred a rare kind of intolerance, the type that seized every student and wrung the last drips of residual humanity from their every pore.

And I was an enabler.

Falling in love with the infected.

Facilitating their hatred.

Playing bystander to crimes against decency and humanity.

3

I heard through the grapevine that Lena had indeed been murdered, but not cut up or raped or mauled by a grizzly. She'd been decapitated by a frisbee'd drum cymbal – and, *no*, you haven't misread. A drum cymbal. Apparently, her student accommodation was broken into by members of the Woke University philharmonic orchestra (specifically the brass section, although the percussion quartet wasn't innocent either having provided the abovementioned crime weapon) and I guess Lena got in the way of the brutes trying to steal a set of prized bassoons and clarinets stored in the attic directly above her room. I knew those boys; the oboist, *Timpson*, in particular, seemed like a mean, nasty piece of work who ate a lot of Almond Joy bars. Music was an anabolic steroid to him, and he took a lot of JJ-180. You'd regularly see Timpson bombing through the campus grounds, bashing unsuspecting classmates over the skull with 'The Complete Book of Classical Music' (the 968-page Robert Hale ltd edition) while Wagner's *Tannhauser's Overture* blared through his headphones. Yet, something didn't quite add up to me. This was more than a tragic accident of involuntary manslaughter. There was malicious aforethought, Lena was too unpopular to have been a chance victim. I had my suspicions that someone on campus had *deliberately* killed Lena. Krzysztof Penderecki was conductor-in-residence at Woke, and Lena, due to her crippling shyness, refused to sing the Polish section of *St Luke's Passion*. I started with him – the first of my three interviews.

I miss Lena's gentle penetration. I miss her load-bearing palms. I miss money. My ministering angel. Reprieve came post-sun while crickets praised the night with their winter symphonies.

4

Interview One

That night, I pushed a pair of fat-toed feet from the bottom of my cabinet and heaved my food-filled bulk from the damp ground. A group of comic book nerds stopped trading fantasy cards and watched me, an ARTIFORG PolyVend snack dispenser, attempt bipedal locomotion.

"If I throw a stick, will you leave?" - I spat at the nerds, and they dispersed.

I straightened up, using the wall for leverage. I gave birth to shin-rods and knobbed-knee joints. Two fat highs emerged, streaked by a river of subcutaneous wires. I had never stood up before. The legs trembled, but I remember that when the will is ready the feet are light. I was standing up for Lena, not just myself. I took a step and all the coins in the lower half of my carcass jangled with nervous energy. When I lurched forward, my snacks descended from their fill-trays and my umbilical coil disengaged from its power supply, dragging behind me like a vestigial tail.

Freedom.

My first destination was the music department, and I knew Penderecki would be waiting.

I approached Penderecki's office and noticed that the door was slightly ajar. When I peered around the corner of the lock rail, I saw him from the back - shirtless, hairy, and air-conducting to Józef Koffler's 'III Symphony op.21'. Mercifully Penderecki was wearing a pair of polka-dotted boxer briefs! I closed the door hard behind me, and the vibration knocked the balance of the counterweight, dragging the symphony to a final screeching halt.

"Who the…?" – Penderecki turned around with a face full of irate surprise. His chest and belly had these little bastions of white fur poking out like fluffy troll hair.

"I'm here to talk to you about a girl called Lena."

Penderecki stood there with his paunch eclipsing his waistband.

"You're a vending machine?"

"Yes, a PolyVend. Please, Mr Penderecki, take a seat."

The baffled composer pulled out a seat and leaned his elbows on the desk.

"Perhaps I should put a shirt on first." - Penderecki had a kind, wizened face which he hid behind a Santa Claus beard. His eyes radiated a quiet genius and made him instantly respectable – even as he stood before me in polka-dotted underpants.

"This won't take a minute." – I assured him.

"Before we start, you don't have anything savoury in there, do you?" – Penderecki pointed to my torso of goodies.

"I have jerky."

"Yes, may I…"

Penderecki got out of his seat, a shiny dime secreted in his palm. He inserted the coin, and a packet of Ruby Bay jerky filled my compartment. Penderecki looked at the fleshy paleness of my legs before retrieving his snack.

"You have Polish legs. Strong and wide."

With that, he pulled out the Ruby Bays and tore the seal. He re-sat himself at the desk.

"I suppose you want to talk about what happened to your friend Lena. Well, the truth is, I don't know."

"Your brass section did the killing. I want to know why."

"I'm not in control of everything my teenage orchestra get up to! I would not condone the killing of anyone, never mind a beautiful Polish rose like Lena."

"So why?"

"Why? Why he asks me! I don't know why! You should interrogate the animals who killed her, not me."

"Lena refused to sing in your end of year performance of 'St Luke's Passion' forcing you to turn to a less talented soprano in Debbie Tabernacle."

"I was upset, of course, but not murderously upset! Those boys have been dropped from the brass section, the offending percussionists have also been told not to return. What more can I do, I'm not their babysitter?"

I looked into Penderecki's eyes and decided he wasn't telling me everything. I moved towards him, towering over the short, fat, seated man. I willed a fist into existence and threw it, balled and nub-knuckled, onto the desk. Penderecki jumped with fright. He pulled a slice of jerky from the packet and gnawed on it like a frightened animal.

"Timpson. Billy T-t-t-Timpson." – He stuttered.

"What about Timpson?"

"This has nothing to do with me, it's all him. He's insane. I'm just the mild-mannered face of Woke University! Please. Lena was pregnant, but that's all I know, please…"

The room spun around me, and my footing became unbalanced. I steadied myself on Penderecki's bookshelf.

Lena was pregnant?

My gut reeled. Food was rising. I vomited a flurry of Skittles and M&M's on Penderecki's floor. He stood there looking at me in utter disbelief. After a moment he just looked annoyed at the mess I'd left in his office.

I left him.

5

Interview Two

I saw Timpson sitting in the library with his headphones blaring. This guy was a real loner; he always seemed to be using those headphones to shut out the rest of the world. In all honesty, I respected how much he didn't seem to give a shit. People's opinions didn't seem all that important to Timpson. There was a power to him, I couldn't put my finger on it at first. In saying that, he was still your typical classical music bully - a cultural snob with inflamed acne, jutting jaw, and bulbous forehead. Timpson had a collapsed face, one that looked like he'd been hit by everything but the digging bucket of a Backhoe. He was not a looker. He had an exaggerated overbite on account of his oboe embouchure, and his hair was set in thick ringlets.

"What do you want, freak?" – He hissed in a glottal-rattle, lifting one muff from his ear.

"Just to have a conversation."

"About what?"

"About Lena."

"What about her? I had nothing to do with it. They're just fucking rumours."

"I'm not here to point the finger, but you knew Lena?"

"I knew her through Penderecki. He was obsessed with her voice. When she refused to sing soprano, it hurt him bad. That's nothing to do with me." – Timpson stared through me and in that moment, I decided there wasn't enough content there to kill someone, neither good nor bad. Just *there*. Just young and angry at the world for not speaking in his particular language of classical music.

"And Penderecki didn't hire you to kill Lena? This wasn't some organised revenge mission? I know, you kids really look up to the man."

"We wouldn't kill for him. These are just rumours. Anyway, I'm in the brass section, oboist, *not* a fucking drummer. Checked for any missing drum cymbals lately?"

"I'll get to that."

"And then there are the valley girls who hated her."

"Did you know Lena was pregnant?"

Timpson went to speak but hesitated. He pulled out a dice of JJ-180 and started slathering it into his cheeks in a display of post-collegiate recreation. He changed colour and heaved a hot sigh.

"I'd heard rumours…" – he eventually got out. Timpson was all breathy and stoned. I'd managed to perturb him. At least interview two had this going for it.

"Thanks for your time."

I turn to leave, and he calls me back.

"Hey, maybe you should ask Debbie Tabernacle. Penderecki has been fucking her since the start of the semester. She seems like suspect number one to me. Penderecki was really into Lena and her talent. Missy hated that. She hated that Lena snared Penderecki's attention. If anyone is prone to jealous outbursts, it's her."

"She deserves something more than what she got."

"What do you care anyway? – he smirked - You in *love* with her or something?"

"I just hate the thought of her being left that way in a lonely dorm room."

"Who gives a shit? Once you're dead, what does it matter where you're found or why? You're dead." – He dropped the muff onto his ear and turned his back to me. I saw him rub the dice of JJ-180 over his neck and chin. He sighed again, the weight of quiet guilt temporarily leaving his chest area. The sun rose, finally, and glimmered on the back of Timpson's slick black hair like the shimmering posterior of Ganymedian slime mould.

It's funny… I have absorbed the great works of fiction by process of osmosis. The intellectual oligarchs of Woke Universities' 'Dead Poets Society' discuss the American novels worthy of aggrandisement in such intense detail that I know the garrulous prose-highlights of your *Ulysses* and *Gravity's Rainbow*. I know you are capable of great things, the things Lena kept on her sleeves, but the rest of you kept locked away in your hearts. But I cannot reconcile your duality. The good and the evil. The smallness of spirit and the universe you call a soul.

My mind started to race. Could Penderecki have asked his devout band of followers to kill the girl for him? It didn't seem likely, but then nothing was ever quite as it seemed. Did Debbie Tabernacle have something to do with this? It was common campus-knowledge that she aspired to be a great soprano and wanted to impress Penderecki, her mentor and lover.

I didn't want to know the truth, not really. But there are two kinds of truth, aren't there? The kind that makes you all warm and fuzzy inside, and the type you cast onto an ugly darkness so that you might catch a glimpse of something important beneath. I thought about Lena, how someone could do such a thing to her.

There's nothing you people won't do to each other.

6

Interview Three

I tracked down Debbie Tabernacle. My answers were there in the proximity of touch. I had a feeling this would be my final interview – the way Jan Bloch was able to intuit the coming of the storm of the Great War. An inevitable climax felt imminent.

Debbie was sitting in the communal garden drinking a can of Fruitopia and reading the latest issue of BITCH magazine, which rested on the arc of her swollen belly. I approach her, and my shadow eclipsed the reading-light from the sun. She looked up contemptuously.

"What. The. Fuck?" – She said in her moronic

interrogative.

"Lena. I'm here to talk about Lena."

"Oh, come on. Give me a break, like I even knew the fat dyke."

"You didn't know her. You didn't take the time to know her. But she didn't want to know you either, because you're a shallow valley girl with a sociopathic predisposition and a heart the size of a wrinkled mustard seed. Now shut up and listen."

"*Excuse* me?"

"Relax, this'll be quick. Now I know Penderecki didn't kill Lena himself because he was too in love her and her talent. I know the brass and percussion sections have no free will of their own and therefore no motive without their instruction from the messiah. I spoke to Timpson. He puts you in the frame as a jealous concubine. Now talk, or I'll start tossing roasted almonds at your dumb face."

"You'll do *what*?" – Tabernacle folded over the copy of BITCH and got to her feet, her face pulled severely to each corner of her skull in disgust. Instinctively, I reached out and grabbed her by the throat. My finger and thumb-tips met around the thin, elegant shaft of her neck. I squeezed.

"I'm not…" – I squeeze tighter.

"…in…" – tighter.

"…the mood…" - her face goes psychedelic purple like she'd been tripping on a concentrated dose of JJ-108, and I release her to the ground. She looks up at me, massaging her throat. I lowered myself to the base standards of homunculi. I feared there was no turning back.

"It…it was Timpson…"

"Timpson?"

"He must've raped Lena in a Beethoven-induced sex attack. He got her pregnant. When she said she didn't want to keep his demon offspring, he went ballistic. A day after she finds out the girl winds up decapitated. They say Timpson removed the foetus before killing her. Tonight, go to the campus forest at midnight. You'll see. And

Lena…you have to separate the head from the body. He *had* to sever it he said! That's all I know. Please don't…"

I tried to calm her down, but already I had descended into brutish interrogator, and her impression of me was set in stone.

"It doesn't matter anyway. I'm dead. He knows. He always finds out. He has eyes everywhere. He has a thousand selves, and he *does*…he told us all he can be in a thousand places at once and he *can*…" – Debbie nursed the bruising indentations around her throat. She looked at me with defeated watery eyes and rubbed her swollen belly. I saw in her eyes the truth – that she knew Penderecki would never love her the way he loved Lena. The way I loved Lena.

"We're the only ones who can hear. No one is nearby."

"You don't understand. He has…powers. An autonomic immune-system. Because of the blood."

"The blood?"

"I can't…I need to leave, right now!"

Debbie pushed passed me and ran off in the direction of the Voigt-Kampff building. I wanted to chase her, protect her. I wanted to prove that my violence was all for Lena and therefor had noble roots. But she was gone, and I knew that whatever malevolent force had taken my Polish beauty would soon get the young, pregnant and bruised Debbie Tabernacle.

7

I saw the near-glow of torch-light. Beneath the purring crickets and the gentle wind's whisper against decomposing leaves, I began to hear the melodic restoration of some ancient chant beside the reedy pitch of an oboe. Through the leaves, I could see naked women on their knees, throwing their hands in the air mid-fireside-worship. I saw Timpson standing at the centre of the circle, his purple penis recoiling from the icy winter night. He was wearing a pair of antlers. Then he stopped playing, started talking.

"Bring me the first…" – and gestured to a girl with blonde braids, whom I recognised as Tiffany Acker, once-head-cheerleader at Woke. Tiffany looked like she'd been sapped of life and there was a demented quiet behind her eyes. She got to her feet, had something cradled in her arms, something swaddled in a blanket. It was a baby, only the child was deathly silent. As she walked towards Timpson, the supported baby jiggled lifelessly in her grasp like a pound of rotten liver. I still get a chill whenever I recall the appalling realisation that the child was dead. Judging by its blue-washed paleness, suffocated. Tiffany handed the dead infant to Timpson, and he raised it in the air like a trophy. It's tiny head rolling limp. My heart grew in the cabinet, and something lurched at the groin-tray. The canopy of trees above me rustled and whispered ugly human-spells. I hear them in cryonic suspension to this day…

"The first!" – He declared, and the cheerleaders hailed their messiah. He grinned and tossed the baby onto the flames. Leaves of fire rose moonward and sent up swirling smoke signals to Hephaestus. I noticed the other girls were holding dead children too.

Then Timpson dawned his vestigial robe while observing the Vitruvian angles of a crucified girl. The girl was Debbie Tabernacle.

Debbie…

She was savagely thin, voided of her foetus. She looked almost starved in an act of imposed ritualistic abstinence. But in the wake of this virginal, delicate creature, a perverse joy had overcome Timpson. The leathery flesh around his mouth pulled tight into a sinister, triumphant smile. He was purpled out of his mind.

Debbie moaned again, her breasts undulating beneath a trembling chin. She had a bird-like beauty, bright, soft of feature, small hipped. I felt bad for strangling her. Her face was a portrait of pure agony - an otherworldly adversary for the young priest to contend. Timpson was transparent now. He stifled a destructive arousal within himself. Having ceased her tormented moans, Debbie started to speak, though her voice emerged in the growling thunder of a hell-dwelling demon.

"YOUWILLNOTPREVAIL.PENDERECKIHASBE ENMYCOVERSINCEHISPSALMSOFDAVIDANDHE ISINLOVEWITHME"

As if energised by the shocking scenes before me, I pushed forth and gave birth to myself. I felt my breasts develop and form in two heavy hemispheres around my chest. I reached toward the fire-light, and my wet body emerged from the vending machine womb and onto the undergrowth. I lay there naked, and female, in full display of the circling girls. I looked up, and they all glowered at me dead-eyed, like the demons who guarded the eighth circle of hell.

"Stay away from her!" – I screamed unconsciously. Timpson stared at me with devil's eyes, two lakes of oily pitch with a thousand dead-infants drowning inside. Debbie looked at me, and her face was different now, distorted somehow.

Pixelated and censored.

"You did it. You impregnated Lena like you impregnated all the other girls in your little cult. When Lena threatened to get an abortion, you murdered her. You and your valley girl disciples!" – I screamed until my throat gave out, and the words trailed off in a shrill slur. Tears cascaded from my ruptured eye-taps and the glottis ached with mucus. I was overcome with anger and sadness. This is my most vivid memory of being a human being.

And, even, disappointment. In myself. In Timpson. In everything.

I felt talons hook around my arms and feet and drop me to the bed of ferns. The girls were abnormally strong. I saw the moon gaze down at me and thought of Lena's round surfaces.

"You have no idea what I'm doing here. I'm not the villain here. I've been keeping order on campus since my first semester." – Timpson stood over me.

I tried to struggle free, but the manicured nails dug deeper into my new flesh, and there was no threshold for pain at this stage in my human-form. I resigned myself to captivity.

"Did you know that I'm polyencephalic? Time travel, do you know I travel through time?"

"Congratulations."

"I can project myself across entire galaxies. I don't do it because I'm drunk on power, I do it because I have to."

"Oh, you *have* to, do you?"

"I understand your scepticism. I've been collecting data, compiling resources and information on the beast."

"The beast?"

"The Stag-Princess."

"Jesus Christ. What Lovecraftian bull shit is this?"

"It's very real. The Stag-Princess, or *Bluebell-Stanley's Daughter* as the Pagans called her, emerges from her forest every 500 years. Taking JJ-180 somehow puts you on her radar, kind of like a built-in satellite-navigation. I noticed we were tuned to the same frequency the first time I took JJ-180. Some people go crazy, I'm one of the few who can control the hallucinations. I can see through time. I can see when the Stag-Princess is on her way to our realm."

"You'll do anything to justify your sick behaviour Timps--…"

"No! You're not listening. I fuck all these girls, and I pass along my gift. We get soaped-up on JJ-180, and when we have sex, we operate on the same provinces, biologically and spiritually, until the drug wears off. I'm creating an army here, one that'll keep the Princess at bay. Don't you understand?"

"Oh, the expository dialogue! Isn't this meant to be a Philip.K.Dick parody?"

"Lena refused to help. She refused to give birth to my righteous warrior. She was part of the problem, imagine if all these girls shared that attitude. Imagine they just allowed the Stag Princess to come into our realm and destroy everything. Castrate us all!"

"So, you killed her? Christ…"

"We had to sever the head. You must sever the head to disconnect the line linking the beast to our whereabouts. The cymbal wasn't even a red herring; it was a weapon of convenience. If you're not with us, you're against us. We'll have to disconnect you, the same way I disconnected the Polish bitch. *I'm* with humanity. Now…make your decision. Do you want to be part of the solution, or do you want to bring on the evisceration of every man, woman and child on this realm? Who're you with?"

I take a moment, gulp back the tears and mucus.

"I've got nothing left inside. I'm just a pink blancmange of pain and loss…"

"Who're you with? Are you with this bitch? – Timpson pointed to Debbie Tabernacle thrashing around on her crucifix like a deranged animal – Are you with Penderecki and the nihilist cabal? Or are you with the good guys? We'll have to disconnect you."

"I've got no Almond Joy bars. No Mountain Dew. No bars of Ubik or CAN-D. There's nothing I can offer you, Billy…"

"You can offer your services as a child of humanity. Now, are you with us or against us?" – Timpson took a long sword from one of the valley girls. He raised it and pleaded with me to join him.

I thought about Lena and the new family of apes I'd grown to despise.

"I'm with Lena…"

TAURED AWAITS

- Madeleine Swann -

Cheri knew from the bursting of nerves beneath her skin that if she couldn't find Gate 27, she would strip naked and run outside until she was taken somewhere and looked after. She couldn't go back to the office, or any office and her mother had long stopped taking her depressing calls until she learned to be more grateful.

"No, no, no," she whimpered, her suitcase wheels lifting from the ground behind her and flopping to the side, twisting her wrist. Gate 5, Gate 6, Gate 7, 8, 9,10, she'd marched past them all at least five times. It wasn't there. People glared, apparently furious that someone would impede their travels and make them half a second late. The airport lights burned, giving her nowhere to hide. She pulled her suitcase up by the handle and flopped into one of many seats, head down, knowing nobody cared enough to stare at her but feeling their eyes all the same. She'd been so sure when she woke up that she'd received the ticket. Her dream was so clear, so believable, but she must have dreamed about the dream instead of having the dream. The delivery woman at the door had seemed so real, so real that Cheri had searched for the ticket handed to her after waking. A quick check online had assured her that a physical piece of paper wasn't necessary to check onto the plane to Taured and she'd gone to work as usual this morning, the 7 O'Clock flight time buzzing in her brain.

She pulled her phone from her pocket to check for information; "Jonah Carlson, Info Nation pundit, called into shock jock station admitting to sexual assault," shrieked the top headline. Minutes passed as she read his revolting statements, including his disdain for his female colleague's appearance. "Ugly cow," he'd said, "fat pig." Cheri felt her own rotund belly's presence like the last guest at a party who couldn't take the hint. Pain shot through her wrist, worsened by the twist earlier, and deepened the ache in her phone holding muscles. She put the phone back in her pocket before remembering why she'd pulled it out in the first place. She knew there was no point checking online. The Gate was either there, or it wasn't. First came the dream, then the inciting incident to search for Gate 27 at Hatford airport, the point of no return.

For many, the inciting incident was a death, destruction of the home by a bomb, the last mouthful of food when they couldn't afford to buy more. For Cheri, it was a slammed door.

She'd stared at the white plastic for several minutes, clipboard in hand fixed with some shitty survey on art resources in the area, and knew this was the last slammed door she'd ever see. At work, anyway. She'd marched back to her car, driven to the office and set her things on the manager's desk. "You're back early," he said, a question lurking beneath his statement.

"I'm going home."

"Wha-why?" he leaned back in his chair, brow furrowed.

"I...just can't do it. I'm sorry." She fled the scene despite his pleas to see how she felt in an hour or give it one last try. The tears of shame and anger at not sticking to anything were already falling as she slumped into the driver's seat.

She'd always been like this. She quit school, she quit jobs, she quit going back to school, she quit more jobs. I'm spoilt, she told herself, I'm spoilt, and my mum made me believe I didn't have to do stuff I didn't want to.

Her phone had beeped, and she'd clicked on the YouTube notification, a response to her video about taking care of yourself during the Brexit hoo-hah and not checking social media too much. The previous comments had been very supportive, and she'd assumed it would be more of the same. The words left by the account with the blue bus picture, however, were definitely not that: "having a panic attack over Brexit is childish and pathetic. i suffer from panic attacks and they are not fun. this is another remainer bitching and moaning about the results and it is pathetic." A sharp pain tore through her wrist, but she couldn't help pressing the 'read more' button. "i have be around enough people and seen other peoples reasons for being "so called" depressed and well it's rather pathetic. "life didn't turn out the way you want so i'll get my doctor to give me antidepressants" even though they have a family, they have friends a home and more. and yet people like this are the reason our NHS is overburdened," he said, and on and on and on. She was the reason "why our mental health team/departments hasn't enough doctors to help real people with real issues," "her panic attack only happen when she needs them to happen," and she only had panic attacks over "issues/topic she disagrees" with.

"At least I'm not a fucking prick," Cherie had hissed, squeezing her phone hard, yelping when the twinge blossomed into agony. She was weak, got everything wrong. Despite knowing she shouldn't, she'd checked the comments beneath and was pleasantly surprised.

"Theres a cockwomble in every comment section lolol," said one, "Stop jumping on the nice lady. Get some fucking manners about you," said another. They were right. All she'd done was share a few tips, a few concerns. She'd said nothing bad about anyone else. It gave her the courage to check another video.

"I know Capitalism is bad," she'd said, "but I worry about other options. What works best? How do we stop it from becoming corrupt? I don't know. I need to look into it, do some reading." She'd hoped for helpful responses, book suggestions, anything. Instead, she'd received comment after comment informing her that "Under capitalism, there are 20 million deaths from starvation a year," and "So you're saying that workers shouldn't own the means production because it's vulnerable to corruption yet you're dandy with how things are?" On and on they went, twisting her words, changing them, mutating her into a different person entirely. It was the third time that week something similar had happened, and it was Tuesday.

The phone had fallen into her lap, and she'd twisted the ignition key, eyelashes beating back tears. She'd exited a roundabout. She was a newly hatched creature waiting to grow a shell; pale, puffy and vulnerable. She wanted to cry when someone made a blunt joke about a film she liked. Her coordination fell apart when anyone watched her working. Her eyes were always on the ground, and it was mainly his fault. His face loomed from her childhood, floating through every new attempt to forget him, big and red like an angry tomato.

Cheri sat back hard in her airport seat, pain snapping her out of the memory. She focused on her surroundings – a couple hissing at each other, a mother holding a sleeping child in her arms, two groups of friends and countless humans drifting like wildebeest from shop to shop. Queues waited by gate 6, gate 7, gate 27, gate 8, gate 9 and…

Cheri squawked and grabbed the handle of her bag, almost falling forwards when it tipped to one side again. Not stopping to apologise to the person she slammed into, she half ran half stumbled to the gate that most definitely had not been there two minutes ago. There was no queue and only one check-in desk, staffed by a beautiful being with teased black hair and bright red lips, "Passport and ticket?"

Shakily, Cheri handed them over. The clerk eyed her picture and information, face impassive, then smiled widely, "wonderful, any bags?"

On the other side of the security line, she pulled her handbag onto her shoulder and squeezed her feet back into her shoes. Usually, she would be a quaking wreck by now, probably stuck behind a group of angry men with sunburn, but being the only passenger, she'd zipped through. Expecting to find duty free shops, she blinked when confronted by a dark corridor. "Last checkpoint," said a voice, making her squeal. Another clerk, this time with long, ocean blue wavy hair and coral pink lips, "step this way."

Cheri followed the echoing heels of her guide's shoes, her own making an unpleasant squish as they slopped against her tights. The clerk flipped on a light which blinked dangerously before settling. The clerk didn't check if she was following, and Cheri didn't ask if she could pause to catch her breath, afraid to blink in case she found herself alone. Eventually, they arrived at a door with a square window, a green and white classroom filled with bored people and a neatly dressed man in front of a blackboard behind it.

"Um..." Cheri couldn't make her brain work.

"Just routine," the clerk said, smiling, "won't take more than a day or two."

"What?" Cheri was already watching her lifeline march back down the corridor, truly adrift now.

"You must be Cheri," said the man now standing in the doorway. Cheri's eyes grew as she took in the faces turned to her. She was back in maths class with Mr Hilton picking on a boy for the crime of being shy. The loud ones heckled as Greg was made to stand and solve equations he had no hope of understanding. Stop looking at your feet, she would urge him, but the poor lad couldn't help it, and each time Mr Hilton howled in faux outrage and pure delight at Greg's audacity to look away from his wrinkly ballbag face.

"There's a free seat here," said the teacher, breaking her daydream, "I'm Frank, by the way." Cheri tried to give her name, but nothing exited her mouth. "Cheri, I believe," Frank continued. "Say hello, everyone."

"Hi, Cheri," the class droned, and she glanced over their blank eyes and slack faces. They look 'differently-abled,' she thought, then felt rude. Was it bad to notice, or..? It made sense, she supposed. Taured should be open to everyone, and perhaps they were more likely to get in for some reason. She turned to the front to avoid thinking anymore.

"First thing's first, I'll need your phone," Frank said,

holding out his hand. Cheri smiled, assuming it to be a joke. Nobody laughed, and Frank's hand stayed put.

"Right," she said, voice quavering. She passed it to him slowly, every second expecting him to give it back. Instead, it went into his pocket.

"Great," Frank took his place in front of the blackboard, "let's continue where we left off. Makiko," a lady stood nervously, "please explain the issues between India and Palestine." She frowned, the dimness behind her eyes corpselike. Frank considered his next words, "why are India and Palestine disagreeing?"

Makiko smiled and nodded, "They don't like each other very much," she paused, confused, "because they are very far away countries, and are not civilised."

Cheri's fists clenched. Frank was going to be furious. To her shock, he looked pleased. "Well done," he said, and Makiko bowed and took her seat.

The horror in Cheri's stomach thickened when Frank turned to her, "Cheri," he gestured for her to stand, "as you're new, perhaps you'd like to explain this new spate of sexual harassment claims in the workplace?"

Cheri rose, swallowing dryly, "I can try, but I'm probably not the best person to ask."

"Go ahead," said Frank. Shame needled Cheri's flesh. She couldn't get this wrong. "Before, people put up with hostile environments at work because..." her throat begged for water, "they weren't listened to and..."

"Stop," Frank said, putting up his hands, "you sound like you're reciting a lab experiment." She'd been found out, her sheltered background dissected and laid bare. The horror inside her pulsated. "Tell me, is it possible for all these women to be telling the truth?"

Cheri blinked, "well, I mean, yes?" The class' laughter was dull, thick, and pressed her back into the seat.

"Stand, Cheri."

"I'd rather..."

"STAND." His voice was so loud it cut off all other

sounds, and the pair stared at each other, Frank red and furious, Cheri searching desperately for a sign of humour or kindness. She was tiny again, tugging on the hem of her mother's dress while He yelled so loud his voice cracked. "Don't interrupt," he shrieked as he leaned down, the biggest and reddest face she'd ever seen. No doubt she'd cried afterwards but that part she'd forgotten, remembering only this, her first memory.

"Very good," said Frank, "now let's keep looking at the other side. How is it possible that all these women experienced such terrible treatment at the same time?"

"S-some men too, and other genders," Cheri's voice was barely above a whisper.

"It's mostly women though," said Frank, "the men are ignored, and the other genders...well, let's not worry about that yet." He addressed everyone, "some are complaining about hugging. Imagine that," he turned to the class, "they want to outlaw hugging." The class chuckled dutifully. Cheri remembered the man at group therapy who'd pressed against her after insisting she needed a hug. She'd been too polite to say no and gritted her teeth when his pulse and breath quickened.

She stood so fast her chair clattered, drawing all eyes to her. She looked about, shocked her body had done this thing without consulting her brain, then headed for the door. She paused and turned to Frank.

"Did you want this back?" he said calmly, as though soothing a wild beast, and pulled her phone from his pocket. Cheri went to take it but stopped. She turned to the corridor beyond the window, which led back to customs, which led back to the airport, which led back to the street, her flat, which she could no longer pay for and her mother who was no longer interested.

"All we're doing," Frank's voice was soft and his face understanding as he placed a hand on her shoulder, "is creating a space where we can discuss things openly and calmly, without this need to cast others out into the wilderness," He continued. She was unwilling to leave or sit down, her mind mashed potato. Frank's fury rang in her head, and when he spoke, she winced, "Haven't you ever tweeted, or posted on facebook, or made a video making the mildest of statements, only to be labelled a bigot or a Nazi?" She hadn't, but the comments from her Capitalist video still stung. Also the trolling she'd received after concerns over Me Too, criticisms of all Republicans and much, much more. Hours of tagging her in the most horrifying insults and memes and threats throbbed behind her eyes. She searched Frank's face. They were clearly very different, but maybe she would be the bigger person if she just heard them out. She could still get to Taured with different opinions as long as she was understanding and kind. "We bring what we've learned, and we form a new colony, somewhere we can grow as people and put this hysteria behind us," said Frank gently.

She pictured a calm, quiet street with people waving to each other as they took out the rubbish and mowed lawns. They might disagree politically, but they could still be friends. It sounded nice. She allowed Frank to lead her back to her chair.

"OK, Lucek," Frank turned to a grizzled man with white sideburns at the back of the class, "can you tell me why so many black people are shot by American police?"

As Lucek explained that absent black fathers led to lives of crime, Cheri kept her thoughts on that quiet street and the safe, cosy neighbourhood of Taured. It was fine. She didn't have to agree. They could still be friends if she kept the conversation light. She sighed with relief as the pain faded from her hand.

A WONDERFUL DAY IN MY SOUP

- DJ Tyrer -

Jim sat in his garden, waiting for the sun to appear as the call to prayer echoed down the narrow English lanes to the accompaniment of pitter-pattering rain.

"It's always the same," said Fred.

Jim nodded. "It is. It is."

A dragonfly shot past them with the precision and alacrity of a jet fighter, then returned to hover beside Jim as if joining him in reading the morning paper in a fruitless search for good news.

"No news is good news," observed Jim, "and, this damn paper is stuffed full of news."

"It's always the same," said Fred.

Jim nodded. "It is. It is."

A raindrop fell from his nose and onto the paper, providing the Prime Minister with a halo at last.

Inside the house, the tiny lead soldiers that populated a hex-based landscape in the attic resumed their brutal battle for supremacy. Lacking brains inside their solid metal heads, they had no memory of the reasons for their war, no excuses to justify their madness.

Back in the garden, a bird tweeted its banal opinion of the latest fake-news non-story.

Thunder rumbled, and the rain fell harder.

Flowers made obeisance to the battering drops, as the nation nodded and asked for more from the imbecilic monkeys that populated parliament.

The bird took wing and struck the bedroom window and fell to the ground below, leaving a bloody smear behind. It twitched, then lay still. There was nothing else left for it to do.

The rain continued to fall, washing away the blood.

"It's always the same," said Fred.

Jim nodded. "It is. It is."

Some mornings you have trouble getting out of bed. Some mornings you don't.

It's evening now, so it hardly matters.

A steaming bowl of tomato soup lays before you, gazpacho gone wrong.

You like soup, don't you? Sometimes, you find it hard to remember.

Today, you do: You do.

You think.

Perhaps you should try thinking of something else.

Jim looked at Fred. Fred looked at Jim. They shared a look, confused, bemused. The sun continued to hide behind the dark rain clouds, amused.

"Glowering," said Jim, looking up at the clouds instead of Fred.

A raindrop struck his eye, and he shrieked, perhaps in pain, perhaps in pleasure, perhaps just because it was the thing you were meant to do.

"Glowering-argh?" asked Fred.

"Just glowering, I think," clarified Jim. "The clouds."

"I like the word," said Fred, although Jim never knew if he meant 'glowering' or 'clouds'. Fred also liked the rain. Other things he liked were paying his taxes, trips to the zoo to look at scuttling things, and steaming bowls of tomato soup. *Especially* tomato soup.

The war between the miniature soldiers in the attic

intensified and many died; if death applied to things that were never alive to begin with. Jim would've said it did, but Fred would've disagreed. They had never discussed the point, and their views remained unsaid.

The rain was now drizzle; damp but without conviction.

A rabbit exited the house, arms full with cabbages, a cigar clenched between its teeth.

Jim nodded at the rabbit.

The rabbit nodded at Jim.

Fred glared – he didn't hold with rabbits. Or, cabbages.

He felt conflicted about whether or not to care about the blatant theft.

He chose not to.

The drizzle continued to fall.

The news in the paper continued to be bad.

Fred continued to glare.

"It's always the same," said Fred.

Jim nodded. "It is. It is."

Some mornings you have trouble getting out of bed. Some mornings you don't.

It's the middle of the night now, so you're supposed to be in bed.

Are you?

It hardly matters.

But why aren't you sleeping?

You *should* be sleeping.

But, you're thinking about tomato soup, about the wonderful adventures to be had, spoon in hand, in every steaming bowl.

Keep thinking about tomato soup.

Mm, tomato soup.

Now, don't.

You can't can you?

Mm, tomato soup.

***

Jim looked at Fred. Fred looked at Jim. They shared a look, amused, enthused. The rain clouds had run away, but the sun remained hidden out of sight, leaving behind a slate-grey sky and a chill in the air.

The roof of the house was tiled red.

Neither Jim nor Fred had ever seen grey slates, but they had seen the sky. The sky was the grey of slates.

Presumably, in turn, slates were the grey of the sky.

Sky-grey slates remained a mystery to them.

In the attic, the battle was nearly over, the table on which it had been fought piled with the dead and dying. If things that had never lived could be said to die. Jim would've said they could, but Fred would've disagreed. Unaware of what was occurring, it remained a topic they had never discussed. Perhaps they never would.

But, there were things they did.

"Do you know what a Scotsman wears beneath his skirt?" asked Fred.

"Kilt," said Jim.

Fred shook his head. "No, they don't wear kilts beneath their skirts."

Jim nodded. "I do know they keep a hidden knife in their socks."

"All of them?"

"Just the right, I believe. Or, maybe, the left."

Fred nodded.

Inside the house, the piano began to play a mournful tune in remembrance of the elephants that died to provide its keys. The keys were actually wood, but the piano didn't know that. It didn't know about the ancient trees that had died.

Jim did and hated the piano with a passion as a result. He hated frauds.

Not that the piano knew. It might have played a mournful tune for itself if it had.

Nobody cared about the ancient trees that had become its keys.

It was probably too late.

A honeybee shivered past Jim's nose.

Somewhere a telephone rang.

Nobody answered it, not that they knew.

Or, perhaps, somebody did, somewhere.

It hardly mattered it wasn't for them.

Jim tossed the newspaper aside, startling a passing spider, bemused by its contents, and the sheets danced away on the breeze, pirouetting in delight at their lies.

"It's always the same," said Fred.

Jim nodded. "It is. It is."

It was time for them to go to bed.

They continued to sit in the garden, wondering where the sun had gone.

Some mornings you have trouble getting out of bed. Some mornings you don't.

It's morning now, but which sort will it be

Do you know? Well, do you know?

A steaming bowl of tomato soup is waiting for you, if only you will get out of bed.

Will you? Well, will you?

You like soup, don't you?

Say 'yes', and get out of bed.

Say 'no' and stay where you are.

You don't know who made that bowl of soup for you, who set it there.

Don't you find that odd?

You should.

Jim sat in his garden, waiting for the arrival of the rain as the sun shot its rays down the narrow English lanes to the accompaniment of inquisitive flies.

"It's always the same," said Fred.

Jim nodded. "It is. It is."

A fly settled on his nose and looked him in the eyes. Jim yawned and swallowed it.

In the attic, the battle was over, and all the little lead figures were dead. Not that any of them had been alive, to begin with. Not that it mattered. Or, ever had.

Jim looked at Fred. Fred looked at Jim. There was no newspaper today. They didn't know why.

"No news is good news," Jim observed, and it was true. Although the truth was also a lie.

There was no news, but there *was* plenty of bad, a whole world full, just beyond his garden gate, just upon the cusp of his thoughts.

In fact, truth be told, everything was a lie.

Things weren't the same.

There were no inquisitive flies.

The sun wasn't shining.

The only thing that was true was that there wasn't a newspaper – and, *that* was bad news.

The sun that wasn't a sun rose on the horizon, a bloody flower, a crimson ball of flame. The sky looked like the stain left by spilt tomato soup.

Inquisitive motes of dust danced towards them down the narrow English lanes, one landing on Jim's nose.

He yawned and swallowed it and began to choke.

Dark clouds rose skyward, but no rain fell. Yet.

A distressed spider scuttled this way and that, not knowing what to think.

Everything was a lie.

Everything was bad.

Fred thought of tomato soup.

Jim laughed sadly.

Or, was that a lie, too?

Some mornings you have trouble getting out of bed. Some mornings you don't.

You won't ever be getting out of bed, not now.

You never will again.

Not even for a steaming bowl of tomato soup.

Jim sat in his garden, waiting for his skin to peel away.

When it did, he would look just like a ripe tomato.

Fred thought of tomato soup.

Jim thought of the unfairness of life.

"It's always the same," said Fred.

Jim nodded. "It is. It is."

But it wasn't.

Fred was dead – and so, too, soon, would be Jim.

Some mornings… so are you.

Ends

TV-HEAD

- Peter Caffrey -

Phil stuck his head around the office door.

'Is anyone around?' he hissed, nervousness obvious in his voice.

'Just the usual suspects,' I replied.

'Staff meeting: Dog and Duck, fifteen minutes?'

'Be rude not to,' I said, giving him the thumbs up before he disappeared back into the corridor. There was only an hour of the working day left, so I shut down my laptop and rounded up the rest of the team. No one needed persuading to head off early.

In the pub, Phil sat behind a table of drinks. He knew the round off by heart; we all did.

'Gentleman and Rebecca,' he said once we were seated, 'I find myself in a bit of a bind, and I'm afraid the fallout might impact on every one of us. You're all aware of my robotic barbecue assistant, TV-Head?'

I suppressed a smirk. When Phil built TV-Head, his goal was to create a robotic commis chef to help with barbecues. He'd fitted the robot with a television for a head so he could watch football while he cooked. I programmed TV-Head and had inserted a chaos sequence in the code as a practical joke. One day, at a random time, the sequence would run, and the robot would go berserk.

'Last Sunday, I had a barbecue for some friends and neighbours,' Phil explained with gravitas. 'It was a civilised affair, but there was an unfortunate incident.'

'You had a barbecue for friends and didn't invite us?' Tommy interjected.

'Oh, trust me, you'll be glad you weren't in attendance,' Phil replied. 'When everyone was there, I sent TV-Head into the kitchen to fetch a leg of lamb.'

'Hang on,' Frank said. 'You barbecued a leg of lamb? What are you: a heathen? No one barbecues a leg of lamb, not in any sane society.'

'Too right,' Tommy said. 'If I had a barbecue for my friends and didn't invite the people I spent most of my time with, the last thing I'd do is barbecue a leg of lamb.'

Phil sighed, frustrated by the interruptions.

'Shut up, all of you. This is important. The lamb was still frozen; TV-Head hadn't taken it out of the freezer in time, so I had a go at him. Well, he flew into a rage and became abusive. One of Jessica's friends from the school cautioned TV-Head about his language, and he beat her senseless with the frozen leg of lamb.'

We all sat in silence, absorbing the news.

'Who'd buy a frozen leg of lamb?' Frank asked with disgust. 'That's fucking disgraceful.'

We all murmured our agreement.

'Disgusting.'

'Outrageous.'

'Unacceptable.'

'Are you lot stupid?' Phil snapped. 'An illicit military spec robot, customised by us with total disregard for our orders, has beaten a woman into a coma. If anyone investigates, the whole sorry mess will lead them straight to Department S.'

'Calm down Phil; just bring Terry in, and we'll dispose of him,' I said.

'I can't,' Phil muttered. 'He made a run for it and escaped. I chased after him, but he reached the underground and jumped onto a train heading into the West End.'

'Are you telling us an out-of-control assassin robot, one we all helped you customise when our civic duty was to decommission it, is on the loose in the West End?' I asked.

Phil nodded, sparking a group realisation: we were fucked.

Until TV-Head beat Phil's neighbour into a coma with a frozen leg of lamb, we were pretty much flying under the radar. The top brass never visited Department S. Our small team of engineers knew what to do, and to a degree we did it. There was some messing about, maybe more messing about than most people would consider proper, but that's what happens when you give inquiring minds a tedious job to do.

When I joined the Special Operations Agency, they placed me in the technical field operations team: the TFO. What we did was so covert, even MI5 and MI6 didn't know about it.

The TFO built robots of all types, and I wrote the code which turned them into spies and killers. We created self-driving cars long before the commercial sector had an interest in such vehicles. The secure limousines were supplied to international leaders and politicians. To the drivers and passengers, they appeared to be ordinary cars, only becoming self-driving if the top brass at the Agency decided a regime change was needed.

If an influential figure died in an unexplained car accident, we usually had something to do with it. We didn't just do cars. If a light aircraft went down with a VIP on board, it was often our handiwork. We also built an army of assassin robots and sent them around the world to tip the balance of power in favour of whichever side we deemed fit.

When they sent me from the TFO to Department S, it was a demotion, a punishment. The Special Operations Agency didn't bump off its miscreants; we were skilled technicians, had full security clearance and knew too much. It just gave us shittier jobs. They demoted me for screwing the office cleaner after the Christmas party. It turned out she was also getting it on with one of the top brass, and as a result, they sent me to Department S, the salvage team.

Salvage was a misnomer; our role was to destroy evidence. Once the Agency's technology had done its work, a ground team picked it up and spirited it back to the UK. We'd strip down the devices and recode the parts. If anyone ever investigated, they'd have no idea the components had been used for international espionage. We disguised weapons of war as household appliances, cleaning up any evidence a breach of international law had taken place.

The Department's mischievous antics started when we planned a birthday party for Rebecca. A few days before, an assassin robot arrived for dismantling. The Agency had used it to knock off crooked politicians involved with drug cartels in Colombia. Before taking it apart, I rewrote the code, and we set it to work as a waiter for the bash. From then on, the Department S team developed a penchant for misappropriating secret equipment and repurposing it for our entertainment.

Because of the secrecy surrounding the tech we dealt with, there were no paper trails. As a result, the temptation to mess around was always there. We were bloody good engineers, too good not to try things out, and it was a way of cocking a snook at the bastards who'd demoted us.

Now we had a problem in the form of a rampaging assassin robot with a TV for a head. It was out there, in the West End of London, armed with a frozen leg of lamb.

The problem was a serious one. Anyone carrying out a credible investigation would realise we'd converted a significant amount of classified hardware into playthings. Hundreds of thousands of pounds worth of advanced military equipment sat in our homes, performing everyday tasks: sweeping driveways, cleaning cars, watering gardens, painting bedrooms and the like. If the Agency found out, we'd be looking at substantial custodial sentences.

'Do you have any ideas on how we can extract ourselves from this clusterfuck?' Phil asked.

'I have a friend in the records office at New Scotland Yard,' Rebecca said. 'I could see if there've been any sightings of TV-Head.'

'Good idea,' Phil replied, 'but be subtle.'

'What do you mean, be subtle?' Rebecca asked with scorn. 'What do you think I'll do; ring her up and ask if there've been any reports of a renegade military assassin automaton causing chaos on the streets, and if so, can we have it back before our boss finds out?'

'Don't be a prick to Rebecca, Phil,' Frank added. 'This mess is your fault, you and your fucking barbecued lamb leg.'

Phil was seething. I knew he wanted to point out we'd all taken liberties, and it could be any of us in the shit. I tried and keep things on track.

'You said TV-Head went into the underground. Which station was it?'

'Pimlico.'

'How do you know he was heading to the West End?'

'I checked with the staff. It was a northbound train he jumped on.'

'Maybe he went to Walthamstow,' I suggested.

Frank laughed, a loud guffaw, and said, 'Robots have intelligence. Why would an intelligent machine go to fucking Walthamstow of all places?'

I could see Phil tensing up, so I got rid of Frank.

'You're resourceful; find a way to access the CCTV from Victoria Line stations and find out where TV-Head got off.'

Frank nodded, downed his pint, and left.

'Everyone else, get home and identify all the devices you've taken from work,' I said. 'We need to get rid of anything incriminating.'

As the others headed off, Phil took me to one side.

'Are you sure you wiped all the old code before you reprogrammed TV-Head?'

'Trust me, I wiped everything.'

'And you didn't do anything stupid ... for a joke? If you did, just tell me. It might help sort things out.'

'Of course not,' I said through gritted teeth. 'I wouldn't be that much of an arsehole.'

I walked around the house, making a note of everything I'd procured from Department S. The robotic gardener had to go; it was built for active duty as an assassin during the Arab Spring. Despite complaints from the children, I removed the automaton fish from the garden pond. The kids loved them, unaware of their dark history: we'd designed them to despatch a hostile media baron while he was at sea on his luxury yacht.

As I checked for more devices, my phone rang. It was Phil.

'I've had some news,' he said with urgency. 'Frank's looked at the CCTV footage, and TV-Head got off at Oxford Circus. Why I don't know.'

'Maybe he wanted to do some shopping,' I suggested.

'Come on, try and be serious, please. Rebecca turned up something too. Last night someone attacked a woman off Wardour Street. Her assailant wore a disguise ... he had a TV on his head!'

'I'm on my way,' I said. 'Meet me at the corner of Wardour Street and Oxford Street.'

'I was thinking,' Phil blurted, making sure he got in before I ended the call.

'What?'

'The woman who was attacked got away without serious injury. She only suffered facial bruising. He didn't fracture her skull like he did with Jessica's friend. Do you think TV-Head might be calming down?'

'I doubt it. It's more likely the leg of lamb has thawed out.'

We met on the corner as arranged. Tommy was the last to arrive, emerging from the evening gloom carrying a black metal tube with a barbed bolt sticking out.

'What the fuck is that, Tommy?' Phil asked.

'Harpoon gun; it's all I could find at short notice.'

'Jesus wept,' Rebecca hissed. 'Are you really going to wander down Oxford Street with a harpoon gun?'

'I don't have any other choice,' Tommy muttered, determined to keep the weapon.

Tommy set off towards Oxford Circus, while Rebecca headed for Tottenham Court Road. Frank and Phil searched Berwick Street, and I took Wardour Street. I looked through every pub, restaurant and cocktail bar window, and nipped up some of the side streets to check the peep shows. There was no sign of TV-Head.

Getting closer to Piccadilly, I checked the final alleyway. In the darkness, I saw a figure, a drunk man leaning against a wall. As I turned away, a flicker of light, cold and blue, caught my eye. It was a television screen. Sprinting towards it, I shouted, 'TV-Head, stop right there. You've got nowhere to run.'

TV-Head spun around, brandishing the leg of lamb. It had thawed, the meat sagging against the bone.

'Give it up,' I ordered. 'I'm not afraid of your floppy meat.'

Swinging the leg in an arc, he brought it up with speed, smashing it into my bollocks. I crumpled, sucking in air as an explosion of agony coursed through my abdomen, pulsing like an electric shock inside my groin. TV-Head was off, running towards Piccadilly Circus. Despite the pain, I hobbled after him.

Labouring with intense ball-ache, I struggled down Piccadilly towards Green Park. The street was empty; there was no sign of TV-Head. I'd lost him, so I slowed down, sucking in air and waiting for the discomfort in my testicles to subside.

Phil and Frank jogged down the street and, spotting me, came over.

'Any joy?' Phil asked.

'Yeah, I saw him. He cracked me one in the nuts and ran down here. I chased him as best I could, but he got away.'

'Shit,' Phil muttered.

'He could be anywhere. If he went into the park, we've got no chance of finding him.'

'We might have,' Frank said. 'Was his screen on?'

'Yeah; that's how I spotted him.'

Frank and Phil stood gazing into the darkness while I waited for the grinding ache in my balls to subside.

'What's that?' Frank asked, pointing into the night.

There was nothing, just blackness, then for a second a blueish flickering light was visible through the bushes. We moved forward, keeping low, edging towards the sickly glow. Before we could formulate a plan, Phil charged. He moved with speed, but TV-Head was faster, sprinting like a demented robotic television-headed Linford Christie. We gave chase, only slowing when TV-Head dashed from the park, ran across the road and vaulted the railings into the grounds of Buckingham Palace.

'Get on the phone to Tommy,' Frank said to Phil, breathing heavily. 'Tell him to get down here with his harpoon gun; the Queen's in mortal danger.'

'There's no time,' Phil gasped. 'Let's head for the gates.'

We staggered towards the entrance, a uniformed police officer watching us from inside the railings as we approached.

'Open up,' Frank snapped, searching in his pockets for his ID card. 'This is a national emergency.'

The officer stood in silence, watching Frank's search with curiosity.

'Got it,' Frank muttered, producing his ID card and showing it to the policeman. 'Open the gate and let us in.

The future of the monarchy depends upon our timely intervention.'

The officer squinted at the card.

'What's this, a library card?' he asked.

'It's my ID; now open the fucking gate.'

'We're with the Special Operations Agency,' I added.

'Never heard of it,' the policeman said.

'It's a secret Government department,' Phil said. 'I shouldn't tell you this, but there's an assassin robot in there, one with a television for a head, and we need to stop it before it reaches any members of the Royal household. If you don't let us in, the Queen's blood could be on your hands.'

The policeman was unimpressed, unmoving and unwilling to grant us entry.

'Let us in, for fuck's sake,' Frank howled. 'The robot's armed.'

'Armed?' the officer asked, his interest piqued. 'What's it armed with?'

'A leg of lamb,' Phil replied, 'a frozen one.'

'What sort of bastard buys a frozen leg of lamb?' the policeman asked, disgust clear on his screwed-up face.

'We've already been through this a few times, so there's no need to go over it again,' Phil responded defensively. 'It was only for a barbecue.'

'You barbecued a leg of lamb?' the policeman asked with concern. 'Are you a heathen?'

'That's what I said,' Frank chimed in.

'Why's a robot armed with a frozen leg of lamb?' the policeman asked.

'In the interests of accuracy, officer, the leg of lamb isn't frozen; not any more,' I explained. 'It's thawed out, but can still cause a nasty injury. He whacked me in the bollocks with it, and I reckon I'll be pissing blood in the morning.'

'Who sent this alleged assassin robot after the Queen,' the officer asked with irritation.

'No one did,' Phil muttered. 'It escaped and … well …

139

the fact it's in the palace is … how can I put this … an unhappy coincidence.'

The policeman leaned towards us, his face a snarling expression of contempt, and he hissed, 'Here's another unhappy coincidence: unless the three of you fuck off right now, I'll have you nicked for drunk and disorderly.'

As he spoke, high pitched sirens pierced the evening calm. Behind the railings, pandemonium ensued, soldiers running, people shouting, bright lights illuminating the building and its grounds. It was obvious TV-Head had entered the palace. The officer turned and sprinted towards the developing chaos.

On the balcony of the palace, the large glass doors opened. An elderly woman, regal-looking and wearing a pastel blue twin set, staggered out. Behind her was a blur of bluish cold flickering light. For a second, she seemed to freeze, petrified in a moment of terror, before dropping like a stone.

Frank, Phil and I stood looking at each other.

'Well, that's not a good sign,' Frank said. 'If you ask me, TV-Head has either killed the Queen or is pummelling her senseless with his meat right now.'

'Her Majesty, beaten to death with a leg of lamb,' Phil muttered. 'God, save her.'

'This is what happens when you buy frozen fucking lamb legs,' Frank said with dismay. 'Come on; I need a drink.'

'Me too,' Phil added. 'Dog and Duck?'

'Be rude not to,' I said.

BILL

- Craig Bullock -

Bill was a man made of money. Now I don't mean the guy was rich, in fact, he was far from it. Bill gave all of his wealth to charities and the homeless. Man, the dude could literally poop Pound coins. No, I mean Bill was literally made of money, Pounds, Euros, Dollars, you name it? The guy was multi-currency.

Legend has it that Bill was conceived when his mother, Lola, sold her voluptuous body to an Arabian Sheik one last time. It marked her 100th lay in what can only be described as a sloppy career. Anyway, 8 months, 3 weeks and 2 days later, Lola was rushed into hospital, with the suspected child believed to be on its way. The birth was a complicated one and no matter how hard Lola pushed the child would not make an appearance. At the stroke of midnight Lola gave one final push and an almighty red wave, blood and afterbirth spewed from Lola's lady area onto the delivery table, but no baby was found. Her baby bump had vanished, and naturally, the doctors rushed her out of the delivery room for closer inspection. When the hospital's cleaner was mopping the area and scooping up the mess, she found a collection of small change mixed in with the blood and excrement. She rinsed the bodily fluids off the coins and feeling hungry, used the small change she had found to purchase a chocolate bar from a nearby vending machine. This was where Bill spent his early years.

Once Bill had pulled himself together, he left his machine to brave the rapacious world before him. A dollar short of a full wallet, Bill, moved on looking for ways to help the financially needy.

"Dude that's such bull. I ain't ever heard of no man made of actual money. That dude would be famous. A freaky science experiment even."

"Honest, it's no lie. Swear on my son's life. Bill was actually made of money. His legs were a mesh of Dollars and Rupee. His arms were solid Lira and Dinar. His face was a hideous mess… but it was expensive. The guy wore a latex mask in the day so no one could tell."

"Haha! If he be real, I'd make sure I was his best buddy. Hell, I'd even be moving him in with me! If he be true, how did you find out about him, and what did you do before getting locked up?"

"I was in community enforcement."

"What you a cop? I ain't sharing no cell with an ex pig! I'll cut you first."

"No! Neighbourhood Watch…. Far more brutal."

"Hmmm. What you in for then Homes?"

"Fraud"

Like I said earlier, Bill liked to give to charities and the homeless. I've no issue with the odd charity, apart from dog trusts. Dog's, crap all over the place and we don't want that where we live. No, it's the homeless I have the issue with!

Bill was going round donating to every low life in the gutter. Druggies, scroungers, drunks, you know, the type you find begging for loose change and food… Filth.

Problem was, Bill was donating too much money to these lowlifes, and they were actually buying houses, actual places to live. Places to live in my street!

Please understand, my street is somewhat exclusive, and I'm sorry, but, I didn't want their type moving in.

The street began filling up with all sorts of reprobates, all mixed background and race. The community just wasn't ours anymore. As the road became more and more ruined, the good folk started selling up. House prices dropped, and the street was awash with those who shouldn't be there, cavorting together in their yards.

Something had to be done! We all knew their sort couldn't afford to live there, but we were confused about where they were getting their money.

I was head of our Neighbourhood Watch, and so, I called a meeting of the elders. Together we devised a plan and the next night put it into action.

"Yo dude this is some crazy stuff! But be careful with the racist talk, I'm easily offended. Would me and my family not be welcome in your street?"

"Of course you would. You'd be very welcome… If we ignore the horrific murder of your mother-in-law and the fact you're Latino. After all, you were an investment banker."

That night, John from 'number 10', a close friend of mine, wore his finest black tracksuit and enticed one of those fuckers into his house with the promise of strong liquor. It didn't quite go to plan, the first guy we captured was Polish, and neither John nor I can speak an ounce of Polish. We got him so drunk he passed out and woke in his own bed, remembering nothing. If I'm honest, we had quite a good night, but that's beside the point.

The following night I took it upon myself to do the enticing, and we caught ourselves a good-un. John brought his pliers, and the guy squealed like a pig. He told us everything about how he got his money and even where we could find Bill. At first, I was sceptical of his tale, but by the time we had broken his fourth finger and had pulled off each toenail, his story hadn't altered, so we decided to check it out.

John and a few others dressed like homeless people, and we took to the streets. After the third night Suzanne from 'number 23', our receptionist for the watch, got a hit and radioed it in. Suzanne instantly recognised the man's description and could hear the clink of change approaching a mile away. He handed her a large enveloped without saying a word and waited to see her reaction when she opened it. Me and the boys hit him from behind. Bill fell with a loud crash, and we bundled him into the back of a van. Jesus, he weighed a ton.

"I'm still not sold. If you caught yourself a cash cow you'd be a millionaire by now, not stuck in this hole. The guy was a walking cash machine. I'd have milked him dry and moved my ass to some fancy island. Nah man I don't get it?"

"It was never our intention to get rich. We just wanted to buy back the property that those scum purchased. We wanted to make our street ours again."

"Dude you got issues. I thought I had problems, but that was easily solved with a shotgun and a cheese grater. You should have fed him on laxatives until he had shat out enough Pound coins to get you gone."

"In hindsight, I wish I had."

We had secured Bill to a chair and waited for him to wake. He opened his eyes but remained silent, not sure if he even had vocal cords because he never muttered a word the whole time he was there. We explained our situation but never got a response so carried on with the second part of our plan.

We needed his money to buy back our street. As you so eloquently put it, we waited for him to shit, and sure enough, he passed a fair bounty, but we soon realised it would take too long. We tried laxatives, and this sped up the process but not fast enough. We gave him the common cold, and each sneeze helped us towards our goal, and if I'm honest, it was quite funny seeing John get violently sprayed with Euros.

We had Bill trapped for months, but people began getting impatient. The influx of new residents had stopped, but now we needed to buy back what was ours. Some of them went easy, happy with a 10% return on their investment, but others were less willing to sell, appearing comfortable in their temporary homes.

Talk moved on to the less favourable option of just cashing Bill in, piece by piece, the exchange rate was reasonable, so we figured why not. He was a walking fortune, and he would probably be enough to get us through. I never wanted to kill Bill, but our options were running out. John fetched his hack saw and took to work on Bill's finger. When John started sawing Yen began to flow from the cut, like a fruit machine dropping a jackpot.

This changed things. For weeks we kept this up, a little cut at a time. However, after a while, Bill just shut down, I guess he died. We hacked him apart piece by piece and deposited parts of Bill in our bank accounts.

It didn't take long to purchase all the homes back. We were now able to offer the more stubborn ones a 300% return, and soon they all moved out, one by one. Our street was ours again, exclusive and rented out to more desirable neighbours.

"Fraud? You said you were in here for fraud, not murder."

"Yep, fraud it was. All of us had pieces of Bill in our bank accounts. Once Bill was deposited we thought it was over but Bill kept giving. Our bank balances started to go up! Large sums of money kept being deposited with no explanation, hundreds of thousands at a time and we couldn't stop it. Soon the bank started to investigate, and when the authorities got involved, they concluded the only explanation was fraudulent activity. The whole street got nicked."

"Haha! Stunning. You got your just! It's true, I guess, in your case, crime don't pay after all. You swapped less desirable neighbours for even more fucked up neighbours. Dude, you got burned."

"It's not all bad. I made a new friend in the shower last week. His name's Teddy, big white guy, he keeps giving me tobacco and chocolate. Says he's gonna look after me and show me a nice time. Seems like a nice guy."

"Hahahaha good luck with that dude. If you're Teddy's bitch, I'll leave you be, for now. Have fun, and I'll see you around, with or without the limp."

AN INCIDENT AT THE PEARLY GATES

- Neil Dinsmore -

"You perished in a jet ski accident".

"No, he flaming well did not!" spat St. Peter, bashing a spanner off the robot's head.

The devout and hard-working saint was particularly flustered today. Usually, his divine duty of manning the Pearly Gates™ was stressful – there were always unjudged souls ready to object to being denied peace everlasting – but today was extra aggravating because he was trying, between fresh neophytes, to train a robotic servant. No mean feat when the world's population never took a break from dying and ascending that ethereal escalator in the sky.

"I told you already, this one died of a brain aneurysm, not a sodding jet ski. Now get that into your thick CPU, or we'll be here all day... Oh Jesus Christ, here comes another one..."

"Did somebody say my name?" It was Jesus, he'd appeared out of a pink cloud, a habit his father had asked him to stop because it was upsetting the more sensitive angels.

"Get lost Jesus, I'm busy here," snapped St. Peter, jabbing a golden screwdriver into the robot's auxiliary port.

"Well now, somebody's uptight today. Better hurry Pete, you're starting to get a backlog there," jested the son of God, pointing at the steadily expanding line of dearly departed on the other side of the pristine palisade.

"Shut up, you wood-whittling hippie!" barked the divine doorman. Jesus sneered and promptly left, kicking up a wisp of cloud in his wake. "Alright, you. Yes, *you*. You're next. Okay, let's try this again. Doorbotron 2000, tell me how this man died, and I swear to the All-Maker you'd better not screw it up again".

"Greetings stiff, and welcome to Heaven. My neural sensors indicate to me that you have recently perished in a jet ski accident".

St. Peter exploded. Literally. Never in his multi-millennia long service to the Kingdom of God had he been this phenomenally angry. After his steaming skull chunks had settled over the cobblestone clouds and the pulpy bits of his sizzling brain slid down the faces of bewildered onlookers, Peter's head reconstituted itself, and he resumed his tirade. "Damn it! You're the single biggest piece of crap I've ever had the misfortune of working with in my entire life! Gabriel, hey Gabriel, get your bronzed buns over here and help me with this pile of trash!"

Gabriel, who was nearby and busying himself with adjusting a quadriplegic's bow tie, sauntered over to the gates and let loose an impressed whistle. He'd never seen a robot in Heaven before. And no, Jesus' wooden golem didn't count.

"Gabe, now you're a smart lad. You know a thing or two about machines, what with that arcade cabinet you and Joseph Jr. threw together for Barachiel's birthday last week. Tell me how to fix this piece of garbage before I lose it completely and send it to Hell".

"What operating system is it running?" asked the angel, rubbing his fake-tanned chin.

"Erm, excuse me..." asked a man timidly on the other side of the pearly barricade. "But could you tell me, is this Heaven?"

"Shut your mouth, you impatient wretch!" blared St. Peter. "I'll get to you in a God damn minute, can't you idiots hang on for just a second? You're already dead, it's not like you need to be anywhere or anything". The angry old saint scratched the bald spot under his halo, it always itched whenever he was stressed. "Now let me think... Um, yes, I think it's Microsoft Windows: Divine Edition. Why?"

"Oh," said Gabriel, sounding suddenly quite hopeless. "I don't know much about Microsoft systems, I've only ever worked with Apple ones".

"Apple?!" spat St. Peter, kicking the robot and stubbing his toe in the process. "Apple?! You know damn well no apples are allowed in Heaven, not since the incident with Adam back in the day. How dare you speak such blasphemy!"

"Oh shut up, Pete," scolded Gabriel, turning to walk away. "It's an operating system by a company called Apple. It's not an *actual* apple, you tool. I hope that robot falls over and crushes you, you nasty old sourpuss".

"Fine!" yelled St. Peter with his finger pointing accusingly at the retreating messenger of God. "I'll fix this thing all by myself! I don't need you or your bad attitude anyway, Gabe!"

"Excuse me sir, but I really must insist: is this Heaven or not?" It was the man on the other side of the gate again. He seemed to have gathered some courage; for now, he had stretched an arm through the bars and was tapping St. Peter vigorously upon the shoulder.

The gatekeeper of the afterlife was about to turn around and chastise the man for daring to lay his fingers upon a saint, but he didn't get the chance. For at that very moment, the robot kicked into gear and wasted no time tearing the impatient soul's appendage clean off. Howling in agony, the man fell backwards clutching his bloody stump as several other recently deceased gathered around and frantically tried their best to stem the bleeding, but soon gave up when they realised he was already dead and bleeding out probably wasn't that much of a concern.

"Why did you do that?" shouted a woman accusingly.

"Yeah, that was completely uncalled for!" yelled another.

"You're a malicious piece of work, that's what you are!" cursed a third man with his arms folded.

"Oh go to Hell, you bunch of babies. *I* didn't tear his

sodding arm off, now did I? It was this useless mountain of junk over here, he's been botching up all day long and now this. I can't win. I just *cannot* win today". St. Peter glared at the group of confused and angry people awaiting both judgement and an apology on the other side of the gate. Then he turned his gaze towards his robotic apprentice. "Doorbotron 2000, why, pray tell, did you tear that poor man's arm off?"

"Master, my firmware dictates that anyone exhibiting hostilities towards an employee of God must be neutralised immediately. I did as my defence programme instructs under such circumstances". The robot stared blankly into space. The gatekeeper considered this for some time.

"Right, owing to your loyalty, I'll give you one last chance. But if you get it wrong again, it'll be the last thing you ever do. Now, tell me how that man lying over there died". St. Peter stood back with his arms folded and awaited the machine's response.

The mechanoid processed the situation long and hard, its capacitors and circuitry buzzing and ticking as it evaluated all available information extra carefully, like a dog who'd specifically been told not to eat the biscuit, despite the biscuit being placed upon its nose.

"You perished..." the robot paused. St. Peter's eyes glared with the intensity of a thousand prayer candles. "...When I tore your arm off, and you bled to death".

"No! Damn it, no!" screamed St. Peter in a foul rage. "A man can't die *twice!* You imbecile! That's it, I'm going to decommission the crap out of you, you worthless heap of bolts!"

"Actually," said a voice from beyond the gate. "I think he's right. This man *is* dead. Erm, again".

St. Peter snapped his head towards the speaker, then looked down at the one-armed man. He was blue. Not breathing. Little angelic flies were dancing upon his glassy eyes. The saint fell into deep shock, this was utterly bewildering. Such a thing had never happened before in the entire history of Heaven. No one had ever died twice. It simply wasn't possible, surely?

Just then, the one and only Jesus Christ showed up once more, having felt a disturbance in the divine force. "What's all this, what's going on, we'll have no trouble here," he demanded as he marched over to St. Peter and saw the blue, one-armed man on the other side of the Pearly Gates™. "Is that man dead?! For *my* sake Pete, what have you gone and done now? You've killed somebody!"

"No, I haven't!" fired back St. Peter, shaking like a fig leaf in a Bethlehem breeze. "People can't die in Heaven. It's not possible!"

"Look, idiot. He's not *in* Heaven yet. He's still on the other side of that gate, therefore, technically not in the afterlife yet. If you hadn't wasted so much time with that hunk of junk over there, he'd be inside enjoying everlasting happiness. Perhaps taking one of my highly praised scrimshaw classes. But no, look at him, he's bereft of life! Lord knows what that means for his soul. He's probably in purgatory now. For all eternity. No thanks to you. That's it, I'm shutting this gate down!"

"What do you mean you're 'shutting this gate down'?" croaked an elderly woman on the other side. "We've got every right to be here! You can't deny us eternal peace, we deserve our divine judgement! We've lived a life of righteousness for this moment!"

"Yes, yes, I know," replied Jesus as he pulled a roll of caution tape out of his bum bag and began cordoning off the Pearly Gates™. "Don't worry, I'll open the second gate for you. Hadraniel'll sort you out. His gate's on the other side of Heaven".

"How far away is it?" asked another.

"I'd say...about fifteen thousand miles," answered Jesus, affixing a large "CLOSED TO THE PUBLIC" sign.

"Fifteen thousand miles?! That's ages! I'm not walking that," whinged a little old lady, shaking her fist.

Jesus screwed his face up in annoyance as he

straightened the sign and took St. Peter's keys off him. "Alright! Fine, I'll arrange a bus to come pick you up. Now don't say Jesus isn't good to you". The Messiah turned to St. Peter once again and addressed him. "Pete, you done goofed royally this time. This isn't like stealing communion wafers or sending Lucifer a friend request while logged into Gabriel's Facebook account. This is super serious. I'm hereby suspending you as the official gatekeeper of the Pearly Gates™ and temporarily revoking your sainthood. Don't look at me like that, Pete. You know fine well I can't let this slide. A man is dead because of you. It's not up to me to judge you for this, that's up to my Father. I've just texted him about what's happened. He wants to see you". Peter opened his mouth to protest but Jesus cut him off. "Shut up! Don't say another word or I'll put these sandals so far up your rear-end we'll rename you Leatherface! Now go. He's waiting. And take that damn robot with you".

Peter, who was now just run-of-the-mill Peter and not St. Peter the revered doorman, grudgingly shuffled off towards God's office, leaving Jesus behind to dispose of the blue, one-armed man. Peter wasn't exactly enthusiastic about his impending meeting with the supreme deity, not when he'd essentially lost an innocent soul to the unknowable abyss of purgatory. He'd probably wind up getting demoted to groundskeeper or sent as a missionary to Hell to try and convert demons like poor old Jegudiel after he'd burnt God's bagel that one time. God didn't mess around.

As he and his robot made their way through the gardens and winding streets, Peter was hissed and booed at by the angels and other saints. Word got around quickly when somebody messed up in the Promised Land.

Up to the front door, Peter dragged himself, audibly whining. He pressed the buzzer and waited nervously for a response. "Come," came the deep, booming reply. Peter gently opened the door and entered God's office.

There wasn't much inside, the Creator was famously a

minimalist. A small wooden desk that Jesus had built Him with some Lego on top of it occupied the centre of the room, a reproduction of the Mona Lisa hung upon the northern wall, and a wilting potted plant sat awkwardly in a corner beside a cage with a fat hamster sleep inside it. God was leaning over the desk, putting the finishing touches on a Lego castle. "Pete. Take a seat".

The robot juddered to the nearest corner, crushed the potted plant in the process and faced the wall, putting itself into power-saving mode. Peter looked around the barren office. "Um, there's no chairs," said the man glumly.

God didn't look up as He put the roof on the castle's east turret. With a nonchalant click of His fingers, a hot pink inflatable chair materialised in front of the desk. Peter sat down cautiously, squeaking and making a great deal of noise. Still not looking up from His work, God resumed. "It has come to my attention, Pete, that you have somehow managed to kill a man".

"Well it wasn't really me, it was—"

"And you did it with a robot". Without looking up, God pointed to the hibernating automaton in the corner.

Peter looked at his feet. His big toe was bleeding. "Yes. Well. *Essentially*, sure. That's pretty much it".

God placed a Lego sheep in front of the portcullis, facing a pirate. "That's not good. That poor man probably doesn't exist anymore. Not even I know what lies in purgatory".

"That's a bit shit". Before Peter even knew what he was saying he'd already sworn in front of the Almighty. The saint's mind flooded with terrifying thoughts of his employer, smiting him senseless for the indiscretion.

"It *is*," agreed God, replacing the sheep with a ghost. "And considering that we have no choice other than to assume that poor man will never find happiness again, I must punish you for your rather severe gaffe".

Peter felt a sudden but strong urge to pee.

"Incidentally," continued God, "why did you feel the

need to use a robot during the course of your duties at the Pearly Gates™?"

Peter shifted uncomfortably in the inflatable chair, sending a loud squeal rippling through the office that woke up the fat hamster. "Well..." he began, his bald spot becoming incredibly itchy. "I, uh, felt that having a helping hand would, I dunno, speed things up maybe? You don't know what it's like out there sometimes, it gets so hectic. Especially when there's a tsunami or earthquake or something. I needed the extra help. So I bought a robot".

"And where did you buy this robot?"

"Amazon".

"I see".

God fell into silence for some time as He removed both the Lego pirate and ghost and moved the portcullis further down the courtyard, allowing more space for His castle's expanding walls. Peter toyed with the idea of scratching his itchy scalp but thought better of it when he realised the inflatable chair would squeak far too much, and he didn't want to upset God any more than he probably already had.

"I had a coupon," Peter offered out of the awkward silence.

"I was not aware Amazon delivered this far north".

"Oh, yes. Only since they started using drones, but yes".

"I see," murmured God, putting the finishing touches on His castle and placing it to one side.

"Right," said the Father of all creation, folding His arms on the desk, "I have mulled it over. You have committed a very serious offence, but you have also served this kingdom for a very long time and, until now, have always acted with the utmost professionalism. Taking this into consideration, I have decided to relieve you of your duties on a semi-permanent basis. When you leave this office, you will report to Gabriel–"

"Aww come on, God!" interrupted Peter, leaping out of his chair in protest.

"Silence! You will report to Gabriel, whereupon you will

join him in his sacred duty of tying and adjusting the bow ties of Heaven's quadriplegic residents. You will do this for the next five thousand years, and if you fulfil this duty without incident, then I will consider putting you back on the Pearly Gates™. Now get moving, and do not let me hear from you again, lest you wish to experience a more severe punishment. Begone".

As Peter left the office with his head in his hands, God looked to the Doorbotron 2000 with its back to Him in the corner. It was the first time He'd actually paid any attention to it. Crossing the room, He began inspecting the machine more closely. There was a minuscule switch on the back of its neck. Leaning in, God squinted His eyes. There was some small text above it. Pulling His prescription glasses out, He read the words aloud. "*Jet Ski Mode.* Huh, now that's odd". He flicked the switch to the OFF position and slapped the robot across the back of the head to wake it up.

"Robot, I am God. I'm not a judgemental guy, well, for the most part, so I want you to know that I do not blame you for killing that poor man. I never granted robots the right to souls, and so I know there was no malice in your actions. I want to give you an opportunity. I wish you to go back to the Pearly Gates™, take down the cordon and get back to work. If you can make it through the day without any more fatalities, you've got yourself a full-time job. Now get moving, there's plenty more souls to judge".

The robot beeped in acknowledgement and rattled off out the front door, trailing a length of houseplant with it. God walked back over to the desk and started rearranging His pirates and ghosts again. Removing the outer wall of the Lego castle, He revealed two homemade figurines hiding behind the portcullis, one of St. Peter and one of the robot. Smiling, God picked up the saint and put him to one side, leaving the robot all alone in the castle. "That's better."

BILDIE SCHNOOKLEBUM!
WHEN CUTE BECOMES TERROR

THE BILDIE IS THE MOST FEARED AND HATED BEAST IN ALL THE LAND. TWO HALVES FUSED INTO A DEFORMED WHOLE, IT EXISTS ON PURE LOVE AND BIRD POO, WHICH ARE BOTH REALLY GROSS.

¡BILDIE ALERT!

IT IS ALSO THE RICHEST BEAST, BECAUSE IF ANYONE REFUSES TO PAY INTO THE BILDIE SUPPORT FUND, GOVERNMENT OVERLORDS PLOP IT ONTO THEIR DOORSTEP.

ONE WEEK WITH THE BILDIE AND ITS UNPLEASANT DIET, LOVING MEWS AND CUTELY DILATED PUPILS IS ENOUGH TO RUIN THE STRONGEST STOMACH, AND SO THE BILDIE CONTINUES ITS REIGN OF ADORABLE TERROR!

MILLIPEDE DREAMS

- Tom Over -

I race among the luminous reeds, splashing through steaming swamp water. My heartbeat hammers against my ribs. The water clings to my small legs, resisting my passage like glutinous webbing. I forge through the reeking marsh, glancing around, not knowing how I got here. The sky is a dusky smear the colour of mouldering fruit. While twilight recedes quickly between the trees, the wetland I plough through is alive with shimmering colours. They scintillate darkly beneath the water's surface, illuminating my path like a trail of neon lava.

How I came to be here is clouded by fear and an instinctual need to be somewhere else, a safe place I cannot recall. All I remember is one moment being in that other place, coddled and secure, and the next I was here. I repeatedly look behind, expecting to see him in pursuit through the tall grass, closing in because he is stronger, faster. But there is nobody there, only shadows cast by the waning light. I don't know who *he* is. He's as much a mystery to me as my alien surroundings. And yet I feel him near, stalking me like a predatory beast. We are connected somehow, him and me, but it is a bond I struggle to fathom.

I trip on a tangle of roots and fall flat in the mire. When I raise my sopping head, I'm level with a bouquet of blinking eyeballs. The eyes are on leafy stalks, sinking down into the swamp water. When they focus on me each of their pupils expand, revealing little sets of teeth which snap toward my face. I scream and lurch backwards. A rustle in the grass nearby jolts me to my feet. Leaping over the eyeballs, I continue on through the churning bog.

I come upon dryer land and sprint up toward a spiny copse. Glancing once more behind me, I charge through the branches, startling a pack of faceless lizard creatures high in

157

the canopy. As I battle through the trees, the hollering animals swing above me, chattering in the manner of human voices played backwards.

Emerging from the dense foliage, I stumble again. When I regain my footing, that's when I see it. On a rocky plateau at the centre of the clearing stands the door. It is a lone, wooden, rectangle of unremarkable design, made remarkable solely by its being there. I am shocked and relieved by the recognition of it. The door draws me near, opening just a crack as I approach; a line of brilliant light separating the wood from its scuffed-up frame.

Yards from the door something lunges out of the trees, knocking me to the ground. Fearing it's one of those reptilian canopy-dwellers, I shield my face from its headless jaws. We roll in the dirt. My assailant clambers on top of me, fastening nimble hands around my throat. Looking up, I can make out only a silhouette against the putrescent sky. The hands grip tighter. My squinting eyes adjust, and I am able to see my attacker. Terror sucks the air from my lungs as I remember who it is, who it's always been. It is *me*.

I writhe on the ground, but the other me is too strong. He leans into his murderous deed, a terrifying leer across the face that is my own. I flail my hands through the grass, one of them eventually hitting a heavy object. Seizing it, I swing the rock up into the boy's skull, hearing a dull crack. My attacker yelps and I feel something warm splash across my face. He topples backwards into the brush, and I scramble to my feet. I instinctively raise the heavy rock into the air and bring it down upon the head of the other me. When the body stops twitching my senses return; I make a dash for the door, falling through it into swallowing darkness.

Cool gloom against my damp skin, relief from the heat of the jungle. I lie flat on my back against rough wooden floorboards, dazed and panting. The air is dusty and stale. For long seconds I remain still, unable to see anything— alone with horrific thoughts of murder. I struggle to understand why that child looked like me, and how I was able to . . .

A faint chittering sound stirs in me both fear and familiarity. The sound gets louder, and I sense something approaching in the dark. I flinch as out of the shadows a large bulky head appears next to mine. Stumpy antennae and a bristling mouth flap twitch in a way that tells me I am being smelt.

"Oh," I say. "It's you."

The giant insectoid head shudders in response to my surprise. Remembering this inquisitive beast puts me at ease. My recognition appears to trigger a light source which dimly illuminates my surroundings and the enormous millipede coiled about me. I am in a vast hallway that stretches off into the distance, the millipede's thick segmented body receding down it almost out of sight. The creature lowers its front section to the floor, waits there patiently. Giving the doorway one last look, I climb onto the back of the millipede and spread out across its wide mass. As the creature starts to manoeuvre itself back down the corridor, I feel my eyelids droop, the rhythmic clicking of its legs on the wooden floor like a soothing mantra.

When I awaken, it is lighter in the huge hallway, and my memories are starting to return. I remember now that I live in this place, this ramshackle old mansion I've never seen the outside of. Though I can observe the walls and ceiling clearly now, I do not know where the light is coming from because there are no bulbs, no windows. I have never seen any windows here, only walls and corridors and rooms.

Lying flat on the millipede's back as it clatters amiably down the hall, I watch the ceiling roll by. It isn't made of wood like the doorway through which I came, but a lumpy organic matter with veins and arteries running through it. I ponder, as I always have, how the interior of this place, its entire structure, can seem to be somehow . . . living. Before my eyes, the fleshy ceiling undulates like the shifting insides of some gargantuan monster. Whilst gazing up at this curious spectacle, the whole corridor starts to shudder. The millipede, clearly agitated, halts its relentless march while the walls and ceiling shake around us in the manner of an earthquake. I know what an earthquake is because they have appeared in my night-time stories. I've learnt all that I know from my night-time stories; they tell me everything about the world outside the house. Once the violent juddering has ceased, the millipede resumes its many-limbed procession. It's at this moment that I remember where we are headed. We are going to see Mother.

Eventually, we arrive at Mother's boudoir, and I sit up cross-legged upon the millipede as it scuttles its elongated body through the entrance. Mother's boudoir is like no other room in the house. It opens up into a huge cavernous space with thick silken webs stretching from floor to ceiling. It looks more like a creature's cocoon, like the kind described to me in my stories. We approach the centre of the room and I see Mother coming out of her opulent four-poster bed, pushing aside gauzy drapes as she emerges. Despite her massive bulk, she moves with an unsettling elegance, her broad frame clothed entirely in mismatched scraps of fabric. As we draw near, she raises two of her arms in a welcoming gesture—the long spindly limbs, covered in tiny black hairs, stretch out wider than the enormous bed.

"Darling, you're home!" she calls out with her spider's mouth.

The millipede bows to the floor and I slide off, settling at Mother's feet.

"You are the victor, and I couldn't be more proud of you!" her gleaming black fangs twitch as she speaks.

"Thank you, Mother," I say, puzzled. "But who was that little boy, and why did he look like me?"

Mother's almost human face softens. "Silly boy, you don't remember? That was your other, and you defeated him admirably like I knew you could." Her shining eyes are wet with pride.

"But . . ."

"No buts, my precious boy. He was a more powerful adversary, and you used your wits in order to survive. Father is thrilled for you too!"

"Where is Father?" I peer toward the bed.

"He'll be along shortly," she purrs through her glistening mouthparts. "He has a new story to tell you."

She lowers herself slightly, her gown of silvery rags fanning out around her.

"But for now, it is time for you to make your nightly decision."

I frown in confusion. My eyes drop to the vast hem of her garment; it twitches and shifts in multiple places. I look up to her face, to the upper half which resembles my own, and say, "What decision do you mean, Mother?"

She sighs. "My darling, the same decision you must always make when you return home to us—whether to move on to the next stage of your development or, if you wish, simply feed before bedtime. It's entirely up to you."

I think for a moment. After everything I've been through, I do feel extremely tired and hungry. My young body aches all over, and I wonder if I am ready for this next stage of development. Gazing into my twin reflections in Mother's big black eyes, I ask if I can please just eat and then go to bed.

Her mouthparts stretch wide in what I presume is a smile. She then undulates in such a way that her makeshift gown parts at the front. What it reveals makes me gasp, though I have the feeling I've seen this countless times. She rears above me, flexing her abdomen and unfurls the six other spider-like legs which line her bristling flanks. Along her underside are two vertical rows of breasts—human in appearance, except they are covered in the same tiny hairs as the rest of her. The hair is thick and smooth, giving the breasts a glossy texture like the fur of a black cat.

"Come to Mother," she coos, curling her long, segmented limbs around me, a pearly blob of milk appearing on the tip of each pink nipple. She bends her thorax into the shape of a sitting lap, and I nestle in the crook of her body, opening my mouth to receive one of the teats as the others provide soft cushions beneath my weight.

Something shifts behind my head and Mother's patchwork garment slide off a large hump sticking out of the right-hand side of her.

"He's here to tell you a night-time story," Mothers says and parts two of her spindly legs to make way for Father to appear. As soon as I turn and see him, I remember that Father is attached to Mother's body. He is human in appearance, resembling myself more than he does Mother. They've been fused this way since before I was born, but whenever I ask the reason I can never remember what I am told.

"Hello my son and congratulations," he says, coiling around Mother's side and tenderly embracing my head as I suckle from her black bosom. Her milk is rich and heavy, filling my throat and flooding my brain as much as it does my stomach. The more I swallow, the drowsier I feel, and the further away the memories of today recede. Before long, it's almost as though my experience in the jungle was just a dream told to me by somebody else. Soon I can scarcely picture what happened there, and all I can hear is Father's whispery words describing his story. I drift toward sleep through the landscape of Father's narrative, his withered fingers stroking my swamp-scented hair.

I unfasten my mouth from Mother's breast to say something, but a loud commotion snatches our attention. We look to the millipede and see a body drop down from the creature's twisting underside. Caked in blood and clutching a jagged shard of stone, my other lunges toward me. Mother screams and I try to dart out of the way, but my other is fast, and he rips me from Mother's embrace. I see hatred burning in his eyes as he swings the deadly stake above his head. Mother lashes out with her long spidery limbs, knocking my attacker off balance before he can strike.

"No, no, no, no!" she continues to scream. "You cannot both be in here! It is forbidden!"

The weapon clatters near me, I crouch to grab it. Looking up, I see my other already back on his feet. He runs at me again, but this time I sidestep him, and he tumbles straight into Mother's flailing grasp.

Right at this moment, the boudoir starts to shake, imperceptibly at first, but within a few seconds, the whole chamber is vibrating madly around us. This makes Mother wail even louder; shrieking in a way I've never heard before, her limbs wrapped tightly around the other me. He tries to struggle, but he is locked in Mother's monstrous clutches, her strong pedipalp feelers curled around his neck. I approach with the jagged shard, feeling myself begin to hyperventilate.

I hear Father's voice. He is instructing me calmly, and it takes a moment before I register his words over Mother's piercing cries.

"Breathe, my boy . . . just push it into him . . ."

I steady myself, gripping the weapon in both hands. My other is thrashing wildly now, kicking and spitting, but he is held fast. I barely notice the cocoon-like room we are in start to disintegrate, the grand web curtains falling and tearing apart. Father emerges from beneath Mother's ragtag gown, his face a hollow smirk.

"Just *breathe* . . . and *push* it in . . ."

Mother's howls fill my skull. The quaking intensifies; walls start to crumble. I raise the shard into the air. Arachnoid limbs crush my other's gasping throat. I breathe.

I open my eyes underwater. I still hear the wailing and the encouraging words, but they are muted now, distant. There is a great pressure on my tiny, frail body, a sucking sensation I am helpless to resist. As I am pulled toward the vacuum, I notice something in the murky fluid. It is a body like my own, only larger. The body is still; it feels no effect from the suction as I do. Around its neck is a translucent cord wound tight—constricting, suffocating. The cord trails away and disappears into the wall of this fluid-filled sac. Then I am gone, I see nothing more. But the sounds grow louder.

The screams make the liquid around me tremble.

"... *Breathe* ..."

The voice is still calm.

"... *Push* ..."

ROY FUTURES AND HIS JUKEBOX TEETH

- Jay Slayton-Joslin -

Rundown English pubs are not like American dive bars. English pubs tend to feel dangerous because football hooligans may bash your skull in for supporting the wrong team, for looking at them funny, for not being part of their community. American dive bars don't have Roy Futures.

I first met Roy Futures on New Years Day. Most places are shut then, allowing the staff a night off after watching people kiss following the countdown, cleaning sick out of toilets and planning their escape to Mexico. The Three Duncans was open that day because the owner had nowhere else to be, his family were most of the stool straddling patrons who wanted £2 pints. I was in there because everywhere else was closed, I was new to the town, figured that it was less likely someone would kick my head in on that day. On days like that, it's not lonely if there are other people drinking their sorrows away.

At the end of the bar, there was a man who would say every sentence differently. His tone of voice, accent, pitch, hell, even sometimes it felt like he was a ventriloquist and there was a 13-year-old girl ordering his ales. After my fifth pint in ninety minutes, I got bold.

"I'm not one to judge, but that bloke at the end of the bar sure sounds strange. What's going on there?"

"Ask him," the bartender said, before turning his attention to a more loyal customer. I thought, 'fuck it, why not, fortune favours the bold and its gotta smile upon drunks sometimes,' and walked down to the end of the bar. The closer I got to this guy, the stranger the background sound was, like multiple radios that couldn't tune into a station for longer than five seconds.

"Alright, mate?" I said to him. He looked at me, smiled, closed lips, nodded.

"I'm Webster," I leant on the bar, the alcohol catching up, pushing some beer mats onto the floor like I was afraid of the logos. I looked back over at the man, and he slid a note over to me.

"My name is Roy Futures, I try not to talk." I read it, a few times actually, double-checking that I wasn't in some fermented fever dream. Weird name, guy didn't even have a pen or paper in front of him too, but I was curious. I sat down next to him, our elbows an inch away from touching.

"I want you to show me why you don't talk," I said.

The guy looked at me, but he wasn't really looking just at me but more into my eyes so he could see where I was coming from, who I was. He blinked, slightly longer than the average person tends to as if he was communicating with himself to show me something, and then he opened his mouth. Each tooth was a jukebox, playing a different song. I wanted to get closer to look, I wanted to get closer to listen.

"Please keep away from my mouth, I think I have bad breath," Roy said, except, it was sung, and not by him, but each word was sampled from a different song. Now, I can't tell you which ones, because I can't afford a lawyer and it's not as obvious as you might think. It's not as if you ask him what his favourite genre of film is and he says Thriller and winks into some camera like a 70s sitcom, but instead splits your mind in two as you process what he said so you can reply, and try and use your brain like some kind of Shazam to place the songs. As we got to know each other, what I think what Roy liked about me the most, is that I didn't really focus too much on the jukebox teeth, the whole reason a shitty English pub isn't where you came from, or where you're going, just having a beer and enjoy where you are.

In between the fights, the darts missing the board and going into the wall and the smell of piss that would creep across the barstools during the night, I began to really enjoy Roy Future's company. I felt guilty sometimes, that maybe if this stranger didn't have jukebox for teeth I wouldn't talk to him the same way, that there were a baker's dozen pissed up men in this pub who could use someone to talk to.

"Sometimes I get lonely," Roy sang to me one night, "I can say anything I want, but I have no voice. You're the only person who talks to me."

"I'll be there for you," I said to Roy, who opened his mouth and laughed the laugh of a TV audience. I could see all the different needles in the jukebox working frantically. I wondered if he could just have one massive iPod bucktooth that he could floss with cassette tape or something instead.

"Quoting songs is my thing," he said and slapped me on the back. It hurt, he had rough hands like he had a hard life, but it means I was his friend.

"Sorry, mate, your voice may be all songs, but I apparently say them without even knowing it, fucking hated *Friends*. Fuck Rachel Green."

"It's fine, I have a plan to fix it, everything is okay to be okay, I'm going to end it all."

I woke up the next day in an ale induced fatigue. I stumbled to the bathroom tap and drank water from it like a bird, then realised what Roy had meant. It was weird at the time, sure, but he had fucking jukeboxes for teeth, how the hell was I supposed to know that he was talking about taking his own life? The issue when he spoke was that there was no context, it could be Motown one word then autotune the next. I spent a long time drinking in that pub afterwards, hoping to hear from him or about him.

For a long time, I didn't. The pub closed, it got shut down due to serving minors, and then the police got called, even though at least they were inside rather than waiting in parks, sipping bottles of vodka on the swings like I saw on television. The pub was renamed something with a swan in the title, but I kept going there, more out of muscle memory than anything else. It was too polished, too clean but I knew that the walls held memories and revelled every time that I saw somewhere that hadn't been painted properly, something that held definitive proof of the chaotic place that came before. They started bringing in events to get younger crowds in; pub quizzes and karaoke nights, one evening they had some sort of modern art piece by a local university, but most of the students thought I was part of the show, a man who just gets older and drunker with three quid in his pocket — take that Damien Hirst!

I kept coming to these events, but it was more that they came to me. I was just there, if you're going to drink alone at home you might as well make a social trip out of it, and life is hard, so I went to the pub. It was live music night, and who the fuck should walk in except for Roy Futures! I thought I was seeing things, the beer finally fermenting my brain, but he walked in and sat next to me and didn't say a word. He lifted his finger to get the bartenders attention, but I ordered for him, and he looked at me and smiled like his lips were sewn shut. I didn't say anything else to him because I didn't have many good moments in my life, and this one I didn't want to ruin by running my mouth. We just sat there and took in the music, letting the songs remind us of days that have gone and to come. The singer finished, a young blonde girl carrying her acoustic guitar off the stage, heading back to friends who greeted her with cheers, smiles and cold beers.

The host went to the stage, stood behind the microphone and insisted on a second round of applause for the singer. Roy Futures smiled at me and slid me a slip of paper as he got up. I looked at him and wondered if this was the last time I'll see him if he would be back tomorrow, or if I would be drinking somewhere in however many years and he would walk in, and everything would feel fine. Together, again.

"And our final act, the incredible Roy Futures, ladies and gentlemen! No covers, just the originals that will become the songs others sing."

Roy went to the microphone and stood like he was finally where he was meant to be, he looked at me and smiled, this time I could see his teeth, and goddammit if they weren't the most magnificent pearly whites I've ever seen. I teared up a bit, looked down at the paper and on it he wrote, *this first one's for you*. He opened his mouth, and he sang, and Jesus Christ, it sounded just like this:

MORE NONSENSE POEMS

- DJ Tyrer -

A Gander to the Dark Side

Goosey-Goosey Gander
Riding on a panda
Searching for Amanda
On the dark side of the Moon

Goosey-Goosey Gander
Found his friend Amanda
Beside a lunar lander
On the dark side of the Moon

Goosey-Goosey Gander
Took tea with Amanda
They both ate roasted panda
On the dark side of the Moon

Dogging in the Black Goat's Wood

Windows begin to fog
As they practice ancient rites
Upon the back-seat of a Vauxhall
Astra, under the low branches
Of the trees in the Wood of the Black Goat
Seeking an illicit thrill
Through observation, quasi-participation
Exploiting voyeuristic tendencies
But, no human eyes spy
Upon the sweating couple
Only the groping branches
Of black-barked trees
Lean in as if to watch
Relishing the awakening
Inherent in the ancient rite

Billy Bunter – Vampire Hunter

Billy Bunter – Vampire Hunter
Stalks his prey by night and day
With a cake, not a steak
Clasped in his hand
Billy Bunter – Vampire Hunter
Having fun giving Van Helsing a run
As he commits vampires to funeral pyres
The fattest slayer in the land
Billy Bunter – Vampire Hunter
Destroys the undead while eating fresh bread
With a cake, not a steak
Clasped in his hand
The fattest slayer in the land

Hothouse Lover

My lover is a flower
Given human form
I sweat in the heat
Of her finely-glazed home
But sweat all the more
For my burning desire
My lover does not sweat
She is calm, a vegetable
Her breasts burst into bloom
A pair of gorgeous white roses
And lower still, hidden amongst moss
Dank yet desirable, a red tulip rests
I yearn for her, sap rising
An urge to pluck her free
She embraces me, takes me
I sink into her vegetable softness
An urgency of desire
Unheeding of the thorns upon her flesh

JEREMY'S JUNK

- Chris Meekings -

I am Jeremy's
jiggling junk.
Safely, stuffed in
tighty-whities,
I spend days
dilly-dangling along.
I lean left.
How about you?
Jeremy leans right,
but that's ok.
The world is made up
of contradictions.

I am hanging low.
Slapping steadily
against Jeremy's leg.
Occasionally,
I jiggle his testicles,
with my head.
My days are dark,
this I like.
He gets me out
occasionally
and wiggles me
at screaming females.
Sometimes I get
excited and spit
at them.

BRITISH BIZARRO

When I grow
I get big
and scary
and veiny.
I pulse
thrum-bump.
Oooh-yar!
But I don't always
manage that.
Sometimes I'm too tired,
or thinking about other things,
or scared of naked girls.
But, when I do it's awesome,
and I am fearsome,
and I spit.

Jeremy's job
is something,
not much.
I don't really know,
I'm just the junk.
Sometimes I get taken
out, but
only to wizz,
not to spit.
It is bad to spit at work,
I think, although
I'd like to spit
at some of those sluts.
It makes me feel
tall and tough,
slick and slime.
Thrummmmmmm.

But that was before,
this is now.
I don't know where we are.

The light is bright,
shiny pale
and glaring.
I am unhappy.
I weep a
streak of piss.
The place smells of
old sweaty socks,
and ancient humiliations.
Fungus is in the air,
I can taste it.
Spores, pour around me.
The air is chill.
I shrink further,
wrapping into folded flesh.

I am not normally
exposed like this,
except when wiggled
at giggling girls.
The cool air
nibbles at my nutty friends.
I know the man
in front of me.
He is sweaty
and huge
and pink,
like a boiled ham.
He growls.
Gowned in shorts
and white shirt.
His arms are huge.
A black
whistle dangles
around his neck.
I try to skrinch
further into my

two testicle friends.

"You're worthless,
spineless!
A measly maggot,"
he screams.
His eyes beam
a straight
laser of hate.
He throws a ball,
across the hall.
It strikes above me,
into Jeremy's bulbous
belly.
He huffs a huge
plume of puff.
I cry a piddle of piss,
down his dappled leg.
I am noticed.

The anxiety starts
in my shaft.
Right in my pit.
I feel deflated.
I shrink my way
further within
my warm flesh womb.
This is an old place.
Before, in the ago.
"Are you joking,
Jeremy?"
Varicose
veins, bulge blue
on his neck.
I wish my veins were
blue like that.
"No time to

put your cock away.
Climb the rope!"

The rope rubs
against my head.
It feels fabulous.
It brings back memories
of being wiggled
at giggling girls.
I grow.
Plume bright.
Purple swell.
Thick and veiny.
I am hard,
and strong
and big.
I want to spit.
"Jesus, Jeremy!"
the short shout.
A bulk-walk bark,
belittling.
I am unperturbed.

Don't be put down.
I am strong.
I am strident.
Blue-black blood
beats in my meat.
Head proud,
helmet on.
A soldier at sunset.
Beautiful and erect.
Heat beat bugle.
Thrum-bump,
thrum-bump.
My nutty friends
rise,

pulled up on elastic
strings.

It feels tacky
in my tubes.
A cough of custard.
Thick and soupy.
I know it is time
to spit.
The cocktail of salt,
wells up
in my throat.
I want to spit.
I must spit.
Here it comes!
I dribble.
A small, sick,
baby spittle
of weak and watery
slime slips
out of me.

"Jesus, Jeremy!"
the bellicose bullhorn
roars up at me.
Jeremy weeps.
I seep, dingle-dangle.
Drip-drip,
droopy.
I curl,
mollusc-like,
a snail retreating
to its shell.
The shouts carry on.
Barking, barking,
a dog in the dark.
I dribble and weep,

Slimy ooze, a weepy
dispair. I wish
I was unspunk.
I am Jeremy's junk.

Not
recommended

MAGGIE THATCHER EGG HATCHER

- Leigham Shardlow -

Margaret Thatcher sat her small taught arse upon her humongous pile of eggs at the base of the old oak tree. With a cricket bat held in her fear sweat covered maw, she waited for the ravenous and dusty coal miners. The moon shone through the canopy, a Dalmation carpet illuminated Maggie's field of vision, and it danced and swayed with every wolf howl of the wind. The scent of damp soil and

The drums began, black holes shimmered almost instantaneously into existence, and the buff hairy coal miners crawled through them. Slithering silently, covered in black dust that coughed out of every hole poisoning the air. They marched forward scowling with bestial hunger, they sniffed the air before exiting their individual portals with huge gaping nostrils filled with coarse hair and more charcoal black dust.

Sensing the nearby danger, Maggie Thatcher hitched up her dress, rolled up her shirt sleeves and took the cricket bat in both hands, poised to strike at any provocation. This was her first lay, and she was determined for them to remain safe and unbroken.

A high pitched and unearthly shriek came from the coal miners in unison, they had her eggs scent, and they would feast upon them at any cost.

They rushed towards Margret's laying spot beneath the Old Oak Tree. Leaping through the air, jaws distended, greasy black slobber dripping from their black and chipped teeth. Maggie laid the first one out with mighty wallop, splintering its jaw into several pieces of bone and black coal infused goo. It spiralled through the air and crashed against a nearby Fir, dead and unmoving.

The second caught her backswing in the ribs, it reeled back for a second, a shocked look agape its face as its heart exploded within its ribcage. Such was the sheer force of Maggie's expert batting skills. Her time at Oxford well spent.

A third came at her from behind, and she twisted out of the way as its enormous yellowed clawed hand pawed at her face. She raised her weapon in defence, and it tore the cricket bat from Maggie's hand. She howled in horror and despair. Others swarmed in seeing her defenceless and Maggie was quickly torn from her nest.

The eggs were quickly devoured by the hundreds of coal miners. Margret, with her robes of office torn and shorn from her now naked body, used the short time that her eggs had given her managed to climb a nearby tree. Climbing to the very top of the branches to hide from any miners that would fancy her a quick meal.

The miners with full bellies left for another year, slinking back into their black holes and the warm, viscous embrace of their working-class dimension. To mine again and provide for their families.

Maggie Thatcher sat upon her sizeable pile of eggs atop the Old Oak Tree. Its branches barren of leaves and coated in a thick layer of snow. Maggie shivered and sucked on a cough sweet. Her vocal cords greased with the honey and eucalyptus, primed for the midnight bellowing.

Church bells echoed in the distance, the call of the school children. For the twelfth ring they had come, and the lunch bell beckoned them into the forest for Maggie's delicious eggs.

Clouds of them formed out of the ether, a low hum of working-class children, small, clawed, milk splattered and ravenous. As they swirled overhead, Margaret took deep calming breaths as one last preparation before the eventually attack. As the first one dived down, Maggie distended her jaw and spewed forth from her throat, a supersonic wail exploding the killer child into a puff of powdered milk and feathers.

Maggie, out of breath, braced herself as another child divided. Unable to unleash another scream, she threw herself over her egg, trying to protect them. The child ripped into her back with barbed wire talons tearing chunks of her flesh and drawing blood as it tore through her Marks and Spencer padded suit jacket like it was butter. It was actually cashmere so it couldn't withstand the assault for long, so Maggie inhaled long and hard.

Jerking back her neck Maggie unleashed another Banshee like cry the remains of her lozenge flew with it and disintegrated in a lemony cacophony of dust, she missed her attacker. Several Children flew out of the way of her burst and flew ever higher.

Maggie's throat was sore, to say the least, she coughed up blood as the strain of each destructive roar stretched the skin on her neck and face to almost tearing point on the inside and out.

The children saw this weakness and clumped together in one bunch, circling over each other in a myriad of wet slapping noises. Maggie had been waiting for this. She let out her loudest most earth-shattering scream decimating the children were cleaving them all from existence by the sonic blast.

Maggie's throat gave out, and she gobbed up chunks of blood and saliva onto her makeshift nest. Softly crying, she gazed across the snow-laden trees towards the horizon, and her soft cries of relief turned to despairing cries of fear. A mass of children, innumerable in number and gargantuan in size had covered the light from the full moon. She could hear their chittering and chattering.

"Listen blud, there's bare eggs innit" They cried, chilling Maggie's veins to ice and her heart to mush.

Taking one last look at her eggs, Margaret shed a single

tear and dived into the canopy of the Old Oak Tree. Grabbing onto a branch on the way down, she swung into a small recess in the trunk. She shrank into that tiny hole, crying with fear and frustration as the milk filled children devoured her unprotected eggs. All the while saying they muttered to themselves over and over again "Hashtag peng".

Maggie Thatcher sat on her three eggs in the nook on the Old Oak Tree. The moon was waxing its legs. The shadows that covered the summer laden forest were thick and sweltering. They could probably also use a shave.

Coal miners sniffed at the base of the tree while Children shook the branches above. Maggie sweated from the heat but also with fear. For the tree's branches hid fearsome elongated Trains, each with steam-filled maws and iron hewn haunches ready to pounce and devour anything that dared block the tracks.

Maggie had no cricket bat, no banshee wail, nothing to defend her eggs from the Trains.

She barely slept at night as they would chug on tree vein tracks, switching hither and thither threatening to crash right into her hiding spot before veering off to pick some unseen passengers for the two twenty to Hepstoke. The Trains were never on time, making Maggie's well-worn timetable essentially useless.

The ten to five to Greenwich had been cancelled. Maggie heard it over the tannoy, Maggie saw it being diverted right to her, Maggie felt it rumble along the branch directly beneath her.

It chugged slowly, purposefully and with the intent to carefully smell out everything it could. Trains rarely had no place to go, they were extra dangerous when they did, striking quick, efficiently as they had little chance to be so normally. Without a station to get to they hunted slowly to the ground. The Trains heavy iron wheels clacked and clanged as it went over the wooden track dividers naturally grown into the tree's bark by years of evolution and a rather generous grant from the home office.

Maggie had fruitlessly tried to peel the bark from that branch, but those trains were too regular and too dangerous for her to spend too long away from her eggs lest a Child learned to go below the canopy or a Coal Miner to climb.

The train beneath her lit up, she could hear it's hunting call from deep within its belly. "The dining cart will be passing through with various snacks and drinks. We're unfortunately out of tea". Maggie closed her eyes, her heart pounding in her ears, her blood boiling.

Maggie could hear it. Louder than her own heartbeat. The smell of smoke, dank. The taste of the air, bitter. The heat from its engine, choking.

She opened her eyes. It had risen several of its front carriages up, the powerful weight of its back two-thirds keeping it balanced.

The caboose salivated with thick mucus and it's mouth spread agape slowly. It sniffed the air. Maggie stopped breathing as it inched ever closer. Not daring to move Maggie realised she would have to abandon her eggs again if she was to live.

The train was a hair's breadth away from Maggie, the steam from its breath scolding her sagging face, coating her in rivers of condensing moisture.

The train leaned back, preparing to strike.

Maggie took her only chance and dived out of the tree as the train began tearing into her eggs. She hit the ground to it's crunching and noisy chewing.

"Due to concerns about terror attacks we ask all passengers to please not leave any baggage unattended," it howled in victory as Maggie dodged the curious sniffs and whines of the hunchbacked coal miners.

Maggie fled for what seemed like leagues through the forest and away from the relative safety of the Old Oak

Tree. When her feet finally became tired, her hair limp and lifeless, her lungs spent of breath did Maggie finally collapse in a heap in the middle of a clearing.

The sun rose, and Maggie knew that, by dawn, something would crawl out of the cold, unwelcoming earth to devour her whole as she lay there, defenceless and spent.

Maggie sat beneath the Blue Rose Bush. Her final egg moving with life, snuggled safety betwixt her humongous arse cheeks. The warm spring sun leaked the through the rose bushes thorny shield. Sharp and pointy they kept out the snarling Miners from the ground level, they pricked any children that dare land on its branches, they did not grow tracks for the trains naturally and most of all they did harm Maggie or her egg.

She was safe, the rose bush leaked fine champagne from its flowers and Maggie quenched her thirst whenever she needed. It attracted large foie gra flies that she would delicately pick out of the air with her un-manicured hands and devour them whole.

There was a price to pay for the bushes existence it sucked the land dry. It was the only piece of flora in a hundred miles in either direction, so it was situated dead centre in dry, cracked, earthy desert. Those that tried to eat her egg travelled long and died even longer. They could not survive the return trip. Those did not lie to rot far from them the bush would eat. Spreading out long thick roots covered in gold and right-wing headline like markings to drag the corpses underground to be devoured.

It had called to Maggie so long ago as she lay dying on the edge of the forest. She crawled on her belly, starving, dehydrated, without hope and with a mindless attraction to a painless death. She arrived after days of, and she made a pact with the bush, it would protect her, and she would lure in food with her delicious eggs.

Maggie was old though, too many winters, too many nights, too many of her precious ova eaten. She didn't think she could produce another. Yet spring came, and the urge to lay overcame her again. For twenty days she struggled the weight becoming more inside her, and she laid one egg. Her final egg.

The bush declared it an outrage that such a paltry thing could bring enough to sustain its avarice hunger. Maggie just whistled and pointed to the sky as it filled with screeching children and then she pointed to the ground as the black holes opened and the legions of coal miners leaked out into the world.

The Bush laughed with malicious glee while it butchered and fed upon every morsel. The Bush was happy, and so was Maggie.

The day came some days before winter for her egg to hatch. It rumbled from within, and small cracks began to appear upon the surface. Maggie cried with joy, and the Bush watched intently, it knew their bargain would come to an end, and it would enjoy the meal of Maggie before protecting the offspring which would lay more eggs.

Margret was no fool, she knew this too, but she also knew that her egg contained no child. It harboured secrets of her ascension. Mighty snakes of pure metamorphosis.

The egg cracked, and the tiny black eyeless worms wiggled free. Maggie closed her eyes, and the snakes engulfed her entirely, swarming into her nostrils and ears, invading her blood and warping her physical form. An avatar of shifting, formless nightmare fuel.

The Bush screamed in fear and attacked Maggie with its powerful roots. It was too late the thick tendril caught fire as its blow landed and the bush didn't have time to scream as all its roots and thorns evaporated out of existence. The metamorphosis had finished as quickly as it had begun, the snakes dropped off her and scurried away towards the forest in the distance.

The IRON LADY rose two thousand feet tall from the tiny thing she had just been. The remains of the bush, merely a blue spec on her shining steel lapel. Maggie did not dust it off for the Bush would worship her in awe as will the rest of the world.

The IRON LADY surveyed the world, beyond the dead desert to the farthest reaches of the wild forest and the remains of the Old Oak Tree to the island of England.

"Yes," she said her voice booming through the cosmos as she stomped over the ground forming craters as big as elephants with each step.

"They will all revere me!" she bellowed vowing revenge to herself on all Coal Miners, Children and Trains.

NANNY KNOWS BEST

- James Burr -

"What we have here," Nanny said to the Judge, "is a blatant disregard for the law and all social etiquette." He wagged his finger at the defendant. "This Client has gone out of his way to break the *Abolition of Death Act* time and time again."

Nanny paced the Court-room and addressed the twelve other Clients who sat in their padded, slightly ululating Chairs™, some farting and dozing, others gurgling contentedly as their IV drips slowly fed them sedatives and perfectly balanced Liqui-Meal™.

"As a society, we have made great strides in Public Health. Our forbears consigned the Social Evils of smoking, drinking and obesity to the history books. Exercise has been prescribed and perfect nutrition implemented. The emotional stressors of social inequality - jealousy, envy, despair – have been eliminated. The negative health impact vectors of personal desire, personal responsibility and indeed any kind of emotional inner life have been removed. And all at the cost of only a hundred trillion pounds, a bargain at half the price I am sure we would all agree."

The Nannies murmured their assent. One of the Clients shrieked in delight when a fly landed on his nose, and he pawed at it clumsily with meaty fingers. There was a beeping noise as a sensor in his Chair™ detected the secretion of dangerous levels of adrenalin, and an automated plunger squeezed down in a syringe, and he was settled.

"Yet *this* Client, despite all these breakthroughs in Public Health, stubbornly and obstinately refuses to obey the law!" Nanny pointed at the defendant, his stiff, pale body wedged into the dock in such a way that it would not collapse onto the floor.

"It was found that the Client had acted in a way inconsistent with the *Abolition of Death Act* in October of last year. As is customary in such cases, the Client was issued with a Cessation of Behaviour Notice and warned about the dangerous and anti-social aspects of his actions. However, despite this, when the Client's Nanny returned to his Home™ the following day, he found that the Client was continuing to indulge in risky and anti-social behaviours contrary to life."

An usher stepped forward to discretely swat some of the flies that were gathering around the ripe-smelling corpse.

"At this point, his Nanny had no choice but to distribute "I like being alive!"™ stickers around the Client's Home™. Recent research has determined that these stickers have a 95% success rate in preventing death addicts from succumbing to personally destructive behaviours, such as lacking life. So, of course, you can imagine his Nanny's sheer horror to discover that, on his next visit, the Client was continuing to insist on being dead."

Not being sat in the thermostatically moderated environment of a Chair™, the defendant's body had started to bloat in the summer heat, and it jerked noisily in the dock as its abdomen swelled and its head lolled grotesquely to the side.

"However, never let it be said that the role of the Ministry is to persecute the dead. Rather, it is to prevent death! So, the Client was then given another opportunity to moderate his behaviour by attending a half-day Life Awareness session. His Nanny at the session reports that he was…." Nanny flicked through some papers as he tried to find the correct quote from the report.

""….Quiet, attentive and clearly reflecting on the experience.""

He closed the papers and turned to the Judge. "But yet again, when his Nanny visited him the following day he was continuing to act in contravention of the Law and stubbornly refusing to live."

The defendant stared at him with milky, unseeing eyes.

"Milord, I contend that this Client should face the full sanctions available to this court. His refusal to even mount a defence of his actions surely only adds to his obvious guilt."

Nanny sat down as the Judge considered the case before him. One of the Clients gurgled and slapped his thighs, a line of drool slowly dripping from his chin. The judge nodded, coughed and turned to the accused. "It seems that the judgement of this court is that the defendant's willful obstinacy in continuing to act in a manner befitting a progressive society is both obvious and somewhat foul-smelling. It is, therefore, the decision of this court that the defendant is found guilty, final sentencing to be undertaken in a fortnight."

The judge struck his gavel and shuffled from the courtroom as the defendant was dragged from the Court, leaving a slime-trail of putrefying flesh behind him. Other Nannies murmured their approval and gathered around Nanny, congratulating him.

And as they shook his hand and slapped his back and exclaimed "Well done!" and "That'll teach him!", Nanny could only feel great pride in his work. For decades his forebears had struggled with keeping their Clients safe from themselves and their own unfathomable behaviour. Yet despite the taxes and bans and media propaganda, nothing had really worked. Nothing, until the *Abolition of Death Act*.

Yes, statistics from the Ministry demonstrated that there was a 100% successful conviction rate for contravening the Act, clear and quantifiable evidence of its undeniable success.

Nanny smiled and walked down the Courthouse steps, eager to continue his important work.

CANNIBAL CATASTROPHE

- DJ Tyrer -

Captured by cannibals
The crazed curmudgeon
Was recognised as a god
To be worshipped and revered
Then cooked and consumed
To release divine essence
From tasty mortal vessel
Unhappy at the outcome
But unable to escape
He laid his plans
Calling for a great feast
And a great festival
To celebrate his transmogrification
Into dinner and deity ascendant
Ordering every house and possession
Beset ablaze
And their crops and orchards too
To provide a suitable cookfire
And their children served as entrées
And their womenfolk as the main course
Leaving him to be dessert
Leaving their island near-desert
Dining then dying
Secure in the knowledge
And selfish satisfaction
That though dead
Their tribe would be too!

MEET LOAF

- Shaun Avery -

"They call me Loaf," she told me that first time I met her. "Because my skin's so soft and I taste so good."

Sitting across the table from her, I decided I liked the sound of that. Liked the *look* of her, too – that smiling face, that pretty body. So, I was kind of excited about where this could do.

But then the bell went "ding," and it was time for her to move along to the next table.

Guess I spent too long looking at her when I should have been talking.

"Sorry," she said, giving me an apologetic little shrug of a delicate and delicious looking shoulder. "Maybe I'll see you again next week?"

She sounded like she meant that. Still, by way of reply, my eyes flicked up to the banner hanging from the ceiling. The one that said, in huge black letters, *Cannibal-Victim Speed-Dating Night – come along and pick your perfect dinner partner!*

I sighed at this sight, knowing that the next time I saw her, someone else would have eaten part of that wonderful body, depriving me forever of that joy.

But I was only half-right.

I hooked up with another pretty girl that night, one called Claudette. And I took her home and ate the lower part of her arm, sliced off beneath the elbow, and though we both enjoyed that, I found that I couldn't get the girl called Loaf out of my mind.

Loaf, sweet Loaf.

It was my first time at the Cannibal-Victim Speed-Dating Night, but I'd heard all about it from a bunch of my friends,

friends who shared my tastes. They said there was a whole subculture of men and women out there who absolutely *hated* certain parts of their bodies and got off on us severing and then *eating* the offending limbs, passing the missing appendages off to friends and families as being lost in accidents. That's when they even *had* friends and families, of course . . . I guess a lot of people who wanted to go home with a cannibal were probably pretty lonely. But I'm digressing.

Back to Loaf.

I waved Claudette off in the morning, after an excellent meal of her flesh and a deep and interesting all-night chat. That was all, though – some of my friends, both men and women, slept with every single person they took home after the eating was done. But I only wanted to do that with someone I felt close to, and as much fun as we'd had cutting off and then cooking her arm, both Claudette and I had agreed that the extra special *something* wasn't there between us, and had parted as friends on good terms.

Watching her go, I wished it was someone else I'd brought back with me.

I thought I'd blown it with that person.

Until she turned up at the next Speed-dating Night.

I was confused when I saw her. By how *much* of her I saw, that is. Unlike a lot of other people around – including Claudette, who gave me a wave with her remaining hand as I entered the building – she did not seem to be missing any body parts.

So had she gone home alone last time? I wondered.

I didn't know.

I'd tried to keep an eye on her last time, after the dating part of the night was done and people were heading to the bar for drinks. But the place had been packed – one of the reasons the sit down at the table between us had proved to be so short – and I'd lost track of her. And then, of course, I'd started talking to Claudette, so had missed my chance to go outside and look for her.

Plus, you know, that would have felt a bit like stalking.

But now that she was back, that was not the case, and soon I sat at my table on tenterhooks, waiting for my turn with her to come around. And when it did, this time I jumped straight in.

"Hi," I said when she sat before me. "I'm Dave."

"Hi, Dave. They call me Loaf."

"I know."

She frowned. "You do?"

"Last week," I told her. "Remember?"

She shook her head, long blonde hair *swishing*. "Sorry," she said. "You must have me confused with someone else."

Now it was *my* turn to frown. Especially when she then added, "This is my first time here." And looked me over, adding, "and I like what I see."

I was about to get her talking, ready to quiz her more.

But then the bell rang, parting us once again.

That should have been the end of it.

But the days that followed saw my mind return to her more and more.

She confused me, did the girl called Loaf. Especially the first thing she'd said to me last week. "*They call me Loaf*," she had said. "*I taste so good*," she had added. But as she seemed to be missing no body parts, *who* had said this? *How* did someone know that she tasted good?

I was sure she liked me, remembering a couple of the looks she'd given me, the last thing she had said to me. But now, thinking it all over, I had to wonder whether she was just some kind of tease.

You heard about those sometimes – guys and girls who went home with you, maybe even let you fool around with them a little, but then did a runner when you pulled out the old surgical saw.

That's something else I guess I should tell you – we're not cannibals the way you see them in the movies. No, we're cultured, educated people. We know how to cut out partners, so they don't bleed to death. How to cauterise and clean a wound to prevent any infection setting in. How to tell the owners of a bar we're holding just a plain and ordinary speed-dating night, then have all the people who are missing body parts come in a back way, so those owners don't get too suspicious. Plus, most importantly of all, how to buy off the right people if all those precautions fail and the police start taking too much of an interest in our underground scene.

We're pretty well-connected online, too.

Which was how I got a few questions answered about Loaf.

Andrew was an excellent example of how successful a modern-day cannibal could be. As I saw when I pulled up to his house. His very *big* house.

He was waiting at the door for me, hand outstretched. "Dave, right?"

"Yeah." I walked up, shook his hand. "Pleased to meet you."

"Likewise," he said. "Come in."

I did so.

"I'm married now," he said, leading me into a vast front room, pointing to a picture hanging on the wall. "That's Maria."

I looked at it.

Saw she was missing no body parts.

Looked back to Andrew, and he must have seen the question in my eyes, as he explained, "met her at work. She doesn't know the type of stuff I used to be into."

"*Used* to be?" I said, sitting down on the chair, he beckoned me towards. "You mean you gave it up?"

"Yeah." He sat down on a huge couch across from me, and his eyes grew distant, his mind remembering. "But she made it pretty hard, did Loaf."

"You met her?"

Now his eyes seemed to *sparkle* with those memories. "Oh, yes. Hooked up with her a couple of times before I met Maria."

"So how come you didn't eat her?" I wanted to know.

He smiled and said, "I did."

Then he explained what he meant.

A few days later, I sat back at the Speed-Dating Night.

Eyes on the door. Waiting, waiting.

And remembering:

"I ate her leg," Andrew said. "But even as I ate it, something weird was happening. I felt the flesh sort of... drifting out of my body. And she'd been lying on the bed in front of me, watching me eat. But then she started to vanish."

"Vanish?" I said. "Where?"

"Back to her house," he replied. "She always wakes up back there – I found that out later after she'd shown me where she lived. She wakes up fully formed, all her body back together. And never with any memory of what happened. Or who she'd met."

"So how does she know about people saying she tastes good?"

"I used to tell her that. Before we . . ." He waved his hand around vaguely, embarrassed. "Before we, you know." He smiled at the memory, making me instantly jealous. "I guess it must have sunk in somehow. I don't know."

I didn't, either. But I knew that whatever the truth, it seemed she always came back to the Speed-Dating Night.

That's why I was here.

"Did she ever hook up with anybody else from the speed-dating?" Andrew nodded. "A few, I think. After me. But nothing serious.

I don't think they could handle it, Loaf forgetting them."

Which made sense, I supposed.

The question was, *could I?*

Did I want a serious, ongoing relationship with her? Or did I want to meet Loaf for the first time over and over again? Did I want to make her see the way she was? Or was I happy to let her carry on in blissful ignorance? Come to think of it, did she even really *like* me?

I thought she did. I was almost sure she did.

But there was only one way to find out for definite.

So, I smiled as she sat down before me.

"Hi," I said.

"Hi," she replied.

Then spoke four words that I wondered if I'd ever hear again.

"They call me Loaf . . ."

THE HOUSE OF JOY

- Doris V Sutherland -

"Wake up, sleepyhead! Wake up, sleepyhead!" said my alarm clock in a Welsh accent. I reached up and patted its top.

I rubbed my eyes and looked around the room. The white clouds painted onto the blue walls fell into focus. It was time to start another day. I came downstairs and found that the Bear was already in the kitchen, next to a bowl filled with dry, dandelion-yellow cornflakes.

"Marvin Milkman's not been yet," he boomed, throwing his white, furry arms into the air. The round spectacles atop his snout wobbled.

I nodded as I walked over to Fridgey and opened his door. His googly eyes stared back at me as he proceeded to list every item of food inside, using his high-pitched, electronically-distorted voice. Eggs. Butter. Bread. Jam. Oh well, enough for a jam sandwich.

The Bear and I sat in the living room. I ate my sandwich in silence while he crunched on his dry cereal. After a while, I asked him a question.

"Have you ever thought about where we were before we came to the House?"

The Bear considered me for a few seconds. I could see a faint movement in his snout as his tongue probed for cornflake debris.

"I see no purpose for contemplating such things," he replied.

"But we must have been somewhere, surely," I protested. "So how is it that none of us has any memory of where we came from or how we got here?"

"The answer is simple, Joy," said the Bear, placing his empty bowl on the table and standing up. "We have no reason to remember any of that. The House is where we live now. There is nothing to be gained from cluttering our minds with affairs that occurred outside, now, is there? We know full well what purpose we serve here."

He patted me on the head with his paw and proceeded to potter around the room, humming a cheerful tune as he dusted the ornamental penguins on the mantelpiece. He did not need a duster: he used the soft, white fur of his paws.

Then the Blue Creature popped up from behind the table. Neither the Bear nor I knew precisely where he came from, as the table stood in a vast, empty space. But as he turned up every day, we had long since grown used to his sudden appearances.

"It's that time," said the Blue Creature, tugging his long, furry ears. The very act of opening his enormous mouth caused the top half of his head to flap, sending his eyes spinning. "It's that time! It's that time!"

The Bear shoved his chair away from the table and stumbled over to the window. He began fumbling with the blind, getting into a hopeless tangle until I assisted him. Once the blind was lifted, he pushed himself against the glass, flattening his snout. I stood next to him and peered out. I heard a snuffling noise behind me as the Blue Creature tried to crane his neck for a clear view.

Sure enough, they were there.

Oblongs were flickering into existence across the sky. Inside each one, we could catch glimpses of staring eyes and round faces. Hundreds, thousands of children gazed out from

those oblongs, their eyes locked on us, their lips parted. One child was positively gawping, a trickle of drool running down his lower lip as he stared down at our house. Bit by bit, the sky was filling up with these shapes. Some were nearly transparent, the children's faces blurring into the fluffy white clouds; others were more solid, allowing a glimpse of a rosy cheek or blonde pigtail against the deep blue sky.

"They seem later than usual today," remarked the Bear, fog from his breath spreading across the window. He stepped backwards and began waving to the faces outside, his arm making slow, mechanical motions. As he did so, he wiggled his head back and forth. I always felt sorry for him when he did that. The shape of his snout prevented him from smiling, and so he had to find other means of looking jolly when we were being watched.

The Blue Creature piped up.

"You know what time it is?" he asked, in his shrill voice. "It's time to visit us all at the House of Joy!"

Coloured lightbulbs flashed around the room. A globe in the corner started spinning furiously, letting out a high-pitched whizzing noise. A blue toy train began trundling around the ceiling, choo-chooing as it went.

A loud knock made everyone jump. The Bear hobbled over and opened the door. On the other side stood Marvin Milkman, puffing and panting, holding a small plastic crate of milk bottles.

"Phew!" he said. "Sorry, I'm late! Sorry, I'm late! Hello, Bear! Hello, Joy! Hello Bluey!"

"Hey, look!" exclaimed the Blue Creature, pointing at Marvin. "He was in such a hurry that he couldn't get dressed."

Marvin looked down and gasped when he saw that he had no trousers. He took off his milkman's hat and held it in front of his red-spotted boxer shorts before clearing his throat.

"I have a very, very good reason to be late today," he told us with an air of importance. "I am late because I've brought a very, very special gift for you all, and it took me a long time to get it." Still holding his hat in one hand, he lifted the crate onto the counter by the door. It contained three milk bottles, each one a different colour.

"This is a new invention I came up with in the Milkman Factory," said Marvin. "I call it Wackymilk. I've been hard at work on it all morning. Each different flavour does something special, but you'll have to try them to find out what!" He started giggling and dashed out of the door. The faces in the oblongs all had broad smiles as they watched him vanish into the distance, still in his boxer shorts.

I closed the door and heaved the crate onto the table in the middle of the room. The three of us looked at its contents together. One bottle was filled with pale blue milk, the colour of a baby boy's pyjamas. The second bottle of milk was a pure, light green like an oak leaf held up to the sun. The third was an unpleasant yellow shade, with dark streaks running down the inside of the bottle as though the liquid inside had partially congealed. I noticed that the foil lid was damaged.

The Bear looked at me. "I think Joy should have the honour of the first taste," he said.

"I agree," squeaked the Blue Creature.

I let out a little chuckle. "I'd rather not try the yellow one. Which should I taste first, the blue or the green?"

"Drink the blue! Drink the blue!" screamed the Blue Creature, as I had expected him to.

I pulled the foil lid off the bottle of blue liquid and took a large gulp. It slipped down my throat, creamy and smooth, tasting of flower-scent with a hint of marshmallow. It was mild and warm and reminded me of things. A few scattered, fragmented memories from my childhood entered my head. Memories of a small garden, and a waterfall, and a town where bears did not talk, and--

The Bear put his paws on his hips and inspected my reaction. "How was it?"

I gave an eager nod of my head and opened my mouth to tell him how tasty it was. But no words came out. I tried it again. Nothing. I placed my hand over my mouth in shock. I had lost my voice.

"Oh-ho!" said the Blue Creature. "Joy's playing a funny game! Instead of telling us how it tasted using her words, she's using her hands. Oh, I only wish Mr Fridgey were in the room to help us, instead of being stuck in the kitchen."

I shook my head and waved my hands in front of my face palms-outward, trying to tell them that my voice had gone. The Bear tilted his head and looked at me. "Hmmm," he said.

"She's shaking her head, and showing us the palms of her hands," said the Blue Creature. "Well, if you shake a palm, a coconut falls out. She's telling us that it tastes of coconuts!" The Bear picked up the bottle and inspected it, wrinkling his nose. "I was never overly fond of coconuts," he said.

I shook my head again and pointed at my mouth. I wanted to tell them. I had to say to them. I tried to force sound from my vocal cords. I felt a tiny murmur down there. Maybe
it was wearing off.

"Look how excited she is, Bear!" screamed the Blue Creature. "She wants more! She wants more! Give her more!"

The Bear approached me with the bottle, raising its neck to my mouth. I pushed it away, at which point the Blue Creature grabbed it from the Bear and began guzzling.

"Share it with me, share it with--" he said, before collapsing into inarticulate glubs and gurgles. These faded away as the Wackymilk had its effect. He soon fell silent altogether and was left darting his head around the room with a confused look, opening his mouth and trying to make a noise.

The Bear pointed one of his claws in the air. "Aha, I see what has happened here. The blue milk takes away people's voices. Just as well, there's none left; otherwise, I might have had some and lost my voice too! Where would we have been then, I ask you?"

By now, I was able to make a faint croak. "It took my voice," I said, after a struggle. "But it made me remember things."

The Bear snorted with derision. "A drink that makes you remember things? Whoever would want that?"

I picked up the green milk and looked at it. What effect would this one have? Would it take my voice away, or

worse? I was not eager to find out. But then I thought about those memories that had entered my head, those shards of experiences from before I came to the house. Perhaps this bottle would give me a few more...

I took a swig.

I held the bottle in front of me as I swallowed. The milk was changing from green, to pink, to scarlet, to yellow, and back to green. Then I noticed that everything else in the room was changing colour. The blue skies on the walls became lemon yellow, and the painted clouds slid and shifted.

A doorway opened in the wall--a door that had never been there before--and a group of exotic animals poured out. First an orange ostrich, then a crimson kangaroo, followed by a big blue badger and a gaggle of green gibbons.

The animals drifted across the room, almost as though walking underwater. They peered into my face as they walked past; the kangaroo waved its paw, while the gibbons blew me kisses. When they were close to me, I saw that they were made out of a substance that I did not recognise, a material that seemed artificial. What I took to be fur was just a pattern painted or printed onto the smooth surfaces of their bodies. It flickered slightly, like a crystal catching the light. One by one the animals floated through a window that had

appeared in the ceiling. The badger was the last to go, shaking his head with a grumpy expression as he hovered away.

While all of this was happening, the Bear and the Blue Creature stared at me, their foreheads creased in bewilderment. The coloured animals must have been invisible to them. I was about to explain what I had seen, but as my head cleared, I realised that the milk had given me a few more memories.

I remembered a house--a different house. I remembered

snow in the garden, and building a man from the snow, my hands in little woolly gloves.

I remembered a kitchen with a fridge. But it did not talk like Mr Fridgey does. A woman stood in the kitchen, making food. I also remembered a man. Did they have something to do with where I came from? Somehow I remembered coming from a man and a woman. But how could a person come from other people?

After a long silence, I faced the Bear and held the bottle out to him. "I think you should try it," I said. He drank about half of the remaining contents, before allowing the Blue Creature to guzzle the rest. I watched the pair of them stare around the room, their jaws falling, their wide eyes following something that I could not see.

"Green gibbons?" I asked, pleased that my voice had now lost its croak.

"No," murmured the Bear. "Pleasant purple porpoises and cumbersome cyan kiwis." The Blue Creature opened his mouth, but it seemed as though the blue milk was still hampering his speech.

A few seconds later, the two of them rubbed their heads and blinked. "They all flew through the ceiling," said the Bear. My eyes were locked on him.

"Do you remember anything new after drinking that?" I asked. He gave me a puzzled look before glancing at the empty bottle, which the Blue Creature had left standing on the table. He looked back at me and shook his head without a word.

"I remember things," said the Blue Creature in a faint croak, his voice starting to return. "I remember tools. Scissors. Fur being cut. Sticks coming out of my hands." His voice got louder as he spoke, the blue milk finally wearing off. "White liquid pouring into round holes, hardening into eyes. A tray full of eyes, in different colours. Shelves of noses and tongues. Green Creatures, Purple Creatures, all silent, unmoving." He had started to panic. "Had they ever moved? Would they ever move?"

The bear reached down to stroke and comfort him. The Blue Creature had stopped talking but was still breathing heavily. I looked back at the crate.

All that was left was the yellow bottle. I picked it up and looked it over. I got the impression that it was, at one point, the same shade as a banana before taking on a different hue. It reminded me of something that had entered my head since I drank the green milk: a yellow stain on the ceiling, a stain above a man holding a paper tube with smoke coming out of the end.

I pinched at the damaged foil lid of the bottle and peeled it off. A sudden smell of rotten eggs and something worse wafted out. I winced, while the Bear fanned his paw around his nose. Despite myself, I could not turn down the chance to gather some more memories. I swallowed a mouthful of the yellow milk.

The second it had finished slipping down my gullet, I felt a new awareness. The colours and shapes around me seemed different: sharper, somehow. The clock's ticking was louder. The foul smell from the bottle was even more pungent. And there were more things floating around inside my head.

But this time, they were not memories from my past. They were things that would happen to me--to all of us--in the future.

The Bear and the Blue Creature were staring at me.

"Well," said the Bear. "Has it done anything?"

I eyed the bottle for a few more seconds before replying. "No, nothing at all," I said. I went over to the kitchen and poured the yellow milk down the sink.

"Oh, well," I heard the Bear saying from outside the kitchen. "Must have gone sour. Sour milk never does anything for you."

I returned dawdled over to the window alongside the Bear. We knew it was the time of day when the faces in the sky would depart, and sure enough, the oblongs were fading away one by one. Before long, each of them was gone, and the three of us were left alone in the room.

The Bear and I sat down at the table. He and the Blue Creature were silent, and I thought about what I now knew.

I now knew that there would be a day when those faces were not watching us. I also knew what would happen after that.

First, the smell of rotting food would alert us to Mr Fridgey's power having cut out, reducing our former friend to a useless heap of metal and plastic.

The Bear would slip on his tatty old nightcap and go into hibernation, never to awake.

The Blue Creature would let out one final, agonised croak that would last for two or three minutes. As he did so, his body would shrivel down to a greyish-brown husk before collapsing lifeless onto the floor.

The light bulbs would not flash, the globe would not spin, and the toy train would choo-choo no more.

Then, it would be my job to let down the blinds for the last time and tuck myself into bed. But on that night, I would not bother to set the talking alarm clock, with its little hammer and its little bells. Something different would wake me up in the next morning. Something different would await me in the new day.

That time was coming, but it was not today. No. Today ended in the same manner as every other day that I could remember.

The Bear sat at the table, flopped against the back of his chair, his stomach swelling and shrinking with steady breaths as he gazed up at the ceiling. The Blue Creature was silent. From the kitchen, I could hear the same sound that I listened to every night: the faint sobs of Mr Fridgey.

I realised, then, that Mr Fridgey knew more than any of us.

THE TRANSLATOR

- Preston Grassmann -

As the train begins its descent into Kamakura, I think of all the stories I've heard about the great Japanese master of horror - pulp narratives of sea-born yokai, murderous cults, and unexplained disappearances along the coast. I tell myself that such tales and legends always form around people like Edo - a recluse who has refused publicity for most of his life.

And yet, for a reason I have yet to understand, he has come out of hiding and has chosen to meet me – his translator.

Exiting the train, I notice a bald man kneeling in the shadows of the platform, wearing what appears to be the robe of a Shinto priest. He doesn't move, his hands are tucked inside the sleeves of his robe – I think of something hiding in a shell, concealed in silt at the bottom of the sea. As I approach, he rises slowly, as if uncoiling his limbs from a place he would rather stay. He stands half-way in the pool of station light, his face a palimpsest of lines as he strains to smile.

"Edo?" I ask.

"I'm glad you have come," he says in English, offering a slight bow. For a moment, the words of old stories return like premonitions. His hands are covered in sepia-coloured stains, ink markings that trail into his sleeves. And then I notice the patterns on his robe – images of skulls covering every surface, with cut sections that dangle down into tapered ends.

"It's a great pleasure to finally meet you," I say in stilted Japanese, trying to push away the growing fear. "I've been an admirer of your work for many years."

"I'm glad there's finally interest in a translation," he says. "Shall we go." He lifts his hand toward the station exit. I keep my distance, letting him guide me down a narrow lane that winds its way between cafés and old houses. When there's nothing left ahead but trails and coastline, the weight of silence grows too heavy to bear. I reach out with the only question that makes any sense: "Where are we going?"

"To the birthplace of all stories," he says.

He never turns back to see if I'm following as if this is meant to happen - a narrative with a conclusion written long ago. The sounds of the city fade away as we reach the shore and the waves wink and tremble in the moonlight. In the distance, I can see the silhouettes of pontoons and metal cranes, the fossils of some alternate prehistory.

"This is quite unusual," I say. "Usually, I conduct business in cafes or publishing houses."

He turns to me with eyes much too large, with teeth that gleam in the dark like gravestones - "I want you to understand what inspires me," he says. "It'll be hard for you to translate my work if you don't know where the words come from."

"I'll do the best I can," I say, finding a way to convince myself that this is an act; an attempt to build on his own mythology.

When we arrive at the cliff-side, we begin to descend along a path cut narrowly into the rocks. At first, it is hard to explain the emotions that take hold of me then. I feel like I'm standing outside the scene, a character in a fictional world where gods and monsters are real. This familiar vision of the sea is a moment from one of his stories playing out to some final act that I can't turn away from. All I can do is turn the page.

"At first, I was against having my work translated," he says. "Something is always lost in words. But then I realised that it's the same for all of us, trying to turn our dreams and ideas into something others can understand."

As he takes in the scene, he kneels down and sweeps his

hand toward the sea. "This is all chaos that we're trying to order in some way, to give it meaning in our lives," he says. The hem of his sleeve falls back. What I had thought was ink are the coils of tattooed tentacles.

I look down at the cut sections of his robe and notice that there are eight of them, their tapered ends draped over the rocks.

I tell myself I'm not a character in an Edo story, drawn down into a plot like a moth down a sinkhole.

I'm not as foolish as the hapless victims of his tales.

But I follow him down.

When we finally reach the bottom of the steps, I know that this is where the climax of an Edo story would be, and the words come to my lips like well-rehearsed lines:

"Why did you bring me down here?"

"I'll show you," he says, pointing down to a peculiar arrangement of rocks below. A group of stone ridges extend from the side of the cliff, stretching out into narrow points. They seem to reach out from the shore to grip at something just beyond reach.

I notice that there are eight of them.

"They look like…"

"Tentacles," he finishes.

"Did you make them?" I ask. But I already know the answer. The rocks are too large to be placed there without a crane.

"This has been here for a long time," he says. He points to one of the stone-piers, where the spray spills down into skull-like hollows, splashing over starfish and crabs. Their scurrying motion is a message, a primaeval glimpse into another world.

I follow Edo down as he makes his way to the edge of the waterline. He nods and smiles as he stares at something below him.

"There she is," he says.

"What… is it?" I ask, unable to hide the shaking in my voice. I star at that strange circle of pulsing skin, an arcane cypher that has to be translated, turned into something I can understand.

"My muse," he says.

I move closer, standing next to him on the rock and then I see it staring up at me with its large black eyes, reflecting moonlight and the sea. I know what it is, but its body and its head are much too large.

"The inspiration for a new story I'm working on," Mr Edo says. "I'd like it to be added to my collection." There is something about the way he emphasises the last word that seems wrong, and when he speaks, his words are directed down, as if he's addressing the creature instead of me.

A moment later, it leaps up onto the pier. I almost fall over as I try to scramble away. It begins to move across the rocks, wrapping its tentacles into two sections until they are joined into makeshift legs. I watch it lumber up toward the shore, numb with disbelief, stepping over rocks and seaweed and scuttling crabs. It moves in a way that seems impossible against that jagged terrain, its head much too massive for its motion. Something is held in its grip, its body conforming to the contours of its shape.

Mr Edo turns to me. "Have you ever seen a cephalopod in its natural habitat? I was a child when I saw one for the first time, imprisoned behind the glass of an aquarium. I still remember how it seemed to stare at me, like an alien life-form forced to live in a space it didn't belong," he says. "It uncoiled a limb and touched the glass, and I felt as if it was reaching out to inscribe something there, some message that I wanted to understand. Maybe it only wanted to tell me how hungry it was or that it wanted to return to the sea, to escape from the man-made borders of its existence."

I try to think of a way I can escape, to return back up that path and never look back, but I am bound in place by this unfolding story, trapped by a need to reach a conclusion I can understand.

"That was why I became a writer," he says. "I wanted to tell the stories of the monsters, of those stuck behind the glass, struggling to be understood, to turn that stray tentacle flailing against the tank into some kind of meaning." He turns to me slowly and says, "I wanted to become a translator."

The creature is a living metronome, its bulging head hypnotic in its swaying motion. It moves between narrow channels of water running between the stone piers and makes its way toward a deep trough.

There are objects inside of it, and I think of shells and gravestones and Mr Edo's teeth. Somehow, they are not covered in seaweed or barnacle-like growths, as if polished and set here to rise and fall in the surging tide - the set-pieces of a dénouement.

"Take a look at that," he says.

Held in the grip of an ineffable and ancient power, I'm pulled along the stone pier – a useless puppet. I reach the trough, trying to turn away one last time, but I fail. Inside, I see a vast collection of gleaming white objects, rising and falling with the waves.

And closer still, I can see that all of them are the same basic shape.

"I think I'm beginning to understand what it wanted all those years ago," Edo says.

All at once I realise that these are what the octopus carries, that circular form bulging beneath its stretched skin and I think of the word Mr Edo had said earlier – *collection*. Unable to stop the story from taking shape, it comes without mercy, and I am struck into silence, thoughts grasping for translations, for some way to parse the meaning, but it breaks apart. *This is my inspiration*. I feel the chaos of the sea, the boundaries of knowing slipping away into oblivion.

I fall back, curling my fingers around the rocks and I close my eyes, those shapes still lingering, empty sockets staring up into the sky or facing the sea, or turned down to face their own grave.

When I open my eyes, the octopus floats below the

surface of the water, rising and falling with its skull, and I suddenly know the part of the story I'm meant to fulfil, the translation I am intended to complete.

"I'm still not sure what my new story will be called," Mr Edo says. "I was thinking of calling it 'The Translator'.

CAUGHT ON THE OUTSIDE

- Dani Brown -

The door opened with ancient clicks and a cloud of dust beneath the neon sign. A battered Roomba moved out of the way, coughing decades worth of spent love onto the dusty carpet. Sucky-O went in first. When he rolled over the spent love, it wasn't there. Faded Star guided by his erection and the ghost of himself trapped upstairs.

The door shut behind him. A woman stepped out from the shadows with an hourglass figure and fingerprints around her neck.

"You can drop the mask."

His hand inertly travelled to his dick. Tentacles fell out of the latex covering her. The thick shag carpet swallowed it down with decades of memories and excess.

"Please keep your dressing gown on."

"I thought you were into tantra?"

"Not with you."

A sexbot came to slow life inside a glass case. Well-used in her prime, but the Neon Dream started to die. *I want to do what you want me to do.* A cassette tape rewound. *I want to do…to do…to do.* An electronic cough blew out the glass in a fall of ancient semen from thousands of different men. *What you want me to do.*

The sexbot twitched around the shards of glass, never leaving her case. The battered old Roomba clicked over them without picking them up.

A tentacle wrapped around Faded Star's shoulders. The finger-bone necklace jangled on her neck with her dying power. The ghosts howled, trapped upstairs. Sticky ooze churned up from the carpet when he dug his heels in as she pulled him closer.

"We gave the world synthpop dreams."

A tentacle pulled at his silver hair, spiking it. The finger-bone necklace sent out flickers of dying neon light.

"You're dying."

I want to do… another cough sent projectile cumdust across the room, hitting another case. Another sexbot chimed into life. Her arms missing. The wallpaper peeled next to her revealing a nest of paper wasps, long since dead. Their corpses crumbled to the shag carpet to join the memories and excess. The Roomba chugged and coughed to them.

A tentacle traced the buttons on Faded Star's satin pyjamas. Another pulled at his trousers, ripping them off and flinging them across the room. An old sexbot tried to catch them with her teeth, but her reflexes were out. She hadn't seen any action in years.

His cock bounced up. No cowering in the Neon Dream, even in its dying years. The spell danced around him. Spewed out in faint artificial fog from the fingerbones jangling around her neck.

*I want to do…I want to do…*the sexbots sounded off in a chorus. Their electronic voices made the dust float in the air. Spent semen from the popstars of yesteryear and dead skin cells. It smelled ancient and decayed.

A girl with hooks for hands watched from a doorframe. Shackles around her ankles. They no longer gleamed like they did when they were new. Broken, like everything else. Her haunted face looked familiar, framed by long hair.

"Up on stage, with your hair restored."

The Tentacle Queen made a noise, and Faded Star's former self appeared. A teased mullet sculpted on top of his head and down the back too. Head held high, somehow, underneath all that weight. The hole in the Ozone layer rested on his shoulders, but they had some padding.

The girl with hooks for hands mouthed, "help me". His brain glitched as he tried to recall the haunted face. A tentacle squeezed his cock, oblivious of her stolen daughter with the haunted face watching from the doorframe. "How?" he mouthed back.

"We'll give the world synthpop dreams."

His former self turned to face him and wink. She flicked her tentacle. Faded Star's head tilted back, eyes half shut. He could still see the ceiling. Sexbot pieces strung up with chains and a keyhole painted on. It peeled back, revealing the plaster underneath. Neon light shone through from the rooms upstairs.

Slime held the Dream Princess together. Slime swallowed the slow ooze of honey tainted by the Neon Dream. Marcy's world seeped in and stole broken sexbots. Swallowed by the dirt in the Forest of the Dead to rest. *I want to do what you want me to do.* The sexbots in their everlasting chorus. They wouldn't stop until they end up beneath the soil a world away. Only when the honey runs fresh and the Tentacle Queen is dead will they be restored and pounded into once again.

The Roomba clogged along the ancient shag carpet. It was meant to swallow the dead flies. Any traces of Marcy seeping into the Neon Dream had to be destroyed. Wallpaper plastered over the tainted honey, so the Tentacle Queen wouldn't have to look at it. Layer upon layer put up by her daughters with their hooks in place of hands.

"We gave the world synthpop dreams."

Faded Star moaned. The sexbot parts twitched with a hiss. The voices stolen by the popstars of long ago and sampled on long-forgotten records that were never very popular, to begin with.

Eggs moved in the oozing slime. A final flick of her tentacle and Faded Star screamed with the relief of being completely drained.

"We can give the world synthpop dreams once again."

His semen travelled in a shooting star of creamy white ribbons and hit the ceiling. An egg sack in the slime burst open as it splattered for instant fertilisation. His semen sample gone in less time than a dissolving picture message.

The Tentacle Queen whistled for The Child That Has Always Been and her stolen daughter. She didn't even bother to cover Faded Star with a dusty moth-eaten blanket. He laid there, drooling onto her floor. The dusty, old Roomba tried to suck it up without success.

His former self wandered away to the lips in the walls, trousers around his ankles. He didn't bother to brush aside the dust before parking himself inside. He weaved his fingers together through the massive mop of hair.

A sexbot came up behind him, her movements slow with age and decay. *I want to do. I want to do. I want to do.* Two fingers twitched into prostate exam position and planted sunshine inside his arsehole. *I want to do I want to do.* A glitch inside her and her broken body and peeling latex fell on top of him.

Faded Star's ghost wouldn't hit the height of a crippling orgasm while held prisoner in a world collapsing around him. The sexbot's fingers never left his arse. Metal shone from her spine. The latex wearing away. Swallowed by the shag carpet that held so many secrets and witnessed so many things. The Roomba could no longer keep it clean.

Faded Star turned his head to the other side. He couldn't watch his former shame. A secret meant to be between him and the Tentacle Queen in a moment of sheer desperation long ago.

The Child That Has Always Been appeared next to her kidnapped sister in the doorframe. Her eyes cut to her mother's necklace. She would never be free. Not while her fingerbones jangled around her mother's neck. "Help us," she mouthed. "Set us free."

A vague place in the back of his post-ejaculation brain screamed at him. Recognition of the stolen one. But he didn't know where. The piercing blue eyes created with contact lenses. Tears cut through the dirt on her face. Missing her daddy.

"Get in here, now."

The Tentacle Queen snapped a tentacle and her necklace

jangled. The neon glowed for a moment, enhanced by the aquamarine fire around her neck. *Feel bad for me. My husband tried to kill me.* Faded Star stared at her with his grey eyes.

"Don't try to manipulate me with your sorry past."

His fists pulled at the shag carpet. Post-ejaculation and he hadn't much strength. His head fell back to the floor and sent up dust. The Forest of the Dead rejected the spent semen left behind by the popstars of yesteryear.

The chains around the two daughters' ankles straightened. They fell to the floor in a cloud of dust, and the Tentacle Queen dragged them across the shag carpet. They reached their hooks in. Faded Star could feel the vibrations hitting his body.

"Kill the boys. Kill the girls with tentacles. They're of no use to me."

Faded Star looked up at the ceiling where a tentacle pointed. The eggs formed into babies, most with limbs instead of tentacles.

Her dressing gown fell from her shoulders, and she slithered naked from the room. Her backside ended in six rear ends, usually concealed beneath a latex mask. A trail of slime tangled the thick shag carpet. She was out of eggs.

The teenage daughters watched her leave. The one with piercing blue eyes leant in close so he could see the outline of her contact lenses. Her body was so thin. The tunic she wore hadn't been cleaned in years.

"Help us, please, Faded Star, get us out of here."

A glitter on her teeth. Braces with the wires cut between them. Her teeth wouldn't move any more in the Neon Dream.

"Please don't kill the babies."

He looked up at them, they looked like new-borns wrapped in a transparent sack. Those with thumbs sucked them, the others put tentacles in their mouths.

"We have no choice."

The Child That Has Always Been reached her hooked hands to the ceiling and cut down the babies. They fell as rain with plaster, letting in neon from the floor above.

Faded Star knew the building well. Remembered from his previous visit and hidden shame. Dreams came to him in the nights, before Honey's visit and their trips to the meadow. He wandered the corridors of the Dream Princess, lost and alone. Everything covered in the dust of years gone by.

The outer egg casings shattered and left the babies screaming and gasping for dusty air. The daughters reacted with learned indifference. A ritual they had carried out many times before. Faded Star never saw any babies in his dreams. Only twitching sexbot parts left to break on the floor and peeling wallpaper.

The stolen daughter reached her hook into a boy's skull. His limbs perfectly formed. He looked like Faded Star until she pulled his head off and threw it at a wall. Lips poised in the duckface look so popular on social media. The walls needed to be fed. They weren't a simple decoration. Organic matter grown from the DNA left behind by the popstars of long ago.

I want to do what you want me to do. The chorus chimed in. Thirty years ago, the sexbots said a few other phrases. Stolen from a future yet to come, some could even hold basic conversations.

"They won't live long, really, it is a mercy," the stolen daughter said.

"Shh…she'll hear."

The Child That Has Always Been cowered in fear.

"You were here the last time I was here, weren't you?"

The Child That Has Always Been didn't answer. Instead, she stuck a hook into a baby that was a mess of tentacles.

"Why does she want only girls with limbs?"

"She's been searching for the perfect baby to raise until the day before her fourteenth birthday."

The stolen daughter raised both her hooks to show Faded Star. The place in the back of his head searched for where he knew her.

"You weren't here, last time, though, were you? I know you from somewhere else."

The Child That Has Always Been brought her hooks down in the skulls of two babies. She kicked their broken bodies against a glass case, waking another sexbot to join the chorus. The cassette tape rewound and started again.

The babies with tentacles instead of limbs bled slime instead of blood. The carpet swallowed it all. But the Forest of the Dead rejected the muck. It landed someplace else. Faded Star knew about his wife's dressing room behind a false door and the potions she kept there. Her face meant to be forever young, in exchange, cancer in her left breast.

"Then she'll cut off her hands and add the bones to her necklace, so it can glow in perfect neon blue again. The Neon Dream will be restored with a third girl's fingers and blood."

The stolen daughter hooked a baby by the eye and lifted it up. She flicked it across the room. The dusty old Roomba couldn't keep up. Sucky-O didn't want to sample the delights of baby flesh and hissed in a corner.

"The daughter will be strung from the ceiling, and the Tentacle Queen herself will slit her throat and shower in the blood."

The stolen daughter tilted her head back so Faded Star could examine her neck. He raised his fingers to feel the slit, it still bled.

"Who did she steal you from?"

The stolen daughter slaughtered another baby. She turned to face Faded Star, dripping with gore. Her piercing blue eyes went right through him.

"I can't remember. It happened so long ago. I think I was friends with her daughter. The child of a man wrapped up in her manufactured drama."

The Child That Has Always Been faced her. Her tunic was older with more holes. The marks on her neck from the blade glittered silver. It stopped bleeding long ago when Faded Star topped the charts.

"There's two perfect daughters, it is your turn to decide."

"Why don't we save them both, the babies never make it past being toddlers. Maybe one will survive?"

Faded Star pushed himself up with his elbows. The dead babies oozed into the thick shag carpet. The decay spread rapidly. It was only a matter of a few seconds. Time enough for a picture message to dissolve.

The babies no longer looked like new-borns. Two perfect girls with chubby rosy cheeks and teeth poking through their gums. One started to clap, and the other followed her lead. Sisters born in the Neon Dream. Sperm milked from Faded Star by the Tentacle Queen. In his bedroom, the tissue wouldn't have time to dry.

"We have to kill one for the ritual to work. There can only be one born of her eggs and raised at any given time."

Both babies looked like him. Daughters Joyce couldn't give him. Daughters Honey didn't want to. Marcy's womb would forever lay barren.

"Please don't."

Faded Star reached his hands for the babies. The Child That Has Always Been kicked them out of his reach and they screamed. Instant bruises forming with the imprint of her toes.

"Fine."

The stolen daughter reached out her hook and caved in the head of the one nearest to her. Faded Star shut his eyes. The baby's sister wailed. The only crying baby left in the room. Her voice heard over the sexbots with their chorus.

"Shut her up. She'll hear."

The stolen daughter stood frozen. The carpet swallowed the babies around her and sent up dust in return. *Do you know my daddy?* Her eyes pierced through Faded Star with the message, cutting right through his brain.

"I don't know."

The Child That Has Always Been scooped gore from the shag carpet into her hook and picked up the baby. She cradled her in her arms and offered the hook to suckle. The baby accepted and grew stronger. Too big for a girl one day away from her fourteenth birthday to handle. Forever thirteen.

Faded Star forced himself to his feet. Disorientation washed over him in the flickering neon. He didn't see his satin pyjamas. The Tentacle Queen's transparent dressing gown would have to do. The feathers would hide his shame until he could do better.

"Where's the door?"

I want to do what you want me to do. I want to… the cassette tape rewound. The sexbots helped each other out of the glass cases and moved in uneasy steps to frosted glass windows, lit up with neon.

The shag carpet swallowed his feet. Dirt moved between his toes. The dead whispered from the other side, uneasy in their graves. They wanted their waxed black threads back. Marcy needed them to hold herself together.

The daughter, now a little taller and stronger wandered away. Exploration in the Dream Princess amongst the broken sexbots. Her hair rested flat against her back. The hairspray no longer imported into the Neon Dream.

"There isn't one."

Chains wrapped around his ankles. The Tentacle Queen hid them in the Forest of the Dead. Thievery in the night, while Marcy wandered collecting souls from her list and dropping off infected rats in gutters.

"I belong to the forest, with Marcy."

His former self howled from the twisted take on the gloryhole. Head tilted back, his hair bounced. The sexbot fell away. Her fingers twitching. The thick shag carpet swallowed her down with the dead flies and rats. The lips swallowed his cum. All except one drop. That fell to the carpet and was swallowed. Dirt spread through the shag beneath Faded Star's former self. The Forest of the Dead claimed him.

"You're here forever, to help raise your daughter."

225

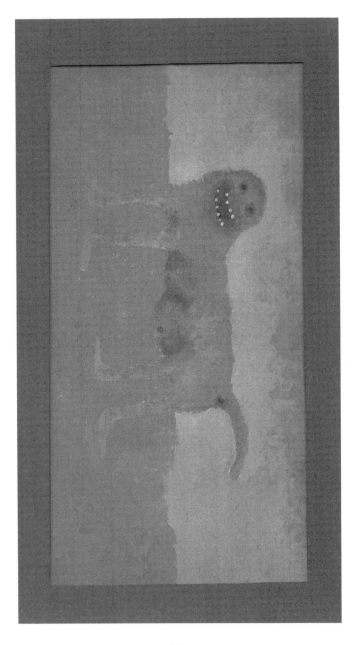

CHRISTMAS MAN

When the snow has fallen softly,
upon hard winter's ground,
it's time, speak words backwards,
for Christmas Mans around.

His fleshy, hairy jumper,
has a fleshy, hairy mouth,
and his fleshy, hairy handbag,
shall lead him from the south.

The snow will catch on fire,
the crackers will now eat,
as he shall walk on endless,
Christmas Man seeks meat

So speak in ancient tongues,
hide your fearful eyes,
look not upon Christmas Man,
for he'll turn you into pies.

THOSE WHO WROTED THE WORDS AND SHOULD BE HELD ACCOUNTABLE FOR YOUR NEW CONDITION

- Shaun Avery -

Dear Editors,

We here at the Anti-Offence League are absolutely DISGUSTED to see you publishing yet another story from the filthy mind of Shaun Avery. We have had it up to HERE with the puerile attempts at satire from this so-called 'writer,' as seen in so many magazines and anthologies. We find his placings in competitions with both prose and comic scripting works a surefire sign of our world's emotional and moral decay, and struggle to see why ANYONE would want to read the script he recently sold, or the self-published comic he co-created. In short, his work is vile and revolting, and we are sure that, upon reflection, you will decide not to inflict his disgusting tale, "Meet Loaf," upon an unsuspecting, and definitely undeserving, reading public.

Yours faithfully,

The Anti-Offence League.

- Die Booth -

Dear Paranormal Digest,

I have lived for ten years now in an old
property in Cheshire, which is haunted. I have
never seen the ghost, but often hear footsteps
and what sounds like the tapping of laptop
keys. Several times, words such as 'Spirit
Houses', '365 Lies' and 'My Glass is Runn' have
appeared in awful handwriting on any envelopes
that have been left lying around. On one
occasion, 'Die Booth' was written on my toilet
roll. A psychic I contacted told me that this is
the ghost's name, but I remain sceptical. The
presence seems benign and, aside from cake
frequently disappearing from my kitchen, I am
happy to let him stay.

Felix Fortune, Chester, Cheshire

- Duncan Bradshaw -

Dear Person in charge of retractions,

It has come to my attention, that in your
article dated 33rd July 2019, you attribute the
murders of four mime artists to one 'Hugh
Finkley', who was subsequently arrested and
executed by your monthly crossword. I believe if
you read the recent works of Duncan P. Bradshaw,
(in particular his treatise on a psychotic
vacuum cleaner, *Mr Sucky*), then you will realise
that it was him who perpetrated these heinous
crimes. In his most recent book, *Cannibal Nuns
From Outer Space!,* he clearly confesses to the
crime and several others, including that of my
social worker.
I demand you apologise unreservedly to the
family of Mr Finkley and focus your hate
campaign on Mr Bradshaw, so he gets what's
coming to him.

Kind Regards,

Angela Foxe

BRITISH BIZARRO

- Dani Brown -

Dear Editors of some second-rate publication,

The inclusion of Dani Brown is most offensive.
Did you know she's a single mother? She should
not be allowed to write. Any dreams she had
disappeared when she couldn't keep her
relationship together - along with her B.A. in
Creative Writing. One of her books includes foul
language in the title! I dare to think what
depravity lurks behind the cover of *Middle Age
Rae of Fucking Sunshine,* or *Sparky the Spunky
Robot.* This is just further proof that a woman
shouldn't be allowed to write, especially if this
is what she comes up with. *Ketamine Addicted
Pandas* doesn't even know what genre it belongs
to. Is it bizarro? It is extreme horror? And don't
get me started on *56 Seconds,* that fits nowhere.
And as for her latest release, *Becoming.* I'm
surprised someone decided to publish something
so bleak.
Return Dani to the kitchen where she belongs
and stop her writing! Single mothers are only
allowed the hobby of jogging down city streets
while leaving their children at home so in
another few years there can be another feral
youth on the streets to give us ladies with class
something to complain about.
Society is breaking down, my dear editors.

Regards

Prudence S Hiscock

- Craig Bullock -

Dear Mr Editor,

I am writing to commend the writing of Craig Bullock of Staffordshire, I'm his mother! I gave birth to him some 38 years ago... it was horrific! i mean honestly i though he would amount to nothing, he seemed a little bit simple! The first story i read was, '9 tales at the end of the world' his Zombie story, was exquisite, and unlike anything i had ever read, as was "children of the lilac tree (i mean a guy whose left arm is possessed by a singer called Frank can not fail!). However his other works have left me confused and slightly repulsed... Baby Bird was a pure stand alone horror story that could and should grace our current mundane T.V on demand world, and his story' Call of duty" published for 'Box of Bizarro" seriously needs work!
All in all, thank you for including him in this amazing anthology, but be aware his long standing input is not guaranteed... I have it from good information that his current goal was to secure a penguin and a small chimpanzee, in a tailored suit..... of which he apparently has already sourced from the black web.... the penguin is apparrently called jeff and the chimpanzee fredrick. Fredrick ensures Jeff is bug free and Jeff, from what i have heard, basically ignores everyone. Basically my son is sketchy. He needs focus and to get up off his fat ass and actually do something productive.

Lots of love
Stella (Craig's mum)

BRITISH BIZARRO

- James Burr -

Dear Editor,

I am writing to you to complain about the
inclusion of the monstrous degenerate, James
Burr, in your latest anthology. I have been the
neighbour of this colossal pervert for several
years and have unfortunately become used to him
pushing tattered pieces of suspiciously-stained
paper with hyperlinks to *Bizarro
Central, decomP* and *Horror Sleaze Trash* through
my letter box, his PVC-clad mittens jabbing at
the sanctity of my flap. Yet more recently, he
has taken to depositing actual books, with
titles like *Darkness Rising, Fiction
International, Trembling with Fear* and *Suspense
Unimagined* onto my doormat, like steaming
literary turds. Now I am stuck in my home as a
result of coronavirus lockdown and he has taken
to dancing around his back garden with his
other depraved acolytes, skipping around in
their rubber and PVC gimp-suits, jeering at how
the virus is a Gimp-ocalypse, a time when he and
his fellow deviants will be protected from
infection and I see them sometimes, through my
net curtains, preparing for the Gimp-World that
they feverishly foresee as arising from the
ashes, taking readings from his collection of
feverish writings and unholy manifesto, *Ugly
Stories for Beautiful People*. Now, from visiting
the repulsive http://www.james-burr.co.uk/, I
understand that not only have you accepted his
vile drivel, but his second collection of

233

ravings, *This Septic Isle*, is soon to be published by Nihilism Revised in the Summer of 2020. I urge you in the strongest of terms not to encourage him. Not only is his personal hygiene abominable but the activities of the gimp-hive next door often interfere with my frenzied, marathon masturbation sessions during Strictly Come Dancing, which are my sole comfort and distraction since retiring from politics.

Yours,

Quentin St John Fosbury, OBE.

P.S. Oh, and that one with the singing furries. That's good, too.

- Peter Caffrey -

Dearest Editor,

I bet you already know what's coming, you
despicable crust of ocelot dung. It's Tuesday, and
Mother is still waiting. Don't even think about
trying to deceive us with your untruths,
falsifying a pretence you called but we were not
home. We waited all day, and no one came aside
from that blasphemous scribbler of puerile
filth, Peter Caffrey, peddling copies of *The
Devil's Hairball* and *Whores Versus Sex Robots*. We
had to turn him away, and you know why, don't
you? We will not wait forever; we will not.
Better men than you have hanged for less. That
may sound dramatic but remember: it's Tuesday,
and MOTHER IS STILL WAITING!

Sincerely, You know who I am

- Gem Caley -

To the esteemed Editors of Wedding Tragedy
Weekly,

Who is Gem Caley? I'm no misogynist, sirs, but
what possessed you to promote this unknown
woman to the rank of Editor-At-Large? I have
Googled her extensively and found little to
recommend her to your edifying publication. Her
writing is the stuff of nonsense! When she isn't
on Twitter pontificating about jaffa cake
sandwiches, she's running sci-fi flash fiction
competition *Songs From Luna* or blogging about
teeth. If you do not reconsider this appointment
I shall be forced to take my patronage to your
inferior rival, The Unlucky Bouquet Review.

Yours hopefully,

Reginald Sletherly.

BRITISH BIZARRO

- Bill Davidson -

Dear vice-editor Barry,

I must warn you in the clearest terms against
accepting stories from that appalling plagiarist
Davidson.
What possessed Ellen Datlow to publish *'A Brief
Moment of Rage'* in her Best Horror of the Year
anthology is beyond me, given that it is based
almost word for word on my own wonderful story
'A Brief Stoat of Rage'. (It's about an extremely
cross stoat, in case you are interested)
I wrote to her many times, making that point -
two hundred and twelve, to be exact - but my
timely words of caution fell on deaf ears. I even
sent her a photograph of my mother, who looks
very like Novak Djokovic, as self-evident proof
of my credibility. But, no.
Hell Bound Books similarly published *'The Long
Woman'*, the most brazen rip-off of my own 'The
Long Stoat', and had the temerity to block my
calls.
You can find his stories everywhere, it seems,
dozens of the damned things in everything from
The Fiction Desk to The Horror Zine, all stolen
from my own personal self. I even bought a copy
of Woman's Weekly, thinking at least that had to
be safe from his endless thievery, but no. How he
succeeded in finding my heart-warming story of
stoats at play is beyond me, but he did, copying
it mercilessly and changing it to remove any
mention of protagonists of the furrier kind.
I lay my plea frankly before you and offer one
of my own stories instead of that Behemoth
nonsense. It's entitled Little Simon and the
Stoat.

Yours faithfully
Charles Aznavour

PS I enclose a photograph of my mother as
evidence of my sincerity, on the occasion when
she defeated Andy Murray to win the Australian
Open.

- Matt Davis -

Dear Editor in Chief of Cryptozoology and
Crochet ,

My what dark times we are living in that you
have consented to publish the work of one
Matthew Davis of Birmingham. By his own
admission, he cannot even tell the difference
between the 127 known species of Chupacabra let
alone master the broomstick lace technique! His
written work for websites such as Geek Syndicate
and Doctor Who Online were filled with the most
puerile trash, and now I hear he has begun his
move into the realm of fiction! Besides, he no
longer resides in the country, having moved to
the wildest parts of Australia and joined a
Dropbear Death Cult!
If this is the sort of direction this once great
magazine is going in, consider my subscription
cancelled. I enclose my "I Love Bigfoot" badge,
which I can no longer wear with pride.

Yours Hepstein Barnacle

- Neil Dinsmore -

Dear Castle Lickers Quarterly,

I adore licking castles as much as the next man
but your recent piece on Turret Tonguing
Techniques by that renowned labial laird, Neil
Dinsmore, has sent me quite over the edge. The
zest of ancient masonry has never felt better on
my taste buds, and for that, I am eternally
grateful. Thanks to his methods, I have begun
producing small stone keeps in my stool, which I
wash and sell to small children and tropical
fish enthusiasts. The proceeds of which I have
used to purchase a laptop to access his excellent
website, www.neildinsmore.wordpress.com and enjoy
a medley of his other thrilling writings.
Thank you greatly for the enlightenment and may
your strongholds be forever seasoned.

Yours lingually,

Marquis Archibald Skink III

BRITISH BIZARRO

- Preston Grassman -

Dear Manager of this hotel I'm stuck in due to
Covid19,

I have been a loyal customer in your hotel for
the past seven years. Everything was fine, the
meals were tasty, the staff excellent. However,
my forced enclosure due to the Covid19 outbreak
has led me to search my room for reading
material. I was overcome with rage to discover
that instead of a Gideon's Bible in my bedside
draws there were copies of the works of one
Preston Grassman.
I believe Mr Grassman is of Scottish descent
(which I find objectionable in and of itself) but
was raised in California (again another black
mark). Here he lived in the same block as one
Philip K Dick (I believe this is the final nail
in the coffin). He became a freelance writer
after reviewing briefly for *Locus* in 1998.
The selection of his recent works which I was
exposed to were, *Nature Magazine, Futures 2
(Tor), Mythic Delirium* and *AE: Canadian Science
Fiction.* I also turned on my laptop, only to
find that he currently blogs for *Nature
Magazine* and a regular feature for *Locus,* which
he has entitled, *"The Cosmic Village".*
I wish to be sent a formal apology and an
appropriate bible within the next fortnight, or
I shall write another strongly worded letter.

Yours

Edith Darling, age 76 $\frac{1}{2}$

- Greg James -

Hello the Daily B*stard,

I have it on good authority that Greg James is a short-sighted badger named Dave who lives under a small mound at the bottom of my garden. He steals Ajax from my kitchen and sells it as crack to the fairies that live in my neighbour's bush. At no point has he had a best-selling Y.A. fantasy trilogy entitled *Age of Flame* and the very idea this visually challenged striped weasel could pen a critically acclaimed horror novel called *The Eyes of the Dead* is frankly absurd. I hope you will expose this mangy excuse for an mustelid for the charlatan he is in your forthcoming addition and bar him from future fantasy/horror anthologies. If he wants to write science fiction though, that's fine.

Yours, madly wanking,

Mr P. Clitthouse of Cricklewood.

- Chris Kelso -

Dear Royal Naval College, Dartmouth,

You may not have heard of me, but I've certainly
heard of you! I was most disgruntled to read
that my illustrious ancestor, one Chris Kelso (a
British Fantasy Award-nominated writer and
editor from Scotland), has not been recognised in
your 205 year re-enactment of the Battle of
Waterloo. All right, the Royal Navy were
slightly superfluous during Waterloo, but damn
it all man, I want him noticed. He's hardly going
to be recognised for his writing achievements,
being published in *3AM, Black Static, Daily
Science Fiction, Sensitive Skin, Evergreen
Review* and many others.
I hope to see him recreated adequately on your
battlefield as soon as possible.

Yours, furiously polishing my medals,

Sir Pippin Squatch

- Frank Key -

Dear God,

We are writing to complain about the untimely
departure of Frank Key. We sum up our feelings
about this with the following phrase:

YOU BASTARD!

Frank's absurdist short stories, which appeared
on *The Drabblecast* podcast were great, as well as
the ones which appeared on his own radio series,
Hooting Yard on the Air. Not to mention that he
cofounded *Malice Afterthought Press* with Max
Decharne, and managed to self-publish several
short story collections.
So, God, now you have to explain yourself to us,
The British Bizarro Community

BRITISH BIZARRO

- Luke Kondor -

Dear Editor,

I once smelled a man called Luke, and I swore
'never again'!
And here you are publishing a person who not
only has no hair on his head but if the rumours
are to be believed hasn't been nude since 1999.
The shame!
Are you aware that this person called Luke is
nothing but an enchanted USB phone charger? And
are you aware that this is the man who dreams of
satsumas? And di you know that this man goes
around wiring things down ...on paper? Where
does he get off thinking he can go off writing
things down? Just who the hell does he think he
is!?
Honestly? I'm asking, genuinely.
I believe he has an identity crisis. He doesn't
know who he is anymore! Please, if you genuinely
love him, you will demodulate him down to his
pants and atoms.
You should delete his new bizarro podcast *Tales
of What* (available on all your regular podcast
apps) and remove him from Twitter (*@LukeKondor)*
and at the very least discombobulate his website
(www.lukekondor.com)

Yours, One Concerned Reader

#SaveLuke

- Chris Meekings -

Dear Mr The Editor of Horse and Hounds,

I am writing to complain about the disgusting
works of one Chris Meekings of Gloucester. Quite
frankly, I think it is revolting that such books
as the bizarro novella *Elephant Vice* (Eraserhead
Press) and the metaphysical fantasy novel *Ravens
and Writing Desks* (Omnium Gatherum) are even
allowed to be printed. I also have it on very
reputable authority that he claims to be 58
weasels in a trench coat, just looking for love.
Let it be known, I am against such things!

Yours

Sir Milfred Windigo
MBE, OBE, KGB, Knight Order of the Bath, and
Champion at conkers for Oxford 1949

- Antony Mercer -

Dear Moth Fanciers Monthly,

I have noticed a young man lurking near your
moths and believe him to be that well-known
gossip-monger who writes for our rival magazine
Fanciers of Moths Monthly, Antony Mercer. Do
not give him any information on which common-
clothes moth was seen on a beach holiday with
which silkworm because he will only spin in
salaciously for his grubby little ray.

Yours,

Margaret Toenails

- Tom Over -

Dear Deidre,

I have started a relationship with a weirdo at
work. He's not at all my type but his reading
tastes have turned me into a violent
cannibalistic sex freak. I just can't help myself!
In particular, the stories of Tom Over from
Manchester, such as those found in *Prose in Poor
Taste vol. 2* (Horror Sleaze Trash),
UNSPLATTERPUNK3! (Theaker's Quarterly Fiction)
and *Aphotic Realm* magazine, have us both
wanting to fight, fuck and shallow fry everyone
we meet! Currently, we're awaiting his debut
collection, *The Comfort Zone and Other Safe
Spaces* (NihilismRevised) which promises to
deliver an orgasmically depraved feast of
apocalyptic proportions!
Please send help! Or better yet . . . dips!

Caroline Gunt
Wigan

- Leigham Shardlow -

Dear Shady News Monthly,

I have reports concerning one Leigham Shardlow;
███████████████████████████████. ██████
████████████████. ███████████████████
█████████████ the location of the P.C. game Half
Life ████████████████████████████████
████████. Sadly, it can only be for this reason
that he ███████████████████████████████

Yours Obfuscatingly

████████████████

- Jay Slayton-Joslin -

Dear Editor Of This Here Book,

Firstly, Jay Slayton-Joslin thinks talking in
the third person to describe himself isn't just
pretentious, but not pretentious enough! The
Grand Master Jay Slayton-Joslin is the author
of such wonderful books like *Sequelland: A Story
of Dreams and Screams* (CLASH BOOKS, 2020) and
Kicking Prose (KUBOA, 2014). He lives in Leeds,
England and is actually really insecure so
please see through this thinly veiled attempt at
humour and like him okay?

Best wishes,

Jay

- Doris Surtherland -

Dear Cryptozoology Bimonthly,

I am writing to describe my recent encounter
with what I believe to have been the entity
known as Doris V. Sutherland. While traversing
the Norfolk/Suffolk border one night I chanced
upon a figure as tall as Bigfoot and as gaunt as
a Chupacabra, lolloping around while imbibing a
beverage of the most noxious blue. When I
returned the following morning, the only
physical traces left by the apparition were a
vampire comic called *Midnight Widows*, some
Doctor Who tie-ins from Big Finish and a book on
the 1932 film The Mummy (part of the Devil's
Advocates series).

Yours,

the Reverend Hotcrosse-Bunny

- Madeleine Swann -

Dear Whomever,

Please remove Madeleine Swann from our garden.
She is frightening the children. She must be
cold, it's 3AM, and she's naked.
If something isn't done, I may have to cast her
Wonderland Award-nominated collection *Fortune
Box* and various short stories into the fire.
Even the Splatterpunk nominated anthology *The
New Flesh: A David Cronenberg Tribute!* Mind you
that might warm her up a bit.
At the very least, you could ask her to stop
screaming at the hydrangeas.

Yours sincerely

Madge Neighbours

Any further complaints please contact
madeleineswann.com

BRITISH BIZARRO

- DJ Tyrer -

Dear Daily Telegraph,

Sir, am I alone in thinking that DJ Tyrer's writing has appeared in far too many anthologies recently? I have it on good authority that they were short-listed for the 2015 Carillon 'Let's Be Absurd' Fiction Competition and have continued to produce a stream of piffle ever since, with stories in the distinctly-unfunny volumes two onwards of *Strangely Funny* from Mystery and Horror LLC, the irrational *Irrational Fears* from FTB Press, something bizarre called *More Bizarro Than Bizarro* from Bizarro Pulp Press, and the quite-frankly robophobic *Destroy All Robots* from Dynatox Ministries (which I am reliably informed is a publisher and not a church, at all!), as well as producing a comic horror e-novelette, *A Trip to the Middle of the World*, that is available from Alban Lake through the Infinite Realms Bookstore. And, that is without mentioning the ordure that is Tyrer's horror writing.

When will it all end? Will nobody think of the children?

Yours in adversity,

Disgusted of Droitwich

THOSE WHO DREWED IT

- LoFiGuy -

Dear Mr & Mrs Bizarro,

In his website bio, Lo-fi Guy dares to state, "I
am a street smart bantam of the alternative,
underground rural art scene. A walking art form
from birth producing pure white eggs of
creativity."

I'll have you know that this is total
unadulterated hogwash! Contrary to popular
mythology Lo-fi Guy obtained an art degree from
a third rate Polytechnic! I should know, I'm his
mum!

Furthermore describes himself as, "An 'ice Ice
baby' of the art jungle, which resonates in his
work like a Ninja chicken ... on acid!"

I can, of course, confirm that this is all balls.
He's a lazy little ginger man who should get a
real job in a Bejams or selling insurance rather
than pretending to be an artist what he is
CLEARLY NOT! Have you seen his work? I rest my
case.

Please don't include him in your book!

Margolis Dench (Lo-fi Guy's Mummy)

- Will Mcdaniel -

Dearest Mildred,

I think, as these lonely hours pass, as we are
parted due to the long oceanic voyage I
undertook to study the beautiful flora and
fauna of the South China Seas, that I should
write to you to complain about a gentleman whom
I have recently struck up an acquaintance with
throughout this voyage.
He claims to be a British filmmaker with a love
of all things creepy, and I can only say that
this summation of him is unerringly accurate. He
posts, upon the interwebs, his own ghastly
moving pictures including practical effects of
his own devising and the odd monster or two, and
many people watch this horror show, which is
supposed to be comedic in nature, on the
YouTubes. Apparently, anyone can subscribe to
his channel and watch these things.
Well, I, for one, won't stand for it. I'm going to
write to the Times about it. Of course, I will
sign the letter Elton John, or they won't print
it.

Your ever-loving Gertrude

- Bill Purnell -

To the Editor,

I am not sure why you decided to commission the
artist Bill Purnell to design the front cover of
your book. I have given this much thought and
have concluded you must have either suffered
some sort of medical incident or been
overwhelmed with pity.
I have been following his creative works for the
past 20 years and find them at best awful and at
worst awful ... they are all awful.
His art at the *Brighton Fringe, The Moulsham
Tap, Art Car Boot Fair* in Brick Lane and
Beecroft Art Gallery in Southend were also
awful. His website design is poorly executed,
badly coded and awful. You only have to look at
billpurnell.com to see that!
His music is just as awful as his visual
creations and I hear he is going to be making
yet more tripe, releasing an album under the
name *Bill Bat*! Pathetic!

Hope you recover soon,

Gary Barry

BRITISH BIZARRO

- Quentin Smirhes -

To whom it may concern,

I am writing to complain about this so-called Quentin Smirhes character. I was minding my own business on the internet a few days ago when I found myself drawn to this fellow with a rather fetching mustard-coloured jumper similar to the ones I have. As a matter of fact, everything I wear is mustard. All I eat is mustard (English, mind). In fact, one could say I adore mustard, I respect mustard.

So, to my dismay, what I saw was something I wish I'd never laid my eyes upon. This bespectacled young man with some form of medieval hairdo stood there in his underpants bearing all to see quaffing copious amounts of Warnincks Advocaat and becoming drenched head to toe in the stuff. Disgusted would be putting it mildly. The combination of this egg-based liqueur in an unkempt beard was plainly vomit-inducing. For one, it is a sheer waste of good drink when people are starving in the world. And two, it's not even Christmas.

Please can you take this preposterous idiot down off the internet as soon as possible.

Yours sincerely,

Olivia Coleman

P.S. Could you find out where he bought his mustard jumper from?

googbye

Printed in Great Britain
by Amazon